KENNA'S DRAGON

Leigh Miller

This is a work of fiction. Names, character, places are either products of the author's imagination, or used fictitiously. Any resemblance to actual persons, living or dead, events, or locales, is entirely coincidental

ISBN: 9798850863838

Cover art by Ashley Simeone (Art by Smashley)

authorleighmiller.com

To A - One set of vows doesn't seem like enough, so here's another.

Love you to the moon and back, forever and always. I'll never be able to repay the kindness, patience and unending support you've given me while I chase my dreams, but I promise to spend the rest of my life trying.

6.20.2023 <3

1

Kenna

This is it. My first day as new-Kenna.

New job. New haircut. New shoes. New me.

Stepping through the front door of the Paranormal Citizens Relations Bureau, it feels like exactly the fresh start I need.

The lobby is open and bright, with Bureau employees streaming in to start their work week. The crowd is a mix of humans and paranormals, and every species from orcs to fae to shifters seems to be represented.

Impossible to imagine just five years ago, when the Paranormal Acts were passed and allowed creatures of all kinds to come forward and join the human world, but standing here today it just feels right. I'm beyond excited to be a part of the organization helping to integrate the paranormal world with the human one and making a better path forward for everyone.

"Good morning," I say as I approach the front desk.

The receptionist looks up and a smile splits his stone-gray face. A gargoyle with rough-hewn features and massive stone-like wings, he greets me cheerfully.

"Good morning. How can I help you?"

I give him the papers my new boss emailed me over the weekend. "Here for my first day. Yvette told me to check in at the front desk when I got here."

"Oh," says the gargoyle, whose name tag I'm close enough to see reads 'Lawrence'. "Welcome! We're glad to have you. This way, please."

Thanking him, I follow as he beckons me around the desk and through a door leading into a short hallway.

"We'll take you back to HR first," Lawrence explains, "to get all your new hire paperwork completed."

I'm starting a new job today as a graphic designer and communications assistant in the Bureau's Community Outreach department, and for me, it's a pretty damn big deal.

I'm twenty-seven, and this is my first Adult™ job. Maybe I should be more embarrassed about that, but all I can feel is excited as I follow Lawrence back to the HR department.

So what if it took me a little longer than most to finish my degree? I finished it, and that's all that matters. Graphic design major with a communications minor, and after years of bouncing around and juggling multiple part-time jobs while I finished school, I've finally landed my first full-time gig.

New-Kenna's got this in the bag. She's professional, smart, on top of the world. Old-Kenna can't come to the phone right now.

Lawrence shows me into a small conference room, lets me know an HR rep will be in shortly, and wishes me good luck on my first day. I thank him again and wander over to study some of the photographs on the conference room wall after he leaves.

The photos show some of the historic milestones for paranormal folk—the passage of the Acts, the opening of the Bureau's headquarters here in Seattle, tons of different events and celebrations marking leaps forward in paranormal integration. The faces in the photos are human and not human, a jumble of both together, sharing the work of helping paranormals find their way in our changed world.

"Kenna," a warm voice says as the conference room door swings open. "Welcome!"

The HR rep introduces herself as Yolanda, and though she looks mostly human, her eyes have the distinct red tint of a vampire's. She helps me fill out my tax forms and all the confidentiality agreements that come with working for a government agency. Once those are done, we head up to the fifth floor so I can get settled in at my desk.

And, to my surprise, my cubicle is decorated with streamers and a welcome sign, and Yvette is waiting with a big smile and a warm welcome.

"Happy first day!" Yvette says. "We're so glad to have you here."

Though I got to meet her during the interview process, I'm struck again by Yvette's appearance. A faun with huge doe eyes and platinum blond hair, she radiates a joy and kindness that immediately puts me at ease. I set my stuff down on my desk, and Yvette starts a round of introductions with the rest of the department.

Susie, a human with brown hair and a petite frame, who works on events and community organizing.

Jax, a wolf shifter with electric-blue dyed hair and a tall lanky build, who runs all the Bureau's digital channels.

And finally Vera, a nymph with light lavender skin and hypnotic turquoise eyes, who handles Bureau PR.

Each of my coworkers greets me with the same openness and enthusiasm, and all of it makes me feel warm and fuzzy as some of my lingering first day nerves slide away.

This is a good thing. I was meant to be here.

Through the whole job searching, application, and interview process, I felt like such an impostor. Which really isn't a surprise, to be honest. I fucked around for all of my late teens and early twenties—with school, with work, with relationships—and part of me still feels like that same old flighty, irresponsible party girl, just wearing business casual clothes and pretending I have my shit together.

I have to get over it. I *know* I have to get over it. And as the morning goes on and I complete some of my orientation and training tasks, it gets easier and easier to believe I really am supposed to be here.

The team goes out together for lunch at a little deli down the street, and that feeling only grows. All of them seem kind and cool and welcoming, and as we eat and chat I start to feel like one of the bunch.

"We better get back," Yvette says as we all stand and head for the door. "All-hands meeting starts at one."

"What's that?" I ask.

"Director Blair's talking to the whole Bureau today," Vera says, holding the door open for me. "About all the crap that's gone down with the government and paranormal policy over the past few months."

I nod, stomach tightening a little at the mention of it.

I've had a front-row seat to a small part of that drama, mainly through one of my best friends, Nora, and her mate, Elias.

Nora was at the center of some of the events Vera is talking about. After Elias recognized Nora as his mate and had the Bureau track her down, it led to Nora's ex-fiance-slash-uber-creep-congressman Daniel Sorenson finding her. She'd been hiding from Sorenson for years, and he abused his position and power to get her info through the Bureau.

And not only that, but Sorenson attempted to fucking *kidnap* her in some deranged attempt to get her back. He was arrested and charged with a boatload of crimes related to the kidnapping and all the other shady shit he was up to, and it caused a massive media firestorm here in Seattle and around the country.

Nora and Elias made it out safely on the other side, together and ridiculously happy, but the Bureau and the whole paranormal community are still dealing with the fallout.

Once we make it back to the office and put our stuff away, it's just about time for the meeting, and we follow the steady stream of employees down to the first floor.

The meeting is being held in the building's cafeteria space, the only room big enough to hold the Bureau's two hundred or so employees.

The room is already crowded by the time we get there, with some risers at the front of the space making a small stage. Loitering near the back, we wait as the crowd hums with conversation.

A couple minutes later, someone who I assume is Mr. Blair, the Bureau's Director, takes to the risers and stands behind the podium. Nora's told me a bit about him, about how much help he gave to her and Elias when they were dealing with everything that went down with Sorenson, but she failed to mention one key detail.

He's really, really hot.

And not just because he's a dragon shifter, but the Director's totally got it going on. Tall, broad-shouldered, and fit, with dark brown hair and a face that's equal parts stern and sexy, he immediately stands out from the rest of the room by his appearance and aura alone.

Power, that's what he radiates.

Power and authority and a magnetism that makes me straighten my spine where I'm standing at the back of the room.

My eyes must also widen, or I must be drooling or something, because Vera laughs softly beside me.

"Yeah, I'd say you get used to it, but you never really do. Man's too damn hot to be the Director of a boring government agency."

Picking up my jaw off the floor, I laugh and shake my head. "Or it's just a requirement for the job, leadership skills and a Greek god's face."

Vera laughs, too, but is cut off a moment later by a hush falling over the crowd.

When Blair finally looks up from the papers on the podium and surveys the room, a jolt of surprise moves through me.

Those eyes. Golden and sharp, with oblong pupils instead of round ones.

Dragon eyes.

"Good afternoon, everyone," he says into the mic, and even his voice is compelling, graveled and deep. "If you'd all find a seat, I would like to get this meeting started."

There doesn't seem to be any seats left, so I shuffle a little to stand at the back of the room by the wall. When I find my place, Blair isn't speaking yet. In fact, the entire crowd is silent, waiting, and when I look to the front of the room, my breath catches in my throat.

Those golden, dragon eyes are fixed squarely on me.

2

Blair

I haven't felt the urge to hoard treasure in almost two hundred years.

Well, at least not in the typical sense. Over the centuries, the jewels and gold and other riches that used to make up the bulk of my hoard gradually became business ventures and investments and bank accounts that could sustain me for several dragon-long lifetimes. Much simpler, really, and less hassle than collecting and guarding shiny baubles.

But when my eyes land on a devastatingly curvy woman with pale, freckled skin and a wild riot of auburn curls, those instincts come roaring back to life.

Steal her. Claim her. Keep her.

It's enough to make the rest of the world fall away completely.

My focus narrows to her, only her, and for a few long

moments I'm not at all certain I'm going to be able to pull myself back from that edge.

Beneath the suit jacket I'm wearing, the muscles in my back cramp and twitch with the distinct, unpleasant sensation of an oncoming shift. My blood heats and the space between my shoulder blades aches with the phantom press of wings beneath my skin.

What the hell is happening?

Still staring at the woman, I watch with eyes locked on her face as she looks from side to side, then back at me like she's not sure it's her I'm focused on.

Of course it's you, that depraved, instinctual voice slithering up from the recesses of my mind wants to croon to her. *Come here, treasure.*

I need to snap out of it. I've never had this kind of visceral reaction to a woman. Well, at least not since...

The sharp sting of memory is enough to jerk me out of my trance and back to the present. I'm not sure how long I've been standing here, staring like an idiot, but it must be long enough if the look on my Assistant Director Cleo's face is any indication. Clearing my throat, I start again.

"I'm sure we're all well-aware of the recent events that have impacted public perception of the Bureau, and I wanted to take the time today to put some of those rumors to rest."

Rumors. More like deliberate lies and PR spin. Still, as I address the crowd and watch the expressions on the faces of the beings who dedicate their days to working in the best interest of paranormals, my gut starts to twist.

All of it—the politicians who'd like to see the Paranormal Acts revisited and revised, if not repealed outright; the public outcry over ludicrous, trumped up morality concerns; the growing anti-monster movement that would see us pushed back into the shadows from whence we came—is weighing heavily on the mind of every creature here.

I don't assume for a moment my words will do much to assuage those fears, but if my leadership can do anything to allay them, it's worth it for me to speak.

Relaying the sanitized version of the events of the past few months in a practiced, measured tone, I studiously avoid glancing in the woman's direction.

She's still there, I know she's still there. The persistent glint of auburn locks out of the corner of my eye teases me, taunts me. A glimmer of temptation meant to bait the beast in me.

I'm not going to give into it, and I'm not going to entertain it for a moment. Not now.

"Nothing will change," I say as I finish giving a brief, bare-bones overview of the challenges facing the Bureau. "Political fights are not *our* fight, and the work we do here will continue day in and day out, as it always has."

A few nods and murmurs of assent weave their way through the crowd, along with some nervous shifting and down-turned gazes. Doubt and frustration and a few threads of anger mingle with that assent, souring the air.

Perception has always been one of my gifts. To look at a face and see the minute details that give me an idea of what a being is thinking or feeling. To see through artifice and outright lies. It's not mind-reading and it's not magick—at least not in the obvious, forthright sense—but it gives me a small window into the minds of others.

And in moments like this it can feel like more of a curse than a blessing.

Add to that the lingering awareness of the redhead in the back, the acute discomfort of instincts I don't have time for right now, and I'm sure my words don't quite hit their mark.

Damn it all.

Today was supposed to be a reset after the chaos of the last few months. After all the ugliness that went down last fall with the former, now disgraced and imprisoned congressman Daniel Sorenson, and the havoc he wreaked here in Seattle, things were supposed to settle back into a sense of normalcy.

They haven't, and it turns out Sorenson was just the idiotic, reckless manifestation of a much larger and more insidious rot.

Still, I'm glad the bastard is languishing in a prison cell, and not just because his ex fiancée now happens to be my oldest friend's mate. I would have gone out on any limb to help Elias and Nora deal with Sorenson, and taking down one of the most outspoken anti-paranormal voices in government was just an added perk.

"If there are any concerns," I conclude, still studying the faces in the crowd and taking great care to avoid looking at one face in particular. "I encourage you to speak to your supervisor, department head, or bring your concerns directly to me. The work we do here matters. The work we do here is changing the future of all paranormals across this country, and it won't be stopped or diminished because of those who refuse to accept that the world has changed."

A few more nods, a scattering of tension released.

I still don't look at her, and do my best to pretend she isn't even there as I thank everyone for their time and step down from the podium. The crowd starts to disperse, and I'm about to make for the exit and retreat to my office to get a handle on myself when a familiar voice stops me.

"Do you care to explain what happened up there?" Cleo asks, nodding toward the podium.

"No," I tell her flatly.

She purses her lips. The shifting expression on her face has me half-convinced she's going to argue the point, but after a few seconds she seems to think better of it and shakes her head. Half-vampire and sharp as a damn tack, I know she's already clocked the way I was staring at the woman and made her own assumptions, but she's also astute enough to pick her battles.

"Fine," she says. "When would you like to discuss the upcoming visit from HHS?"

Health and Human Services, the Cabinet department which oversees the Bureau, has upped their oversight in recent months. They're sending a Deputy Secretary to meet with us about some changes they'd like to see in our organizational structure, and just the idea of it makes me itchy.

"Tomorrow at 11?" I ask her. "I can have Ruthie clear my calendar through lunch."

Cleo nods, pulling out her phone to put the meeting in. While she does, I unconsciously glance toward the back of the room.

The woman is gone, but instead of relief, all my instincts kick into high gear. Where is she? Flipping rapidly through my mental catalog, I remember seeing her standing near Yvette, our Community Outreach Director. Is that the department she works in? If today's her first day, her paperwork should be on file, and when I get back to my office, I can...

Gods above.

Enough. This is enough. I'm not the mindless creature I'm acting like right now.

I gave Elias so much grief for the way he seemed to lose his mind the moment he first spotted Nora. A mating bond does strange things to a monster, and with the instinct riding me now, I regret every bit of ribbing I gave him.

Not that this is the same thing, though. This woman is not my mate. She can't be.

I've already found my mate.

Found her, and lost her, all over two centuries ago.

So whatever this instinct is, it's something I need to leave well enough alone. Perhaps it's just a rogue synapse firing, or some rebellion in the base, lizard part of my brain that hasn't been exercised enough since I stopped shifting regularly. Temporary insanity or the misplaced urge to hoard, all directed at some innocent bystander.

An innocent bystander with hair that glints like a flame and a full, delicious body that makes me want to sink my claws in.

"Tomorrow at 11, then?" Cleo asks, again snapping me out of the madness that's gripped me. She glances in the same direction I'm looking with clear knowing and disapproval on her face.

"Yes," I say gruffly, and turn to go.

Back upstairs in my office, however, the instinct doesn't go away. No, it only heightens with each moment the woman is out of my presence. Madness, utter, misplaced madness, but it's enough to have me pacing up and down the length of the room, mind whirring and skin burning from the inside out.

Unable to deny it, I open the door and stick my head around the corner. "Ruthie?"

From her desk, my forest sprite assistant's head snaps up, her curtain of mossy hair falling back from her face. "Yes, Mr. Blair?"

Since she started working directly with me a couple of months ago, I've told her a dozen times 'Blair' is more than fine. Ruthie, however, has the formal manners of the old fae from where her sprite family line originates. That heritage also gives her a deep well of empathetic instinct that makes her all too preceptive at times.

Like right now.

She frowns as she looks at me, tilting her head to one side as her black eyes sparkle with concern. "Is everything alright?"

"Everything's fine," I tell her, hoping I sound more convincing than I feel. "I need you to look up a new employee for me. One who started recently in the Community Outreach Department."

Nodding, she turns back to her computer. "I'm only seeing one new employee in that department in the last year. Kenna Byrne."

Kenna Byrne. Well, the Irish name would certainly explain the red hair and the freckles.

"Good. Can you connect with her boss and have her send Kenna up?"

"To your office?" Ruthie asks, confused.

"Yes," I tell her, fully aware of how odd the request is. As Director, I'm not in the habit of personally greeting our new hires.

"Of course. I'll reach out to Yvette and have Kenna come right up."

A whispered thread of sanity in the back of my mind warns caution, and if I were a better man, I would listen to it.

But I'm not wholly a man, not right now.

With a decisive silencing of that whisper, I retreat into my office and wait to see what kind of enormous mistake I'm about to make.

3

Kenna

"Hey, Kenna?" Yvette's voice startles me out of the anxiety spiral I'm having at my desk.

"Yeah? What's up?" I ask, even though I'm pretty sure I already know.

"I just got a call from Director Blair's assistant. She let me know he'd like to see you upstairs in his office."

There it is.

Stomach sinking, I nod and stand from my desk. "Did she say what he wants to talk to me about?"

Yvette shakes her head, and for the first time today, all the sunniness in her face is gone. "She didn't. I'm sure everything's fine, though."

I'm not convinced. Not after what happened downstairs before the meeting.

Even now, I can still feel the weight of Blair's golden gaze on me, the intensity of being the focus of such sharp scrutiny.

Something Nora once told me about him sticks out in my mind, though I can't remember exactly how she phrased it. Something about Blair being preceptive—beyond the normal, human concept of the word. Some instinct that lets him get an immediate beat on people.

Maybe he got one on me, and maybe he didn't like what he saw.

Impostor syndrome sitting heavily on my shoulders with each step I take, I follow Yvette to the elevator. She's quiet, but then again, what can she really say right now? By the strange tension in the air and the odd glances I get from my new coworkers as we leave, it's not hard to guess being called to the Director's office on your first day is not a normal occurrence.

They all saw Blair looking at me. Vera was the only one to ask about it outright after we all got back to our cubicles, but let the topic drop when I told her I had no idea what it was about.

Although, I suppose I'm about to find out.

Yvette and I reach the top floor and walk up to a desk outside an office door with Blair's name and title printed on it. The forest sprite sitting behind the desk looks up, immediately locks eyes with me, and studies me for a moment before some sort of understanding spreads across her face.

What she thinks she understands, I don't know, and Yvette apparently doesn't either as she shifts uncomfortably next to me.

"Hi, Ruthie," she says. "Mr. Blair wanted to see us?"

"Just Kenna," Ruthie says brightly. "And he'll be right out if you want to take a seat."

Yvette frowns, but covers it up quickly as she turns to face me. "Alright. Well, I'll be downstairs in my office if you need to drop by after you're finished."

Yeah, if I'm not fired and frog-marched out of here.

I don't say that though, and as Yvette heads back to the elevator, it's just me and Ruthie sitting in silence outside Blair's office.

"Today's your first day at the Bureau?" she asks.

"Yeah, it is." And maybe my last.

"Well, you don't have anything to worry about. With Mr. Blair, I mean. He's—"

I don't get to find out what Mr. Blair is, because the office door opens and the dragon himself steps out.

"Ms. Byrne. Please come in."

The rumble of his deep voice is even more compelling now than it was downstairs in the meeting. Standing on legs that feel oddly like jelly all of a sudden, I walk to his door. He holds it open for me, and as I brush past him I almost imagine I hear the slight catch of breath in his throat.

Blair follows me inside, closing the door and gesturing to the chairs in front of his desk. "Please, take a seat."

I do, watching warily as he circles around the desk to sit across from me. And damn if I don't feel like a kid called in to see the principal, waiting to hear how many days of detention I'm about to get.

The whole vibe of Blair's office just adds to that tension. The space is large and open, and its top-floor location gives it great views of the city. With dark walls and carpeting, a wide mahogany desk, and heavy, expensive furniture, it's impossible not to feel out of place here.

Shifting a little, not sure what I'm supposed to do with my hands or where I'm supposed to look or what I should say, I settle for meeting Blair's golden gaze where he's sitting silently and staring at me just like he was during the meeting.

It's a mistake.

He's even more handsome up close, and I can't stop myself

from taking a full inventory of his solemn, serious face.

Blair radiates authority from the firm line of his jaw to the sharp cut of his cheekbones to the unyielding focus in his gaze, with a few scatterings of softness tossed in like an unexpected afterthought. His full lips, the slight crinkles around the corners of his eyes, and the faintest hint of gray in the dark brown hair at his temples.

In human years, I'd say he looks about forty, but what that equates to in dragon terms, I can't even begin to guess.

Not that I have any spare brain cells to dedicate toward guessing. Not when he's still looking at me without saying a single word, studying my face in that keen, uncanny way of his.

It makes me want to squirm. The fact that I'm able to sit so still, keep holding his gaze even when I feel a flush climbing my cheeks and a fluttery, panicked pinch in the center of my chest, is a freaking miracle.

It doesn't last for long, though. My flush deepens under his continued inspection, and before I'm able to stop myself, I open my mouth to blurt out the first thing that comes to mind.

"Am I being fired?"

The question surprises him out of his study of me, and he shakes his head. "No, you're not, Ms. Byrne. Unless you've done anything on your first day that merits dismissal?"

Is he… teasing me? No, that's absolutely not it. Not when it's still so damn weird that I'm here in the first place, and when he's not smiling or giving me any indication this is a friendly chat.

It's kind of bullshit, if I'm being honest. I didn't do anything. He was the one who made it weird by singling me out in a crowded room. And now I'm the one being made to sit here and feel uncomfortable?

New-Kenna doesn't like this. New-Kenna's not going to be

a damn doormat, even for a creature as powerful as Director Blair.

"Why am I here, then?"

Again, the absolute lack of filter seems to catch him off guard, and he frowns. He doesn't answer me right away, though, not for a few long, painful seconds that I have to keep sitting here and internally squirming.

"I wanted to apologize," he says finally. "For what happened at the all-hands meeting today."

Alright, now we're getting somewhere. I still want to hear him say it, though.

"What do you mean?"

A slight twinge of discomfort crosses his face. It's the first time he's looked anything but distant and aloof since I entered his office, and it gratifies the petty, irritated part of me to see it. If I'm going to feel awkward over this, then he should, too.

"If I made you uncomfortable, I apologize."

Well, that's half an answer. "By staring at me, you mean?"

Another pinched expression. "Yes."

"Why did you?"

If he was uncomfortable before, he's practically cringing now, and for the first time, I feel a little bad for him. Maybe it was something embarrassing.

A sudden suspicion strikes me, and I speak before I can think better of it.

"Was it like, a mating thing?"

Blair's golden eyes narrow. "What do you mean?"

"Well," I say, cheeks heating again, "I have plenty of friends who are paranormal, and know a few who are mated. Not to mention one of my best friends, who I think you might know, too? Nora Perry?"

His brow furrows. "You know Nora?"

"I do. I met Nora when we were working at a bookstore

together. That job… well, that job didn't really work out for me. But I got a best friend out of it, so it wasn't all bad." I realize I'm rambling and try to get back on track without really knowing where I'm going with this. "But what I mean to say is that I know it happens fast, recognizing a mate, and I was wondering if that's what—"

"It wasn't," Blair interrupts, tone firm and commanding and completely shutting down the idea.

Oh.

Fuck me.

Did I just insinuate the goddamn Director of the Bureau might have thought I was his mate? No. Absolutely not. I did not just do that.

"O-okay," I stutter, grasping helplessly at any mental straw I can to salvage this. "Sorry. I didn't mean to imply—"

"It was a simple mental lapse," Blair says, cutting me off again with an impersonal, no-nonsense tone to his voice. "But I realize it might have come across as something else."

My scrambling internal panic flat-lines. Um, okay, let's not soften the blow or anything.

Silence falls between us, and this time it's my turn to study him. Tilting my head slightly to one side, I let myself take my time and process the details of him. Handsome, yes, but also closed-off and distant, despite what should be warmth in his golden eyes. Instead of flames, they're like hammered gold—metallic, cold.

It makes me question Nora's opinion of him. She's always had such nice things to say about Blair, hasn't she? How kind he's been, and how helpful.

Maybe it's just me that rubs him the wrong way.

"Alright," I say. "Thanks, I guess, for clearing that up."

His mouth opens, then closes, like he thought better of whatever it is he meant to say, and we lapse into silence again.

It really is a shame he's being so standoffish. Sure, the whole mates thing was far-fetched, but a part of me is really, really curious to know the Blair Nora talks about, the *dragon* Nora talks about. By the way she tells it, he's pretty damned impressive in his shifted form. Fearsome enough to team up with Elias and swoop down to save the day when Daniel Sorenson had Nora at gunpoint last fall.

Not that I'm supposed to know that. Blair's involvement was hushed up and Nora swore me to secrecy.

Regardless, I'd like to know that Blair, not this one who looks like he'd rather be anywhere but here. Which is still pissing me off a bit, considering this little meeting was entirely up to him. We could have just pretended nothing happened.

Well, *he* could have pretended nothing happened, and I could have kept my head down and my panic to myself, even if no part of me can forget those few long moments that passed between us.

His eyes were different, then. Burning instead of frozen. Locked on me like I was the only person in the room. He can call it a mental lapse or whatever, but some part of me knows it was more. Maybe not a mating thing, if he's so adamant that it wasn't, but something that definitely didn't feel quite human.

Just the memory of it pricks at something in my chest.

"Anyway," he says gruffly. "I just want to apologize again. I didn't intend to make you uncomfortable."

My heart sinks even further. That's all I'm going to get, isn't it? An impersonal apology and a dismissal.

I mean, it's not really surprising, but it makes that sharp, unexpected ache kick up even harder. I rub my hand absently over the spot where it hurts, and Blair's keen golden eyes track the movement. He frowns even more deeply, and I take that as my cue to go.

"Alright," I say as brightly as I can. "I'm glad all of this is settled. I guess I'll head back to my desk."

Another awkward beat of silence, indecision on his face, and I stand without waiting for him to answer.

"Nice to meet you, by the way," I continue, straightening out the mint green blazer I picked out for my first day. The one that feels more like an uncomfortable costume at this point. "Nora's told me a lot about you, so it's good to put a face to the name."

He makes a noise that's not quite decipherable as an answer, and my discomfort doubles. God, this is awkward.

Still, new-Kenna doesn't back down, and she doesn't let the grumpy asshole of a dragon ruin her first day at a new job.

"I hope you have a good rest of your afternoon," I tell him with my best, brightest, fakest smile before turning tail and heading for his office door.

Why in the world I feel the sharp sting of tears behind that smile, and why my chest feels like I've got a ton of bricks sitting on top of it, I don't want to think about right now. No, all I want is to flee back to my desk and finish the rest of my day and pretend like I belong here.

"Kenna." Blair's deep voice stops me in my tracks.

Kenna. Not Ms. Byrne.

The sound of my name in his rough, graveled timbre sends a shot of unwanted awareness all the way through me. Awareness of him—his power, his aura, the inexplicable compulsion that makes me turn back around to face him.

"Yeah?"

"I..." he starts, and then trails off.

What does he want? He's dismissed me, dismissed the possibility that what happened between us during the meeting was anything more than some kind of mental fog on this part. Why can't he let it go?

A few more long moments pass, and he remains silent.

God, I don't want to do this. I don't want to be here anymore. Staring him dead in the face for three seconds, five, ten, it's clear he's unwilling or unable to say anything more, so I turn and leave without another word.

4

Blair

Inviting Kenna to my office was a mistake.

Big surprise, that.

What did I think I was going to accomplish? Convincing myself it was all in my head? Coming to the conclusion that she is not, in fact, utter hell for my sanity?

As soon as the door closes behind her, I'm out of my seat. An unconscious sway in my body tugs me in the direction she just left, but I let out a harsh curse and cross to my office windows instead. I stare out at the gray Seattle day without really seeing it, counting my breaths and trying to focus on reigning in the instinct pulsing through me.

I need to shift. Preferably sooner rather than later.

Only... would that help, or make things worse? How long has it been since I allowed myself to shift fully to my other form?

The answer comes to me immediately. It's been since last fall, the night I took Sorenson out and let Elias and Nora make their escape. A necessary shift, one I don't regret for a moment.

Before that… it had been years.

Occasionally I allow myself a half-shift, just to stretch my wings and work some pent-up energy out of my system. Full-shifts, though, are few and far between. Letting myself go entirely, letting the dragon out and ceding some portion of my humanity and control to his whims, it's not something I indulge in lightly, and nor is it something I should be entertaining now.

Kenna Byrne is dangerous.

Not that she means to be, and not that she shoulders any of the blame for my temporary insanity, but left to his own devices my dragon would still follow her, steal her, hoard her. So perhaps it's best not to give him the leash right now.

I've never lost control, not entirely, and there's only been one time I've come close.

Still staring out the window, my mind is thousands of miles and hundreds of years from here. Another place, another time, another woman who would have done herself a favor by staying far away from me.

Despite all the time that's passed, I seldom let myself think of the woman I recognized as my mate.

Lizzy.

With her long black hair and her crooked smile, with the sense of adventure that made her more than willing to hop aboard a pirate's ship and sail into a new life with a dragon she barely knew.

Before I met her, Elias and I had spent decades of our lives marauding, untethered, sailing to distant shores and co-captaining a crew of monsters. Both young and arrogant, cocky and flush with the confidence that comes with being at the beginning of a centuries-long life.

There had been nothing, absolutely nothing that could have prepared me for the instantaneous reorientation of my life when I met her on that fateful day in port.

And Lizzy, for her part, had taken it all in stride. She'd been fearless, right up until the day her choice to be with me got her killed.

When we were attacked by two French ships, we were outnumbered, out-gunned, and when Lizzy fell, the entire world seemed to fall apart with her.

In the aftermath, my dragon had full reign. Ships burned and vengeance was won. And even all these years later, I can't say I regret allowing it.

What I do regret is everything that came before. All my sins and all the irreparable harm I caused. The price Lizzy had to pay for my mistakes.

Like it always does, time has stolen away the finer details. When I think of her now, it's more tattered emotion than actual memories that fill my heart and soul.

I know Lizzy's smile was quick to appear and filled with mirth, but I can't remember the shape of her lips or the sound of her laugh. I know her eyes were blue, but whether they were closer in hue to the sky or the sea I can't say.

Even the grief of losing her has become blunted by the unstoppable corrosion of the centuries I've lived without her. An ache, rather than a stabbing pain, a well filled with guilt and regret rather than acute heartbreak. That forgetting, too, feels like a betrayal. Another sin added to the long list I'm sure the gods will have me answer for one day, if indeed they do exist.

It's too much to contemplate right now, and feels entirely too discordant and shameful to be thinking of Lizzy when Kenna just walked out of here.

I don't do this. I don't lose control. I don't give into the baser parts of myself and let them steal my reason.

Still, the memories of the last half-hour hang heavy in the air, along with the last traces of Kenna's scent. Seeing the tentative hope on her pretty face, the way her eyes lit up when she started talking about Nora and her friends and the way she's seen them find mates, it puts a strange, leaden weight into the bottom of my stomach.

Perhaps Kenna does have a mate out there somewhere. I wouldn't doubt it. With that open, honest air about her, the way she wears her heart on her sleeve, if anyone would be the perfect candidate to be a monster's mate, it would be her.

I won't acknowledge the fact that the idea of it bothers me, not when I'm the one who shut down her questions with such finality.

I can't acknowledge any of it. Not here, not now, not when I barely have the mental faculties to keep a handle on myself, much less dive into introspection and soul searching.

A soft knock on my door draws my attention back to the present, and I gather just enough composure to clear my throat and call out to whoever's on the other side.

"Come in."

It's Ruthie, and as she pokes her head around the door, her face falls with concern. "I have HHS on the phone for you. Line three."

"Thank you, Ruthie," I say, irritated at having to speak to anyone from the department, but happy enough for the distraction. "I'll take the call shortly."

She nods, lingers in the doorway for a moment, no doubt full to the brim with questions, but leaves with a soft snick of the door behind her.

Taking a few last moments at the window to compose myself, I breathe deep and shove all of that misplaced instinct back to the far corners of my lizard brain, where it belongs.

5

Kenna

The rest of my first week at the Bureau goes off without a hitch.

I don't see Blair again, and none of my coworkers bring up the awkwardness from the all-hands meeting. By the time Friday rolls around, I'm feeling almost as confident as I was at the beginning of the week that the Bureau really is the place for me.

All in all, I could have had a worst first week.

The work they have me doing is right up my alley, even if it doesn't push me all that far out of the box creatively. Flyers and posters for Bureau events, graphics for digital campaigns and the website, internal publications about the work and initiatives going on this quarter. Easy peasy.

I've still got a couple of side-hustles on the back burner, and plenty that I want to achieve with my art, but it's pretty damn nice to finally have a steady, healthy paycheck coming in.

When I first enrolled in college at eighteen, I was a visual arts major, with a concentration in illustration and digital design. I'd had it in the back of my head that I was going to grow up and illustrate childrens' books, comics, art for video games. As it turns out, though, that kind of work is scarce and opportunities don't just fall out of trees and land at your feet.

And, as it also turns out, twenty-year-old Kenna was a lot more interested in boys and partying than going to class. I'd always had a wild streak as a teenager, but moving far from home for university and getting a taste of true freedom was just fuel for the fire.

I dropped out during my junior year, spent the next few years bopping around part-time jobs and casual relationships and being generally unbothered by any kind of adult responsibility.

My parents were disappointed. My perfect older sister Jenny was horrified. I, however, was having way too much fun to care.

Until a couple of years ago.

I don't really know when the exhaustion started to set in, but by the time I was twenty-four or twenty-five, the whole routine started to feel stale and empty. Men, late nights, shitty dead-end jobs. A lot of my friends had graduated, moved on, started getting married, and I was just... stuck.

It took me another year and some change to finish up the degree—shifting to design with a communications minor—and at least as long to shake the rest of my flighty, partying ways.

Well, I've almost shaken them. Because what's life without causing a little trouble now and again?

Late in the afternoon, most of my coworkers are winding down for the day and chatting back and forth over the tops of our cubicles about our upcoming weekend plans.

"What about you, Kenna?" Susie asks. Out of the bunch, she's the softest spoken, and also happens to be dating one of the Bureau's accountants—a tall, handsome orc.

"I've got plans to go out tonight," I say, keeping the details deliberately vague.

While things aren't as weird as they were on Monday, I'm still not sure how appropriate it is to tell my coworkers I'm going out tonight with a wolf shifter I met on a dating app.

"Fun!" Jax chimes in, poking their head over the other cubicle wall. "Hot date?"

Well, so much for that.

"*A* date," I say with a laugh. "Hotness level TBD."

The joke earns me a good-natured chuckle from them both, and after a few more minutes of conversation people start packing up to head home for the weekend.

I'm staying late, both to finish up a couple of projects, and because I'm heading straight from work to my date. I packed my clothes for tonight in a backpack and brought it to work with me. Since I'm meeting my date at seven, it wouldn't have made sense to take the bus forty-five minutes home, only to get ready in hardly any time at all and catch a ride back downtown.

A little after six, I head into the bathroom to change and fix up my makeup.

Standing there and looking at myself in the mirror, I wonder for about the hundredth time since I accepted this date whether I should cancel.

There's no reason I should cancel. Absolutely none. This guy seems great. A real adult with a real job who's taken the initiative and made all the plans for tonight. Cute, too, if his pictures are accurate.

This is a good thing. Just like this job. Just like the steps I've taken to move my life forward these past couple of years.

I'm not going to cancel, and I'm not going to let the small but persistent whisper of doubt in the back of my mind stop me from enjoying it.

Finishing up in the bathroom and stowing my backpack under my desk with plans to leave it there until Monday, I take one last deep breath, power down my computer, and grab my purse before heading toward the elevator.

The office is nearly empty this time of night, only a couple of lights still shining from the other departments on the fifth floor. It makes me slightly uneasy, but luckily it only takes a few seconds for the elevator to arrive.

Unluckily, it's already occupied.

I don't know who looks more surprised, me or Blair, but I do know that I don't imagine his sharply indrawn breath or the way his golden eyes flare wide when he sees me standing there.

He looks… disheveled. Suit coat unbuttoned, tie slightly loosened, hair a bit mussed like he's run his hand through it a time or five.

My legs wobble forward without me consciously telling them to. Some dim part of my brain reasons that getting on the elevator with Blair is bad, yes, but it would be even worse to stand here like a statue and let the doors close in my face.

Or to turn and run in the other direction.

Standing as far away from him as I can in the confined space, I glance at the buttons and see he's headed for the lobby, too.

As we begin our descent, the awkward tension in the air is thick enough that if I reached out, I might just be able to touch it. It makes me antsy, jumpy, so goddamn uncomfortable that I do the unthinkable.

I open my mouth and talk to him.

"I hope you had a good week."

Blair makes a noise in the back of his throat that might be a yes, but also might just be him hoping I shut the hell up.

"I did," I go on, fully stress-rambling now. "Even after Monday. My week was good."

Stop. I need to stop. Why can't I stop?

"So," I continue, unable to dam up the mortifying stream of words coming out of my mouth. "Everything is fine. Totally cool. Work here has been awesome, and I even have a date lined up tonight, so there's absolutely nothing you have to worry about when it comes to..."

When I glance over and see his expression, my words die in my throat. Blair is utterly stone-faced, golden eyes burning a hole through me. A slight twitch near his side catches my attention, and I look down to see his hand clenched into a fist at his side, knuckles white.

Okay. No more small talk.

Fixing my eyes forward, I stay absolutely silent until the elevator comes to a stop at the ground floor.

When the doors open, I bolt. I cross the lobby toward the exit, only glancing back once over my shoulder to find Blair still standing in the elevator, eyes fixed on me as I make my escape.

6

Blair

She's going on a date tonight.

As Kenna hurries away from me through the lobby and toward the front door, the sudden, insane urge to give chase rises in me like a blaze.

Follow her. Catch her. Steal her away.

The dragon in me is already thinking of the best place to hoard her. He'd take her somewhere comfortable and safe, somewhere we'll always know where she'll be, somewhere we can always find her.

Fuck. *Fuck.*

I stay rooted in place, fighting every instinct that would send me after her.

She's going on a date. Tonight.

That's fine. A completely normal thing for a young, single woman in her twenties to be doing on a Friday night.

Fire burns beneath my skin. The muscles in my back ache and clench, demanding a shift that I absolutely will not, *can not*, let happen. It's there, just there, in the edge of insanity that whispers in the back of my mind.

The freedom in the shift. The ecstasy of letting that side of my nature take over.

It's been years since the urge to shift rode me like this. Godsdamn it.

The elevator doors close, and I curse under my breath, smashing the button to open them back up. It doesn't work, and the elevator rises toward whatever floor it's just been called to.

And, somewhere below, Kenna Byrne is headed out into the Seattle night on a date.

I can still smell her in the close space. Her scent has hints of ginger and citrus, along with a dark floral note that smells like sex and temptation.

I concentrate on breathing through my mouth until the elevator glides to a stop and the doors open. George from Finance and Mikayla from HR are standing there, waiting to get on—standing a little *too* close to be strictly platonic—and they spring apart when they see me.

But far be it from me to worry about inter-department fraternization right now. I don't spare the time for more than a cursory nod and clipped greeting before exiting the elevator and acting like I meant to be here.

The third floor is almost entirely empty this late in the evening on a Friday, and thank the gods for that. Walking swiftly between the empty rows of cubicles, I head for the back stairs, throwing open the door and pausing on the landing to take a few deep breaths.

Kenna is going on a date tonight.

The outfit she was wearing... black jeans so tight they looked painted onto her skin, and a barely there red tank top under her leather jacket. High heels that made her generous ass and hips sway as she scurried away from me into the lobby.

Where's she going, dressed like that? Who's she seeing? Is some godsdamned male going to have the privilege of sliding those jeans off her later?

It tugs on the wild, feral thing beating against the inside of my chest, and the insistent press of wings beneath my skin makes my muscles burn and ache.

Irrational. I'm being completely fucking irrational right now.

It's none of my damned business where she's going or who she's seeing.

It's what I keep telling myself, what I keep mentally repeating as I jog down the stairs toward the ground floor. I fully intend to head straight for the parking garage and get in my car, drive home, and lock myself safely in my condo for the evening.

Until I open the front door and catch a whiff of her scent on the breeze. Faint, but there, following her to wherever she's going.

A whisper, a taunt, the barest essence of her.

It draws the image of her face to my mind, the deep green of her eyes and the rosy apples of her cheeks. A pair of sinfully full lips I can just imagine turned up in a smirk or bitten to deep red temptation. Her shoulder-length auburn curls and the stubborn tilt of her chin.

On a date with someone else.

I told her we weren't mates, made it clear we weren't *anything*. I was a cold, unfeeling asshole to her. I'm the one with the problem, and I don't need to make it hers as well.

Yet the urge to shift, to follow her, just to *talk* to her so I can try to understand what's going on here, won't leave me alone.

Turning my face to the sky, I wish like anything I could let myself go, take to those skies and soar high, give the dragon his freedom. All the way to my car, the thoughts don't stop spiraling, hounding me, making me want things I have no business wanting.

And even when I'm in the driver's seat, hands clenched hard enough around the steering wheel to make my knuckles white, I can't shake them.

I can't stop seeing Kenna in all her devastating, ruinous glory, walking away from me like she has every right to do.

7

Kenna

My date with the wolf shifter is not going great.

And that's being generous.

Throughout dinner, Dylan regales me with every last detail about his weight lifting and bulking routine between taking big, bloody bites of his rare steak.

I'm no vegetarian, but I almost want to become one with how queasy my stomach gets watching him.

After that, I'm treated to an expletive-filled monologue about the state of the wolf packs in the Pacific Northwest. It would be kind of interesting to learn about, actually, but Mr. Wannabe-Alpha struggles to get through a single sentence without interjecting how badass he is, how all the other packs cower in fear, how he's going to be pack leader in a few years.

God, he looked good on paper. Or, well, on *screen* in the dating app I found him on. Good degree. Good job in finance. I can even admit he's hot, despite the personality. The perfect guy for new-Kenna. If only he wasn't so absolutely insufferable.

I spend most of the date bored and uncomfortable, resisting the urge to check the time.

Old-Kenna probably would have taken him home anyway. Chances are with as self-involved as he is, he would have been a shit lay, but hey, it would have been worth it to find out.

I might have even still given into the urge tonight, let new-Kenna slip a little and let old-Kenna have some fun, if it wasn't for one tiny, annoying fact.

I can't get a pair of sharp, golden eyes out of my memory.

It's pretty damn inconvenient, too, after how much of an ass I made of myself in front of Blair earlier. The way he just stood there and stared at me as I ran away from him like an idiot, the way he didn't say a single freaking word.

"So," Dylan says as we walk down the street outside the restaurant after we've finished dinner. "Where to next?"

Home, I want to say. A bath and a glass of wine and a few episodes of a fluffy sitcom on my laptop in bed sound really, really good right now.

"It's late," I say, shrugging. "And I've had a long week at work. I should probably—"

"There's a great little cocktail bar around here, a couple blocks away. We should go."

All at once, I'm exhausted. Exhausted of this date, exhausted of this whole damn week. So, so tired of being polite Kenna, adult Kenna.

I'm about to open my mouth and tell him that no, I don't want to go have a seventeen dollar drink with him, when a cyclist comes careening around the corner. Dylan grabs me, drawing me out of the way and spinning me so I have my back pressed up against the side of the building.

If he were a dude I actually liked, his quick reflexes might impress me. I'd probably take this as my sign to kiss him and ask if he wants to go to his place or mine, but right now I'm just irritated to be so close to him.

"You're so fucking hot, Kenna." He leans in close, his breath warm and damp and unpleasant on my neck. "If you're not up for a cocktail, my place is just a few blocks from here."

Not a chance, wolf-boy.

I'm about to shut him down when his wet, steak-flavored lips land on mine.

Yup, I'm definitely becoming a vegetarian after this.

I brace my hands on his shoulders to push him back, but he must take that as me encouraging him as he presses harder into me, tongue darting out to smash against my firmly closed lips.

Gross. This is so gross.

Pushing with all my strength, he takes a stumbling step back, eyes wide with surprise. I'm just about to lay into him and give him a ration of shit and a lesson on consent, when a booming roar from above has us both looking skyward. Dylan jumps back another step, looking around for cover, and I'm about to do the same when the roar pierces the air again.

A bright flash of golden scales is the only other warning I get before I'm plucked off the sidewalk by two massive, clawed feet.

8

Kenna

I've been kidnapped.

I've been kidnapped by a damned dragon, and as he drags me higher over downtown Seattle, it takes a few seconds of stunned paralysis to actually realize what's happening.

"What the fuck are you doing?" I shout, hands scrambling over the claws holding me.

Holding me, *just* holding me, not sinking into my flesh or bringing me up to what I imagine is a huge, fang-filled mouth. Which, I mean, small blessings.

The dragon, of course, doesn't answer.

He does tuck me in closer, and I feel a growl rumble through him. I'm pressed up against his scaled belly, kept sheltered from the worst of the wind, and as we climb higher still, I do my best not to look down.

It's not that I've ever had a fear of heights, exactly, but

there's a hell of a difference between being in a tall building or an airplane and only having a set of huge black dragon claws standing between you and plummeting to your death.

When I do glance down briefly, there are tiny figures of people standing on the sidewalks below, pointing toward the sky, aiming their phones' cameras at the spectacle. There are some distant calls—for help maybe, or just of shock—but all of those fade as we climb higher, over the tallest downtown buildings, before the dragon banks sharply and starts heading out of the city.

As the shock starts to wear off, a wave of fear and panic crashes over me.

I know who this is—well, I'm almost certain I know who this is, and it would be a pretty big damn shocker if I'd somehow wound up on the radar of *two* dragons—but I have no idea what he wants or where he's taking me or what he means to do with me.

Blair wouldn't hurt me, would he?

His wings snap fully open as he stops climbing and levels out into a smooth glide, and I glance up to find them spread wide against the backdrop of the night sky. Despite my fear, my eyes widen with something that feels like awe.

Beautiful, this dragon is beautiful.

Golden scales and massive wings, and even his claws are polished to an obsidian-dark shine. Terrifying, too, and probably even more so if I could get a look at his face.

I try to talk to him a couple more times during our flight, asking him where we're headed and what he's going to do with me, but the dragon either doesn't hear me or chooses to ignore me. I'm inclined to believe it's option two, because although I don't get any response, I feel him rumble a couple more growls and squeeze me tighter, like he's nonverbally trying to tell me to shut up.

The flight lasts maybe ten or fifteen minutes, and my

stomach lurches as we begin a dive back down to the ground. Wind whips through my hair, and even though he's still got me held close, I clutch onto his claws and feel him cradle me tighter still.

When the dragon finally sets me down, we're in a forest clearing somewhere that seems like it's far away from the city.

Dark pines tower above us, framed between their branches by a canopy of stars more breathtaking than any I've seen in years, maybe not since the last time I visited home in Idaho.

I take a few stumbling steps over the grassy, mossy ground, and the dragon flies to the other side of the clearing before touching down.

Steadying myself, I get my first good look at him and my breath catches in my throat.

A giant, horned head covered in more of those golden scales, looking like some kind of fairytale creature that would have been guarding a tower with a princess in it. A long, spiked tail, whipping impatiently behind him. A body that's even more massive than I realized when he was carrying me.

He's not looking at me, just standing there huffing, muscles twitching, shaking his head from side to side in irritation. But when I take a step into the clearing, breaking a twig under my foot, the dragon snaps to attention like he's getting ready to strike, and his focus zeros in on me immediately.

My entire body freezes. I know those eyes.

Much larger now, but they're the same shimmering gold that tracked my retreat earlier this evening, the same ones that had me pinned in place that first day at the Bureau.

"Blair?"

The dragon doesn't make any sound where he's crouched low to the ground, but his eyes flicker slightly, the only acknowledgment I'm going to get from him.

The only thing I'm going to get from him period, apparently, because a moment later he stands back up and turns his huge, graceful body away from me, toward the darkness of the forest.

"Hey!" I call after him, taking a couple more tentative steps into the clearing. "You're not just going to leave me out here!"

The dragon doesn't respond. Because of course he doesn't.

I pull my phone out of my jacket pocket—to do what, I'm not sure, call 911? Call an Uber to take me home?—and find it completely out of range of cell service.

Great. Just perfect.

"Blair!" Is it wise to shout after a retreating dragon? Hell if I know, but I'm absolutely livid right now. I've been kidnapped, and I'm not about to be left for dead in the middle of some forest. "Hey! Lizard! I'm talking to you!"

A tremor runs through his enormous frame, and when he whips back around to face me, his golden eyes are burning as he lets out a low, ominous snarl.

"Oh. Shit."

The dragon stalks closer, body moving in hypnotic, sinuous waves, and forked tongue flicking out to scent the air. I should back away, maybe try to run, but fear and panic keep me rooted to the spot.

How much of Blair is in there right now?

I don't want to be a coward, and I don't want to look away, but as he comes to stand just a couple of feet from me, I can't help it. I close my eyes, fight the shudder that's threatening to break over me, and although I'm not a praying woman, I silently send up a request to any gods who may be listening not to become a dragon's snack tonight.

"That male is lucky to still be alive," a rough, hissing voice rasps out into the night air.

My eyes fly open, and I'm face-to-face with Blair.

Only... it's not Blair. Not quite.

He's more man-shaped now than dragon, and his face is almost the same, but he's taller, broader than his normal human form. His skin is also accented with more of those golden scales, and two enormous wings spread from his back.

He's in a half-shift, if I had to guess. Terrifying and awe-inspiring as he stares at me with molten eyes that burn from the inside out.

He's also naked. Very naked.

The scales covering his shoulders and biceps flash in the moonlight as his thick muscles contract and relax. More scales scatter across his chest, wind down his flanks, and wrap around his lower abs, flowing right into...

Nope. Absolutely not. I'm not finding out if he's got a scale-covered cock.

Belatedly remembering he's just said something to me, I pull my gaze back up to his face. A shiver races down my spine as I'm pinned in place once more by those fire-bright eyes.

"W-why?" I stutter.

"He kissed you," Blair says, voice still deep, but with more of a hiss than his usual graveled timbre. "Without your consent."

Oh, so that's what we're doing out here? Letting Blair play white knight?

I shake my head, trying to sort through my racing thoughts. "And what? *Kidnapping* me is somehow better?"

A harsh, rumbling sound echoes in his chest, and I freeze up again. Maybe it's not a great idea to antagonize the snarly dragon man.

But... fuck that. I know monsters, and they don't act like this. Blair is a rational man when he's not in this form. A cold bastard, yes, but rational. Not like this.

"I'd like to speak to the human version of you, please."

A flash in those golden eyes, but he doesn't answer me. Which… perfect. Just great. Back to making an ass of myself in front of this dragon and getting absolutely nothing in return.

Well, almost nothing. Because even though he doesn't speak, Blair leans closer to me, and I swear I can feel the heat of him radiating across the distance between us. His wings flare wide, blocking out the light of the moon and reminding me just how far from human he is right now.

I can't make myself move away.

I can't do *anything* as he inhales deeply, leans closer still. And when I impulsively follow his lead, swaying into him, I know I'm in trouble.

I need to snap the fuck out of it. Now's not the time to realize I'm still attracted to him when he's half-reptile, and I need to remember I'm beyond pissed at him right now for pulling this stunt.

"Where are we?" I ask, taking a step back.

Still no answer.

"I need you to take me back to Seattle."

Nothing.

I'm not sticking around for this. We didn't fly *that* far, and there's got to be a road around here where I can flag down a car for help.

"Fine," I tell him. "Don't talk to me, then. I'll find my own way home."

Turning on my heel, dread rises in my stomach over the fact that I truly have no idea where I'm going or what I'm about to do. But even though I'm probably standing on more pride than I should be right now, I head toward the cover of the trees.

"Kenna." That harsh, hissing voice stops me in my tracks.

"Come back here."

9

Blair

For the first time in my existence, I'm not able to pull out of my shift.

Not fully, at least, and even in my half-shift, I still feel half out of my mind, half lost to the dragon. It's making it difficult to put my thoughts into words, difficult to do anything but keep my eyes trained on the woman walking away from me.

"Kenna. Come back here."

She freezes, but doesn't turn around right away. As I wait for her to decide what she's going to do, hot shame washes through me.

I didn't mean to do this.

I made it almost all the way home. I parked in my condo's garage downtown, got out of my car, and caught the scent of her somewhere nearby.

Even then, when I followed that scent to a little plaza

across from a block of busy bars and restaurants, I didn't mean to approach her. Stalking her to where she was walking down the street with her date was bad, but seeing the male she was with push her up against a wall, kiss her even though she was struggling, it broke the very last threads of my restraint.

Still, I had no right to take her.

I know it, and Kenna knows it too as she finally comes back to stand in front of me, livid anger vibrating through her.

"You don't get to do this, Blair."

I don't like hearing her say my name. At least, not that one.

Blair.

It's what I've mainly gone by for the last two or three hundred years. It's become natural to hear and even to think of myself using that name.

It's not the one I want her to use.

Why it should matter at all to me, I don't know. Not that I have time to contemplate it, not when Kenna's still laying into me with devastating precision.

"If this is some kind of shifter instinct thing, you need to figure it the fuck out. Deal with whatever shit it is you need to deal with, and leave me out of it."

The mouth on this woman. If all her profane ire wasn't directed at me, I'd almost be amused by it.

"You say it's not a mating thing, fine. Then don't get all dickish and agro and possessive like someone else just picked up the toy you wanted to play with... Are you even listening to me?"

I am. Sort of. Because it's pretty damned hard to concentrate on all the different ways she's insulting me when she's still all wind-rumpled and pink-cheeked from flying here, and when those jeans she's wearing cling to her thick thighs like a second skin.

She snaps her fingers in my face, and the motion of it makes her breasts bounce in a way that draws my attention immediately.

I'm being an ass right now. I'm being a beast right now.

The more elevated side of my brain knows it, but that side isn't really in charge at the moment.

"Un-fucking-believable." Kenna throws her hands in the air in frustration before turning around and stomping away from me toward the forest at the edge of the clearing.

"Stop," I grate out. "Do you even know where you're going?"

She whirls back around. "No, Blair, I don't know where I'm going. And do you know why that is?"

I huff out a breath, not answering her rhetorical question.

"No? Not even a guess? I'll clue you in. It's because some fucking dragon kidnapped me and brought me out into the middle of nowhere and won't have a normal conversation with me to try to figure all of this out."

She steps closer to me while she speaks, not afraid for a second, temper growing hotter and more vibrant with every word. By the time she finishes her tirade, she's only a few inches away from me, poking her index finger into my bare chest. My skin burns at the contact.

Kenna is close enough that I could pull her to me, kiss the rest of those insults off her lips, wrap her riot of curls around my fist and—

"*You* did this, asshole," she continues, cutting off that particular train of thought with incandescent anger flowing off her in waves. "And now you refuse to be reasonable and control your damn shift so we can talk. So I'm going to find someone else who can help me."

Magnificent. Kenna Byrne is magnificent.

She's also a big damn problem right now, and one of my own making. Slowly, the primal haze is receding and reason is taking back over. With it comes the stunning clarity of just how badly I've fucked up.

I kidnapped her. Plucked her right off the street in the middle of downtown Seattle and carried her away like some kind of war prize.

And what a prize she is.

Staring at me with her hands on her hips and embers kindling in those beautiful green eyes, she looks as if she'd like to set me ablaze in my own dragon fire.

Joke's on her, though, because I'm already burning. With shame, with regret, with the lingering remnants of the fiery instinct that made me take her in the first place. I'm being charred from the inside out, and I don't know how to make it stop.

Patience finally snapping, she shakes her head and lets out a short, scorn-filled laugh. "I'm outta here. Have a nice flight back to the city."

I can't think, can't concentrate, can't speak. My throat is clogged with self-loathing, and the weight of the mistakes I've made tonight press down on my chest like a load of cinder blocks.

I need to get out of here. But I need to figure out what to do with her first.

"Stop," I hiss, and she does, turning back around and opening her mouth to chastise me some more.

Shifting back into my full dragon form, I take a few stalking steps forward. Kenna's eyes go wide.

"Oh no," she says, backing away. "Oh no, you are absolutely not going to—"

She doesn't get to finish her sentence before I snatch her up and carry her away into the night.

10

Kenna

Blair really needs to learn how to use his words.

He plunks me down on a very familiar doorstep then takes off again, not even giving me the courtesy of a roared goodbye.

"Yeah? Well fuck you, too!" I holler as he flies away into the night.

I turn to knock on the door, but it's already opening. I'm met by Elias, Nora's mate, looking at me utterly confused.

"Kenna? Is everything alright?"

For the first time tonight, it hits me—really hits me—just how messed up all of this is. Slowly, I shake my head.

"What happened?" he asks, brow furrowing in concern.

I gesture vaguely at the sky. "Blair. Blair happened."

"Ewan Blair?"

Ewan. Seems strange to associate that name with him. I

think I've only ever heard Nora use it a time or two, and just assumed he always went by Blair.

"Yes," I say. "He, uh, kidnapped me."

Elias's mouth falls open in shock.

Before he can answer, though, Nora joins him in the doorway, eyes darting over my face and expression drawn with concern. "Kenna? What's wrong?"

I must look a little worse for wear after my two flights, or maybe it's the exhaustion of the last few hours catching up to me. Whatever it is, I shake my head, unable to find the words.

Nora's outside a moment later, wrapping her arms around me. "Hey. It's alright."

I take a deep, shaky breath. "I'm fine. Really. Just dealing with a nuisance dragon who has an impulse control problem."

"Blair?" Nora asks, just as shocked as her mate.

It almost makes me want to laugh. Apparently I'm the only one the dragon loses his mind over.

"The one and only. Can someone give me a ride back to the city?"

Nora glances around, sees that there's no additional car in the driveway, and then turns her eyes skyward. Elias does the same, a deep frown on his face.

"He didn't... bring you all the way out here, did he? And just leave you?" Nora asks.

"Bingo," I tell her. "And unfortunately, the Uber back to Seattle would be a little outside my budget."

"I'll drive you," she assures me. "I'm just... what happened?"

"I'll tell you about it on the way."

She nods, heads back inside to get her keys, and I give Elias one last weak smile before heading to get into the passenger side of Nora's car. Slumping against the seat, I stare blankly out the window, watching as Nora reappears, kisses Elias, and walks to the car. He stays in the doorway as she goes, watching her the whole way, then waving as we pull out of the driveway.

The sight of them puts an ache in my chest. A happy one, considering how winding and challenging their path to each other was, but also one that twists and tightens unexpectedly somewhere in the vicinity of my heart.

Pulling out of the long, gated driveway and onto the road, Nora keeps glancing over at me nervously.

"You don't have to tell me anything you're not comfortable sharing," she says. "But I'm honestly shocked that Blair would be so..."

"Impulsive? Reckless? Brutish?" I supply a few adjectives.

Nora lets out a sigh. "That's not the Blair I know."

"Yeah," I say, trying not to let the bitterness creep into my voice. "I guess I'm just special."

Nora makes a small, concerned noise in the back of her throat. "Did he... hurt you? Do you want to go to the police?"

I shake my head slowly. "No, he didn't hurt me. And... I don't know. He seemed like he really regretted it, like he knew he fucked up. Or, at least that's what I'm assuming. He was barely able to speak to me."

"That still doesn't give him the right to just take you."

"He gave me back, didn't he?" I say with a small, hollow laugh.

"Kenna," Nora says warily.

"I know."

What I know, I'm not exactly certain, but I don't think I want to get Blair in trouble. What I want more than anything is just to talk to him, for him to explain what's going on in that thick dragon skull of his. But with how our last few interactions have gone, I'm beginning to think there's little to no chance of that ever happening.

Sighing again, I lean my head back against the seat and close my eyes. "He kidnapped me when my date tried to stick his tongue down my throat."

"What? The shifter?"

I told Nora and Holly all about my hot date when we got together last night for our weekly thirsty Thursday wine night at Holly's place. They'd been encouraging, supportive, just as impressed with the wolf boy's credentials as I had been.

"Yeah. The shifter. Total dud, actually. And not too good at realizing when a woman doesn't want to be slobbered over."

"Shit, Kenna. I'm sorry. But how does Blair come into it?"

"As soon as the wolf started mauling me, Blair was just... there. Shifted. Swooped right down and carried me off."

A startled laugh breaks from Nora's mouth, and she immediately pulls one hand off the steering wheel to stifle it. "I'm sorry. Truly. I don't mean to laugh. It's not funny."

An exhausted, slightly hysterical giggle rises in my own chest. "It is *kinda* funny."

As we continue on toward Seattle, I tell her the rest of it. How Blair locked onto me that first day at the Bureau, our conversation in his office, the elevator ride.

"And he claims it's not a mating thing?"

I grimace. "Absolutely, unequivocally not a mating thing."

Glancing over at Nora, she still has her eyes on the road, but her brow is furrowed in concern.

"What is it?" I ask.

"Blair just has... a complicated history when it comes to mates."

"Care to elaborate?"

She shakes her head slowly. "I don't know how much I

should say, and it's not really my story to tell, but there's... baggage there. A lot of loss and grief."

I don't press her for more details, but even that little bit of information feels like *something*. Some small part of the tangled, infuriating puzzle that is Ewan Blair.

"It doesn't give him a pass, though," Nora continues. "Even with what he's been through, he knows better than to act the way he did tonight."

"Agreed."

"These shifters," Nora says, exasperation creeping into her voice. "Centuries old, and they still act like fools sometimes."

The corners of my mouth quirk up in an unlikely smile. "Maybe, but at least yours comes with some fun accessories."

Nora snorts. "Again, Kenna, you're never going to make me spill on my sex life with Elias."

"Alright," I concede. "But you're still a lucky, lucky woman to have found him."

Ever since Nora and Elias got together, and ever since they dealt with all the shit with her ex, Nora has been different. Lighter, more confident, at peace. I liked her immediately when she moved to Seattle and started working at the same bookstore I had been, and seeing how much she's come into her own this last year has been wonderful.

"I know," she says, and the soft affection in her voice makes my chest ache again.

We're mostly quiet for the rest of the drive, and when we pull up outside the old Victorian home I rent a room in, Nora looks over at me.

"Is there anything else you'd like me to do?" she asks. "Talk to Blair maybe, find out if he—"

"No," I cut her off, mortification rising in my throat at the idea. "No. It's fine. I can deal with the dragon."

She doesn't look convinced, but must decide to let it go for now as she gives me a small smile.

"Call me, okay? If there's anything Elias or I can do for you."

I nod, thank her again for the ride, and head inside.

The Victorian is the first place that's really felt like home since I left Idaho. Painted a vibrant turquoise, with bright white accents and plenty of intricate wooden scrollwork and trim that make it look like a dollhouse, the outside is almost as whimsical as the tenants who make their home inside.

My friend Fran inherited it from her late aunt, and has filled it up with misfit humans and monsters looking for a place in the city. As I step inside, she calls out to me from where she's sitting with her partner, Bruno, in the living room just off the entry.

"How was the date?"

A lump settles at the base of my throat, but I swallow around it. "It was, uh, fine, I guess. Uneventful."

"Bummer," she says. "Hope the next one's more exciting. Wanna talk about it?"

I shake my head. "Nah. I'm pretty tired. Think I'll head up to bed."

"Alright. Good night."

Thankfully, I don't run into any of my other roommates as I head upstairs, and when I close my bedroom door behind me, all the rest of the wind goes out of my sails. I slump against the door for a few long moments, breathing deep and pressing the heels of my palms against my eyes to try to keep a sudden wave of tears at bay.

Fuck. Just... fuck.

I don't want to cry over Blair. Damn dragon. I didn't ask for this, and all I wanted was the chance to talk to him, understand him a little, and he couldn't even give me that.

Kidnapping me was insane, yes, but he at least owed me an explanation.

He *owes* me an explanation, and I mean to have it.

All of this is insane. From that very first day at the Bureau, there's been something between us. Something beyond simple attraction or interest. Something that made him irrational enough to pluck me off the sidewalk, and makes *me* irrational enough not to hate him for it entirely and still want to get to the bottom of this.

Letting out a sigh and stripping off my jacket and my shoes, running a hand through my wind-tangled hair, I start mentally formulating my plan for Monday.

That damned dragon owes me some answers, and he's not getting off the hook this time.

11

Blair

Cleo slaps a newspaper down on my desk on Monday morning. There, in a story on the front page, is a blurry image of a golden dragon snatching a woman off the sidewalk.

"Care to explain?"

I glance down at the paper for a second before turning my gaze back to my computer. "The Mariners are looking good this season."

"I wasn't talking about the sports section."

I know she wasn't, just like I know I'm not about to acknowledge the write-up below the fold about how they still haven't identified the rogue dragon who kidnapped a woman in downtown Seattle Friday night.

My name hasn't come into it, mainly because there are very few people who know exactly what I am. Even when Elias and I went public as the founders of Morgan-Blair—the company Elias now runs—we didn't disclose what kind of shifters we were, exactly. Cleo knows, but she's one of the few at the Bureau who do.

Some might call it dishonesty, but frankly I don't see how it's anyone's business what's lurking beneath my skin.

Kenna's name hasn't been brought up in the press, either, and thank the gods for small blessings. She doesn't need to be dealing with that, too.

"Blair." Cleo's voice is hard, and when I glance up at her, she's scowling at me. "What the hell is going on?"

It's a mark of the years we've spent in contentious cooperation that I don't bat an eye at her language. She can speak to me however she wants, doesn't mean she's going to get an answer.

"It's handled," I say, crossing my arms over my chest and leaning back in my chair.

"Doesn't look handled." She sits in one of the chairs across the desk, red eyes flashing with irritation. "Looks like a big damn mess."

"It's not a problem."

That might be a lie. Might not be a lie, either, since I didn't have any cops showing up at my door this weekend to arrest me. Just a call from a very confused and disappointed kraken, though even for Elias I didn't feel the need to explain myself.

No, the only person I owe an explanation to is the same one who still has the power to blow this whole thing up in my face.

And I wouldn't even blame Kenna if she did.

I couldn't help but look her up on the Bureau's internal chat software this morning. There, right next to her name, was a little green checkmark letting me know she's here in the building, working down in the communications department. I haven't seen her, and even reined myself in from calling Nora to find out how she was on Friday night after Elias let me know Nora drove her home.

It's been burning me up all weekend. The guilt. The shame. The lingering, insane urge to seek Kenna out, apologize to her, an urge that would probably just lead to more harm than good.

Cleo shakes her head. "Blair—"

"I'm not discussing it," I say firmly, shutting the conversation down. "How are preparations going for the visit from HHS?"

She purses her lips, but lets it go. "Good. Just waiting on final confirmation from Harrison on when he and his staff will be arriving."

The HHS Deputy Secretary has been a pain in the ass the last few months. Demanding increased transparency about Bureau activities, hyper-critical of every cent spent, despite that money having been allocated to keep our programs running.

"Any idea how much shit he's planning to shovel our way?"

"Harrison's going to be a problem," she says, all business. "He's ready to come in here and swing his arrogant damn prick around, work the PR and public perception angle. And let me tell you, this little kidnapping story isn't going to play well into that. Not even after all the shit with Sorenson last fall."

Nonsensically, the whole Sorenson ordeal stirred up even more anti-monster sentiment, rather than highlighting the depth of hypocrisy within the US government when it comes to paranormal relations. But it turns out having a sitting congressman use confidential Bureau information to stalk and kidnap his ex girlfriend didn't do anything to sway those who already had their minds set against paranormals integrating into human society.

"Allow me to play devil's advocate for a moment," Cleo

leans forward to rest her elbows on the desk. "What if there was a way for us to beat these bastards at their own game?"

"I'm listening."

"A whisper campaign," she says, lip curling back in a satisfied smirk that shows one of her gleaming white fangs. "Planting some of our own stories, riling up public support in favor of paranormals. Gods know there's enough out there that we could dredge up."

A pang of unease moves through me, and Cleo jumps on it immediately.

"None of it will be traced back to the Bureau. Trust me. I know how to do this right."

I don't doubt that for a moment.

In another life, Cleo was a ruthless executive in the corporate sector. Back in a time when she wore veneers to hide her fangs and contacts to hide her red eyes, and never let her half-vamp status be known to anyone other than her family and closest friends.

Still, that doesn't mean I'm not wary about putting those special talents of hers to use now, not when the lives and futures of so many depend on the decisions we make here.

"I can put Ophelia on it," Cleo adds when I don't reply right away.

Despite myself, the suggestion draws a short laugh from me. "You think it's time to call out guns that big?"

Ophelia—Cleo's younger, fully human sister—doesn't work for the Bureau. At least not in an official capacity. By all technicalities she's an independent contractor, but in reality she's one of the best assets we have when it comes to private investigation. Despite not being paranormal, the woman's got an uncanny knack for finding the unfindable, and moving in circles no human should rightly have access to.

Cleo grins. "She's getting bored. It's been, what? Four or five months since we gave her anything juicy? She's more than ready to get back in the field."

"I'll think about it," I relent. "Hold tight on it for now."

She agrees, and we move on to other topics. We spend the next fifteen minutes discussing the HHS visit, and a few changes to some of the benefits programs we've been providing for paranormals looking to enter the human world, but when a soft knock sounds from the other side of my office door, we both turn to look.

"You've got another meeting?" Cleo asks.

I frown. "Not that I'm aware of."

When I call out to whoever's on the other side to come in, Ruthie sticks her head in.

"Mr. Blair. I have Ms. Byrne here for you."

The weight of both Ruthie and Cleo's gazes settles on me like a brand, putting me directly under the guilty spotlight I've earned for myself.

"Give us a moment," I tell Ruthie, and she nods before shutting the door softly behind her.

Cleo shoots me a skeptical look, waiting, judging. "I thought you said it's taken care of."

"It is," I say brusquely. "And I've still got you on the calendar for later this week to finalize everything for HHS."

Taking the hint, she lets out a long, exasperated breath, gathers her things, and stands, shaking her head with unmistakable disappointment.

"None of this is going to be for shit if all this mess blows back on the Director of the Bureau," she says, holding up the newspaper in her hand. "You know that, right? What a disaster this could be?"

"I'm aware."

With a final admonishing look, she turns to go.

"Cleo," I call after her.

"Hmmm?" she asks, one eyebrow raised.

I stand. "I forgot to say congratulations. On you and Stephanie's anniversary."

A slow, wry smile spreads over her face. "I'm surprised you remembered."

"Of course I remembered. I was at the wedding, wasn't I?"

Cleo laughs and shakes her head. "It would be a lot easier to be mad at you if you didn't say shit like that, you know?"

"I know. And tell Steph I said hi and congrats."

"I will," she says, giving me a wave over her shoulder as she turns to go.

Before the door fully closes behind her, Ruthie appears again, followed by the one person I'd been hoping and dreading to speak to today.

Like she can sense the tension that springs up immediately in the room, Ruthie leaves silently, shooting me a glance of concern as she goes.

The door closes behind her with the finality of a death knell.

As soon as Kenna and I are alone, a lick of that same flame from Friday kicks up in my veins. Hot and urgent and undeniable, I try to shove it down the best I can, even while I drink in the sight of her.

She's wearing a dress today. It's a little gray number that might almost be matronly with its high neckline and elbow-length sleeves, but the way it's cut to hug every one of her ample curves undermines that modesty entirely.

My palms and fingers itch to reach out and touch, but I clear my throat and gesture toward the chairs in front of the desk. "Would you like to sit down?"

Kenna doesn't budge, just tilts her head and studies me. "So, I'm going to get to speak to human Blair today?"

That little bit of sass makes my palms itch even more. "Yes. And I meant to reach out to you, to offer an—"

"I think we're beyond another apology." Her green eyes light with temper, and she walks over to stand across the desk from me. "Don't you?"

Gods, the things that temper does to me. Just like Friday, her spark seems to catch against my own. Two lit matches that might send us both up in flames.

Shaking my head, I make myself concentrate.

"I was out of line," I tell her. "And I take full responsibility for that. I was... not myself."

She frowns. "What does that mean?"

"It means I should have had better control of my emotions and my instincts. I didn't, and none of that's your fault."

Kenna's eyes flicker at the admission, but beyond that she doesn't give an inch. And good for her. She shouldn't give an inch, not a single damn millimeter, not with the way I've behaved.

She lets out a short, humorless laugh before she speaks again. "I know it's not my fault. I just want to understand why. Why is it me that's got you like this?"

I don't know how to answer her.

"Or, fine, whatever," she continues when I don't speak. "If you don't want to tell me why and don't want anything to do with me, fine. But that means you have to leave me the hell alone. Nothing like Friday night can ever happen again."

Leave her alone? The dragon in me bristles with displeasure at the idea.

Coming out from behind the desk, I circle it to stand in front of her. "Is that what you'd like, Kenna? For me to leave you alone?"

"I'd like for you to *talk* to me and explain what's going on here."

The fact that I didn't get an immediate 'yes' to that question is... bad. Bad for me, bad for her, bad for my self-control. I take a deep breath, trying to think how to even begin explaining my actions, when she speaks up again, changing the topic entirely.

"Do you know what was all over Twitter the last two days?" She fishes her phone from her pocket and flashes the screen at me.

There are photos, videos, news stories about the dragon kidnapping in downtown Seattle this weekend. Fortunately, all the images that have come out are grainy and blurred, with nothing other than the flash of red hair even hinting it's Kenna.

I've seen all the coverage, of course, but confronted with it here, now, facing the woman who's borne the brunt of my recklessness, hot shame washes over me once more.

"And that's not even the half of it," Kenna goes on, shoving her phone back in her pocket with a disgruntled huff. "Apparently my date must have reported it, because I had two cops show up at my house this weekend, asking me if I wanted to open up a case and press charges."

A shot of ice moves through my veins. "What did you tell them?"

Kenna studies my face for a moment, keeping me on the hook before she answers. "I told them I didn't want to. I kept your name out of it."

Some of the ice leeches out of my blood, but I shake my head, not fully comprehending. "Why? It would have been well within your rights."

Her eyes narrow, and she takes a step closer to me, close enough to touch if I were foolish enough to reach a hand out and feel the heat of her. "Is that what you want me to do? Get you arrested? Would that be preferable to actually talking to me about what the hell happened on Friday?"

How can I talk to her about it when I hardly understand it myself?

She's still watching me, eyes sharp and keen on my face as if she can read me just like I read everyone else. It's unnerving, her inspection. Like she's cutting through the layers of distance and protection I've kept wrapped around myself for years, decades, centuries. Like she can see the man and the dragon beneath.

"So are you going to?"

"Going to what?" I ask, realizing I've forgotten the question.

"Talk to me about it."

Her tone is different now—lower, softer. As she speaks, she takes another half-step toward me until there are only a couple of inches between us.

From this distance, I can see flecks of gold in her green eyes, the little crinkles at the corners that show how often she must laugh and smile.

"I don't know what to say, Kenna. Other than I'm sorry."

"Just sorry?" There's a hint of challenge in her voice now. "That's all? You're not going to admit why you took me in the first place?"

That challenge tugs on something deep and dark in the far corner of my psyche.

Gods, this is madness. The same madness that made me take her on Friday. The same one that made hers the only face in a sea of hundreds I could see that very first day.

I need to step away, to move back, to reclaim some semblance of sanity and self-control. But as the silent seconds tick by, I don't. I can't. Not with her question and that challenge lingering between us. To retreat would be unthinkable. A defeat my dragon can't allow.

"Why, Blair? Why'd you do it?"

"Because I wanted to."

She inhales sharply, and I smother the sound with my

mouth.

Kenna tastes just like she smells—citrus and ginger and a dark note of desire. She freezes for half a second before melting into the kiss, hands shooting up to clutch at my shoulders as she parts her lips for me. The harsh sound I let out is one of pure want, pure pleasure as I savor the taste of her, stroking my tongue deep and swallowing her own little moan when I wrap my arms around her.

She presses closer to me, body soft and yielding beneath my hands.

Perfect. Just perfect. Like I knew she would be.

Still, a moment later, she pulls her mouth away from mine. Her eyes are glazed, breath coming hard and fast, and she takes a few seconds to gather her thoughts enough to speak.

"What are you doing?"

"I don't know. Fuck, Kenna. I don't know what this—"

Kenna isn't gentle when she kisses me. With her hands fisted into my hair and her sharp little teeth nipping at my lip, I groan into her mouth and surrender.

12

Kenna

New-Kenna has left the building.

I'm kissing a dragon. Full-on making out with Director Ewan Blair himself.

This isn't what I intended when I marched up to his office to demand an explanation for Friday, but any thoughts about what I meant to happen fly out the window as soon as his lips and hands are on me.

I tug at his hair, fit my body into the hard contours of his, and he groans into my mouth before pulling away slightly.

"Just a little ember, aren't you?" he says in a rough whisper. "Ready to spark a flame and burn me to ash."

I don't know what he means, but he buries a hand into my hair as he speaks, wrapping my curls around his fist. The expression on his face is almost pained.

Still, when he drags my face back to his, kisses me rough

and deep, it's not hesitation I taste. No, it's want and need and sex. It's dark spice and the faintest hint of smoke, hot and stirring and altogether too tempting.

His other hand splays over my ass, lifting me up onto the desk. Blair knocks my knees apart with one of his thick thighs and steps between them, using the hold he has on my hair to tip my head back and deepen the kiss.

God, it's good. Maybe the best kiss I've ever had. Blair is demanding, relentless, not giving me anywhere to hide as he plunders me. He's taken total control and I don't mind it for a second. I melt into him like my body already knows how right this is, how easy, how good it would feel to let go and burn with him completely.

Between us, the hard, insistent press of his erection bulges against the fitted gray slacks he's wearing. When the position I'm in has my dress sliding higher on my thighs, he presses himself deeper between them.

I moan at the contact, bucking my hips and straining into him. He pushes right back, breaking our kiss to look down and watch himself grind into me. When he meets my gaze again, his gold eyes are nearly glowing with excitement, but whatever it is he sees on my own lust-hazed face makes those fires dim.

"Kenna," he whispers, reaching up to curl a hand around my jaw, brushing his thumb over my tender bottom lip. "I'm —"

"If you say *sorry*, so help me god, I'll—"

"Fine," he says roughly. "I'm not sorry. But this is... not the best place to be doing this."

Shit. Right. We're at the Paranormal Citizens Relations Bureau. In the Director's office.

Funny, how easy it was to forget that.

Especially when Blair's still standing between my thighs with his hard-on pressed against me.

My face flushes with shame and embarrassment, and he steps back. I follow, hopping down from the desk and tugging my dress back into place.

"Do you have a mirror somewhere?"

He moves silently to a door at the side of the room and opens it, revealing a coat closet with a mirror inside. Walking over to stand in front of it, a small, pained whimper slips out of me.

I'm a mess. Hair a tangled nest, lips red and kiss-swollen. Blair's still standing behind me, and when I meet his eyes in the mirror, they're burning again. He looks away quickly and crosses to his desk.

"I think I have a comb in here."

He hands it over, and I spend the next couple minutes silently, awkwardly trying to fix myself up. The mindless haze is receding, and shame is creeping up to take its place.

This is exactly what I didn't need to happen.

Blair's still hovering in the middle of the room, hands in his pockets, not doing anything, not saying anything. The tense silence stretches on long enough that I want to jump out of my skin.

How did I fuck this up so spectacularly?

This job, this opportunity, it was all supposed to be the chance I needed to grow up a little, stop pulling shit like this. Yet here I am.

Only this time, it feels worse. It feels bigger and more dangerous, something that might send my whole life up in flames if I'm not careful. Because even now, even when I'm choked with the self-loathing of it all, I'm still aware of him. *Too* aware of him. Skin humming, body aching, mouth swollen and tingling with the taste of Ewan Blair.

"Kenna," Blair says, voice tight and hesitant. "I—"

"I need to get back to my desk. This was... let's just forget it, alright? No more kidnapping, and we'll be square?"

I'm letting him off the hook when I shouldn't be, but I truly, truly can't deal with this right now. I shouldn't be doing this. Not with him. Not here. Not when I finally have the chance to be someone different than I've always been.

I can't reason any of this out, not when my heart's still racing and my mind feels fuzzy and empty. Not when my pussy is damp and aching for him, and when part of me wants nothing more than to launch myself at him and get another taste.

Taking a deep, steadying breath, I paste the widest, brightest smile I'm able to summon onto my face. "Sound good?"

"If that's what you want, Kenna."

"It's what I want," I tell him, still with that bright smile that's making my cheeks hurt. "So, see you around, I guess."

Blair, apparently with no desire to say anything else, just nods. Taking that as my cue to go, I turn and head to the door before I can make any more life-ruining mistakes.

13

Blair

My office still smells like Kenna Byrne.

Even three days later, her scent lingers in the air. With each deep inhale I'm reminded of the taste of her, the press of her warm, willing body against mine.

It's distracting as hell, but I don't know what to do about it other than ignore it and wait for it to fade.

I need to let it fade. I need to forget about it. I need to stop looking for her each morning when I walk through the lobby and stop checking the Bureau chat software to see when she's online.

I also need to send the suit I wore that day in for dry cleaning. I *will* send the suit I was wearing for dry cleaning. The fact that it's still hanging in the back of my closet, bringing the faintest whiff of her into my home, doesn't mean anything at all.

None of it does.

I'm not sure what's more pathetic, spending the last three days covertly savoring the scent of her, or lying to myself about doing it.

Because as hard as I try and as much as I want to, no part of me can stop thinking about Kenna Byrne.

Still, knowing how precarious all of this is, and understanding what the consequences for myself and the Bureau still might be, I at least need to try to keep my distance. Besides, it's what Kenna implied herself, isn't it? The kiss was a mistake. All of this was a mistake, and one that we have absolutely no business repeating or dwelling on.

Thursday morning rolls around, and that's exactly what I've done. I haven't seen her. I haven't spoken to her. I've done everything I can to put her out of my mind completely.

Well, at least until I find a meddling kraken waiting for me in my office when I arrive.

"Remind me to have your visitor's pass revoked," I grumble to Elias as I store my coat in the closet—the same closet where Kenna tried to fix herself up after I made such a mess of her—and sit down at my desk.

Elias just smirks at me, looking completely at home in the space where he knows full well he's always welcome to stop by for a visit.

Once upon a time, Elias and I shared an office. Back in the early days of Morgan-Blair Enterprises, well over a century ago, when we'd both dedicated our lives to building a company founded and run by paranormal creatures of all types.

Elias is at the helm of the company now after my departure a few decades back, and has taken Morgan-Blair to heights we never could have imagined all those years ago. He's also taken the truth about the company and those who work there from the shadows into the light. He's deftly guided it forward through immense obstacles, and in defiance of those who'd rather not do business with a monster-run organization.

Building Morgan-Blair with him was good work, meaningful work, work that felt like atoning after the era of our lives that had come before. The one that cost me my mate.

Though our paths have woven together and apart over the two and a half-centuries we've known each other, and though we still carry some of those shadows between us, I count Elias Morgan as my closest friend.

Regardless, it doesn't mean I'm thrilled to see the kraken this morning. Especially considering how well he's always able to read me, and given the fact it was his doorstep I plunked Kenna down on Friday night.

Elias, the smug bastard that he is, inhales deeply and arches a brow at me "New cologne?"

"What do you want, Elias?"

He shrugs. "Can't I just stop by for a friendly chat?"

"Thought you were too busy for that these days."

"Fair enough. My free time has been in shockingly short supply these past six months."

Though I grumble a little at that, it's with no true malice. Of all the things I could gripe at Elias about, him finding his happiness with Nora will never be one.

"Something else interesting about having a mate," Elias goes on with a knowing tone to his voice, "is that she introduced me to her friends. One in particular who I think you might—"

"If you're here to lecture me about Kenna Byrne, you can save your breath."

I don't mean to put as much char in the words as I do, but whatever Elias hears in my voice, it makes his smile fade.

"Blair," he says cautiously. "You kidnapped her."

"I'm aware."

He lets out his breath in a disbelieving huff. "That's all you have to say? Because, as I seem to recall, you had some very choice words for me about violating a woman's autonomy last fall, even in pursuit of a mate."

"She's not my mate."

The words fall with a weight and finality that ring discordantly through me.

It's also enough to shut Elias up. His lips press into a thin, skeptical line as he leans back in his chair and crosses his arms over his chest.

"This isn't like it was with Lizzy."

At my use of her name, Elias goes absolutely still. He's aware, as am I, that this might just be the first time I've spoken it aloud in more than two hundred years.

"How's it different?"

"It just… is." It's a non-answer, but it's the only one I can give.

If I'm being honest with myself, I can't exactly remember how it was with Lizzy. The shape of it is there, of course—the immediate connection when I met her, the complete devastation when she was gone—but the finer details have been lost to time like so much else has.

"But you're drawn to her. To Kenna," Elias prompts gently.

Something in me bristles at the mention of her in such close proximity to Lizzy. It's wrong, somehow, to compare them, to dredge up a ghost and hold her like some sort of standard to a living, breathing woman.

"It's just different," I say gruffly.

"So what made you take her?"

The million dollar question. If I knew, maybe I'd be able to deal with it and leave her alone. If I knew, maybe I'd be able to stop the persistent ache in my muscles and the fire in my blood that flares every time I get another whiff of her scent.

"Blair," Elias prods when I don't answer.

"Damned if I know," I mutter. "Old age, maybe, or the fact that I don't shift as much as I used to. Some kind of instinct gone haywire."

Elias chuckles. "You've barely reached middle age. Don't try to tell me you're headed into your golden years."

Dragons and krakens both have unfathomably long lifespans, though my kind live time and a half what a kraken might expect.

Fifteen hundred years. Fifteen hundred *long* years.

It almost makes me envy Elias's short millennium.

Not that he'll have to do his full time, not since Nora. A mating bond with a human usually halves the years we ancient creatures have left and gives the excess to the human at the other end of the bond. A steep price to be paid, certainly, but for the possibility of living out those years with the other piece of your soul by your side? The cost is nothing.

Gods, if Lizzy had lived... the two of us would indeed be nearing our golden years by now. But Lizzy and I never fully bonded. We'd been waiting until we left the ship and started our lives together to take that last step to solidify our bond.

So perhaps that's my punishment, too—living the rest of my centuries alone with myself and my guilt.

I shake off the morbid thought.

"I've spoken to her," I say, ready to put the matter to rest. "To Kenna. We've settled things."

"Have you? And she's what? Just fine with the fact that you scooped her off the street and dragged her off to the middle of nowhere and then abandoned her at our house?"

"It's settled." Another beat of finality, shutting the door on whatever other questions he might want to ask. Oldest friend or not, I don't feel the need to explain myself to the kraken.

Elias lets out a long, exasperated breath. "Fine. I'll tell Nora to stop worrying, then."

"She's worried? About Kenna?"

It's a slip I didn't mean to make, and I mentally curse myself as his provoking grin returns. When he opens his mouth to speak, I cut him off.

"Forget I said that."

Elias just shakes his head and stands. "Fine. Whatever you say."

"I'll walk you out," I tell him. "I need to speak to Ruthie before heading down to the first floor."

"Great. I meant to ask her about the tea blend she sent home with me the last time I was here. Nora's been craving it."

That draws a raised eyebrow. "Oh? Anything you need to tell me?"

Elias laughs as we leave my office, and the joy that spreads over him at talk of his mate makes his whole expression lighten. "No. You're not going to be an uncle quite yet. We're a few years away from that, at least."

The thought rattles around in my head as we approach Ruthie's desk, brightening my mood a little. A dragon uncle for a half-kraken baby. The idea would almost be absurd if it didn't fill my chest with happiness for my friend.

After I've spoken to Ruthie, and Elias has secured the promise of more of whatever enchanting blend she had for him before, we cross to the elevator to head back to the ground floor. Elias is off to Morgan-Blair's downtown office, and I'm headed to Accounting to review some of last quarter's financials in preparation for the upcoming HHS visit.

As we step out of the elevator, my eyes scan the space without me willing them to, some newly honed instinct making it impossible not to look, to try to catch a glimpse of...

A flash of auburn catches my avaricious eye from across the lobby, and my gaze zeros in on her immediately. Like she can feel the weight of that stare, Kenna turns to look at me, stumbles a step, then catches herself and hurries toward the stairs.

Beside me, Elias follows my gaze before huffing a quiet laugh. "Keep telling yourself all those excuses, friend."

14

Kenna

It's Friday, and I swear I can still feel the imprint of Blair's lips against mine from days ago.

His body, too, where it pressed against me. The brand of his hands on my hips. The insistent thrust of his cock between my thighs.

I've only seen him once since then—yesterday, when I stumbled over my own feet after I saw him in the lobby—but those golden eyes are never far from my mind.

New-Kenna really needs to get her shit together.

But apparently that's too much to hope for, because I'm still thinking about that devastating kiss when noon rolls around. I'm startled out of my thoughts by a huge orc in a polo shirt and khakis passing by my cubicle. Looking up, I watch him continue on to Susie's desk. She jumps up immediately, grinning at him.

"Ready for lunch?" the orc asks, and she nods.

"Oh," Susie says brightly as they get ready to leave. "Kenna, I want to introduce you to Jonah. He works in Accounting."

The two of them are barely touching, but the way she leans into his side and the hand he has resting gently on the small of her back communicates volumes.

Good for them. They're freaking adorable together. With Susie's tiny, slender frame tucked into him and the way Jonah towers protectively over her, it's so obvious how into each other they are.

It's also completely out in the open that they're dating, and the reminder of that is... probably way more interesting to me than it should be.

Does the Bureau allow coworkers to date? Obviously Susie and Jonah are getting away with it, so maybe it's no big deal. Maybe it's... nope.

I stop that thought right there. Whatever the rules are around intra-office fraternization, I'd bet my left foot they absolutely wouldn't apply to the Director getting it on with an entry-level graphic designer.

"Do you have plans for lunch today?" Susie asks.

I nod, appreciating the implied offer, but I've already got an emergency vent sesh with Holly I've been looking forward to all morning. "Yeah, I'm meeting a friend downtown."

They head out, and I follow a few minutes later, waiting for the elevator to arrive.

Like it does every time I leave the safety of my desk, an electric awareness skitters over my skin.

Am I going to run into him? Where is he right now? Up in his office? Coming down to leave for lunch?

The elevator opens, and it's empty.

Ignoring the tiny pulse of disappointment that moves

through me, I hit the button for the lobby.

Ten minutes later, I walk into a little bistro down the street from the Bureau and find Holly already waiting at a table near the back. It's a place that serves only vegan food, which is fine with me after my steak-flavored kiss from wolf-boy, and right up Holly's alley.

"Hey," she says when I sit down. "Is Nora coming?"

I shake my head. "She's got noon class today."

It's been awesome to see Nora get her groove back with summer courses at a local university, finally finishing the degree her asshole ex convinced her to drop out of. Elias is, as always, her biggest cheerleader, but Holly and I are a close second.

We give the server our lunch orders and Holly turns back to me as he goes.

"So," she says. "The dragon. Let's hear it."

We missed our thirsty Thursday last night since Nora was closing at work, so I haven't yet been able to fill Holly in on all the details. I do now, and by the time I'm finished telling her about the awkwardness at the Bureau, the kidnapping, and the kiss in Blair's office, her eyes are wide and she's got her elbows leaned on the table, hanging on every quiet word.

We're close enough to the Bureau that it's not totally out of the realm of possibility someone from work might overhear. Not wanting to take any chances, I'm leaning in too, keeping my voice down.

"Fuck, Kenna," Holly says, and it's a testament to just how bananas all of this is that she's using profanity. Since she went all peace and love and zen on us, her swearing has pretty much gone out the window.

"Yup," I say, leaning back and taking a sip of kombucha, which, I admit, I was pretty skeptical of, but Holly's converted me.

"And it's not a mating thing?"

"You know, funny you should ask..."

That launches into a whole dissection of Blair's behavior and his flat refusal that this is anything more than some kind of passing fascination for him. Like me, Holly doesn't look like she quite buys it.

"What does Nora think? Has she talked to Elias about it? Or to Blair?"

I shake my head. "I asked her not to. She did... mention something. Something about Blair's baggage when it comes to having a mate."

Holly frowns. "What does that mean?"

"Your guess is as good as mine. Nora didn't think it was something she could share."

She chews on her lip for a moment in contemplation. "I suppose that's fair, if it's something personal. And, anyway, the more important question is how you've been doing through all of it."

"I've been... fine, I guess."

She opens her mouth, and I can almost hear the words before she says them.

"No meditations," I say, "and no affirmations. I would just like to wallow, please."

Holly shakes her head and gives me a rueful smile. I'm game for vegan food and kombucha, but I've got to draw the line somewhere. Granola girl, I am not.

"Fine," Holly says, a rare wicked smile turning up the corners of her lips. "No woo-woo. How does hitting a few bars tomorrow night sound instead?"

I grin right back at her. "Now you're speaking my language."

Walking downtown between bars on Saturday night, I breathe the night air deep.

This is exactly what I needed. Operation 'Cheer Up Kenna' is in full swing. Not only with Holly, but with all my roommates, too.

My friends. Some drinks. A bit of trouble in the air.

I used to live for nights like this, and even though I can be new-Kenna all I want when it comes to work and getting my shit together, there will always be a little of that party girl left in me.

"Where to next?" Fran calls over her shoulder.

She's got her arm looped through Bruno's, with our other roommates Lexa and Wes strolling ahead. Holly and I trail behind on our way from the first bar to wherever the night's going to take us.

"You pick," I tell her. "I'm good with wherever."

I've already got a slight buzz going from the fizzy, champagne-based cocktail I started the night with. Not drunk, but just sparkly enough to feel the promise of the evening.

"You might live to regret those words," Fran says with a laugh.

Wes and Lexa chime in with their own suggestions, and the conversation devolves into good natured jabs at everyone's favorite watering holes.

They're a ragtag bunch, and I love them to death.

I met Fran and Bruno during my first attempt at college, and had no idea they were both paranormal. Fran's a nymph with a rich umber complexion and silvery hair I always assumed was dyed before she confided in me it's a striking feature all the females in her family line possess. Bruno's a big, burly bear shifter with a massive beard and an even more massive soft spot for Fran.

Fran was an art major like me, and also my suite-mate freshman year. We stayed close even when I dropped out, and when Fran inherited the Victorian from her late aunt, she immediately extended the offer to move into one of the spare bedrooms.

Holly was the long-suffering computer science major who had the misfortune to be suite-mates with a couple of rowdy art students, but she came around eventually. She went right from college to a job in big tech and a fancy apartment with her ex, Cody, so she never moved into the Victorian with us.

Wes, a vampire, and Lexa, a human, came on as roommates later. All of them became the support system I so badly needed back in the 'fuck around' portion of my early twenties, right before 'find out' showed up to slap me in the face.

And even now, when I'm finally navigating my way into responsible adulthood, I wouldn't trade their friendship for the world.

Tonight's got all the makings of a hell of a good time. Everyone's in a great mood, and it's blessedly not raining on us.

Well, tonight *had* at the makings of a hell of a good time, because we're just about to head down another block to a little hole-in-the-wall bar when something makes me stop turn and to the other side of the street.

There, at the entrance to some swanky hotel, a tall, broad figure steps outside, holding the door open.

It's Blair.

He's not alone, either, as he walks out under the hotel's canopied entrance with a tall, slim blond by his side.

They're too far away to make out their conversation, but when she leans in to say something conspiratorially close to his ear and Blair tosses his head back laughing, I freeze in the middle of the sidewalk. And when he places his hand in the center of her back before opening the door to the town car that's just pulled up, a wave of gut-twisting envy makes me feel nauseous.

"Kenna?" Fran calls over her shoulder. "You coming?"

From across the street, Blair closes the town car's door as the woman disappears inside. Like he could hear Fran from where he's standing, his head snaps up and his eyes meet mine.

If I was frozen before, I'm made of stone now.

"Kenna?" It's Holly this time, and when she follows my gaze to where Blair's now heading across the street, I hear her suck in a breath. "Is that..."

"The one and only."

"Oh, shit."

Oh shit, indeed.

"Do you want to go?" Holly asks, quiet enough so only I can hear. "I can tell him to get lost if you don't want to deal with him."

Silently, I shake my head and watch Blair approach in long, confident strides. Even in his human form, he moves with a power and authority that radiates from him without him having to say a word, with enough magnetism that the rest of my friends stop where they'd been walking a few yards ahead and turn to watch the scene play out.

"Kenna," he says in his deep, graveled voice when he stops just a couple of feet away, eyes searching my face. "I didn't expect to run into you tonight."

That makes two of us, but I'm still too tongue-tied to do more than nod in response.

Blair looks... different than he does at the Bureau.

No tie with his black suit, shirt unbuttoned at the collar. More relaxed, at ease, and about a thousand times more dangerous for my self-restraint.

And the way he's looking at me... golden eyes running up and down my body for a moment before meeting mine again, sends a shock of desire all the way through me.

Ten seconds.

Ten fucking seconds was all it took for me to feel like I'm right back where I was on Monday, all worked up into knots over this dragon, somehow unable to wrench myself free from the intense hold his stare has on me.

And maybe Blair can see he has me, too, because his eyes sharpen and a small, knowing smile turns up the corners of his lips before he speaks again.

"Do you want to get a drink with me?"

Acutely aware all my friends are staring, a flush climbs up the back of my neck and over the curve of my cheeks.

A small, idiotic voice from somewhere dangerously close to the center of my chest shouts *yes! Yes, of course I'd like to get a drink!*

Or, maybe not in my chest. Maybe that voice is somewhere decidedly lower as Blair leans a little closer to me and I get a whiff of the smoky, spicy scent that clings to him in a way that makes me think it's not just his cologne.

I'm saved from doing or saying anything truly catastrophic by Holly's hand on my arm.

"Kenna?" she says. "A word?"

Breaking Blair's gaze, I let her tug me a little way down the sidewalk.

"Are you, uh, going to take him up on that offer?" she asks in a low voice.

"I'm considering it," I whisper. "Am I an idiot?"

I expect her to be my voice of reason, to tell me no, absolutely not, under no circumstances should I let the stern, sexy dragon shifter take me out for a drink. But Holly surprises me by glancing over my shoulder at Blair, then looking back at me with a wry smile on her face.

"Well, we were planning on making some bad choices tonight."

I might only imagine it, but I catch the slight sound of a

huffed breath from where Blair's standing a few yards away.

"And you can always call if you want to meet back up later," Holly says. "Wes is still planning to DD."

"I'll make sure she gets where she's going safely," Blair cuts in, and I know I wasn't imagining his last reaction. Damned dragon's been listening to us.

I glare over my shoulder at him. "Private conversation, buddy. And I haven't said yes yet."

Blair just huffs another amused breath and turns to face the street, pretending like he's not listening anymore.

I look back at Holly, and she arches a brow at me in silent challenge.

"You're supposed to be the rational one, remember?" I whisper.

"What can I say?" she asks with a shrug. "He's got a good aura."

Blair chuckles, and I fight the urge to snap at him again.

"Besides," Holly says, whispering now. "Life's short, Kenna. Have your fun if you want to."

There's something a little sad about her words, and when I look at her more closely, that sadness is echoed in her expression.

I'm not totally clueless about where it's coming from. The man she thought she was going to marry walked out of her life a little over a year ago. It's been one of the hardest things for her, feeling like those years with Cody were wasted. I reach out and squeeze her hand in understanding.

"Not the time for a heart-to-heart," she mumbles.

I nod before finally turning around to face Blair.

He's looking right back at me, hands resting casually in his pockets, chin tilted up and golden eyes gleaming with unmistakable challenge.

This is a bad idea. This is the worst idea. This is something new-Kenna would never do, not in a million years.

But old-Kenna? Apparently that bitch is pretty hard to kill, because looking at Blair dressed down, with a little stubble over his jaw like he didn't bother shaving this morning, and that teasing glint in his gaze, no part of me wants to turn down his offer.

No, the longer I look, the more tempted I am.

When it comes to Ewan Blair, I'm in big, big fucking trouble.

15

Blair

Offering to take Kenna out for a drink wasn't something I did consciously.

No, as far as I'm concerned, one moment I was helping my friend Ari into her car and the next I was standing here in front of her, my offering hanging in the air between us. It wasn't even a choice to be drawn to where Kenna was standing in another pair of painted-on jeans and a tight, low-cut top that's got her breasts pushed up so high they're threatening to spill right over.

With the temptation she presented beckoning me forward, I could no sooner have resisted than I could have stopped the beating of my heart or the rush of fire in my blood that consumed me as soon as I was near her.

Now, though, with all her friends watching and Kenna still standing silently in front of me, I begin to realize this might not have been the best idea.

And even beside that, my evening with Ari already had me on edge.

Ari's a cambion I've known for decades. She's the President of the Paranormal Advancement Society, and although she's a friend and a peer whose counsel I've always valued, our conversation tonight was grim. It's not only the Bureau that's been feeling the ramifications of shifting public sentiment around paranormal integration, and after spending a couple of hours commiserating with Ari, seeing Kenna was like an unexpected candleflame held up against my dark mood.

An ember, just like I called her in my office after she kissed me. Burning brightly and sending all those shadows skittering away. And gods above, I'm not strong enough to turn away from her right now.

I want Kenna to say yes. I want to take her somewhere, talk to her, spend a little more time basking in the light and the heat of her.

At the same time, I know I have no right. Not tonight. Probably not ever, with the way I've behaved toward her.

I'm about to open my mouth, rescind the offer, and tell her to have a good night with her friends—even if the idea of her going anywhere looking like that makes me feel like dragon fire is crawling up the back of my throat—when she glances over at the woman next to her. They share a few seconds of silent conversation before Kenna turns back to me.

"Alright," she says. "I'll get a drink with you."

The dragon in me roars his approval, and all of those reservations burn to ash in the glow of her acceptance, but I merely give her a nod. "I know a place near here."

She turns briefly and says something into her friend's ear before pulling her into a hug and sharing a short laugh. The other woman walks away to join the rest of their group, leaving Kenna and I alone.

"You didn't have to accept," I tell her, nodding after her friends. "If I'm ruining an occasion, you can still turn me down."

Kenna shrugs. "Well, since the whole point of this night was to distract me from thinking about you, and now here you are, it seems a little too late for that, doesn't it?"

Her candor catches me off-guard.

"You—" I stutter, lost for words, but Kenna doesn't seem to expect a reply.

"You said you know a spot?" she asks, looking at me expectantly.

I nod, still feeling off-balance as I cup a hand around her elbow and steer her toward the next intersection. Instead of bristling at the touch like I might have expected, she leans into it for a moment before shifting slightly to wrap her arm around the back of mine.

I glance down at her in surprise, but she just shrugs again.

"It's getting a little chilly. I didn't bring a jacket, and you're warm."

She's cold? I reach up and start to slide off the suit coat I'm wearing, but Kenna stops me with a hand on my arm and wry humor in her voice, rolling her eyes at me.

"Not necessary. Unless you're dragging me all the way across the city, I'll be fine."

The dragon grumbles his disapproval at that, and I can't help but agree with the beast. Still, knowing we're only a block and a half away from our destination and not wanting to start an argument with her when we've barely begun our time together, I let the matter rest.

Reaching the bar a couple minutes later, I open the door for her and Kenna throws me a questioning look.

"What?" I ask, stepping inside behind her.

"Just not the place I would have expected you'd pick."

"Why not?"

Kenna looks around the interior of the bar. Dimly lit and not too crowded, it's outfitted with dark wood floors and dark walls, gold light fixtures turned down low. Shadowed, private booths perfect for intimate conversation line the walls.

Glancing at me again, Kenna shakes her head. "No reason, and I guess a place like this is good for no one to see or recognize us."

I frown. That wasn't my intention in bringing her here. I just like this place. I know the owner, and the bartenders always make a good drink. That Kenna assumes I'd pick it because I wanted to hide her...

Well, she's not wrong, per se, but the idea still sits uneasily in the bottom of my gut.

Before I can say anything else, Kenna walks further into the bar and chooses an empty U-shaped booth near the back. We slide into opposite sides, and are saved from immediate conversation by a server coming to take our drink order. Kenna gets a gin and tonic and I ask for whiskey neat.

When the server retreats, though, we're left with nothing to do but stare each other down. Kenna has her chin jutted up slightly, a challenge in her green eyes, clearly expecting me to fire the opening salvo.

Which, fair enough, I was the one to invite her out with me, after all.

"Tell me what brought you to the Bureau."

She cocks an eyebrow. "That's really where you want to start?"

"If there's another topic you'd prefer, by all means," I allow, throwing an arm up on the back of the booth.

Kenna tracks the movement, eyes fixing on my arm for a moment before she fidgets a little where she's sitting.

Closer? No, not closer. She's skittish, still understandably skeptical about what I want and what motivated me to ask her out. There's no chance in hell she's moved closer… even if I can suddenly picture her sliding over, tucking herself against me, pressing the side of her luscious thigh against mine, parting her legs just enough for me to drop a hand and…

"No," she says, snapping me out of it. "That's fine."

She thinks for a moment. "The Bureau, the whole graphic design and communications thing, it was more of a backup plan than what I actually wanted to do," she admits, then frowns. "Shit. I shouldn't have said that. You're like, what? My boss's boss's boss? I shouldn't be—"

"I'm not the Director tonight," I tell her, and her frown deepens.

"Easy for you to say," she mutters.

I reach over and take her hand gently in mine. "Should we call it a night, ember? Would you rather forget any of this happened and just go back to me being your boss's boss's boss?"

Her eyes flicker a little at the nickname and her hand flexes slightly in mine, but she shakes her head. "No. I don't want to call it a night."

A small spark of triumph in my chest. And a warning.

The line we're dancing over is dangerous. Perhaps more for me than for her, but I'll be damned if I'm able to remember that now. Not when Kenna's fingers relax in mine, or when her full lips quirk up into a small, mischievous smile.

"Tell me what you wanted to do instead," I say. "If the Bureau was just your backup."

She pulls her hand away before crossing her arms over her chest and giving me another challenging little look. "Illustration."

Another surprise. "What kind of illustration?"

"Digital character work, mostly. I've also worked with

physical mediums, but most of it comes back to digital."

We talk about that for a few minutes—where she went to school, what she ended up getting her degree in—though I can tell she's not being completely transparent about some part of it. Which part, I don't know, and I've got no right to press, so I file the detail away for later.

She seems to relax as the conversation goes on, and when the server drops off our drinks and Kenna takes a long sip, I try not to stare at her mouth.

"What about you?" Kenna asks. "What brought you to the Bureau?"

It's my turn to give her a challenging smirk. "I'm one of the Bureau's founders."

Her eyes widen for a moment before she laughs softly and shakes her head. "Of course you are."

I can see the wheels turning in her mind, but I'm suddenly not in the mood to talk about work anymore. Just the mention of my role at the Bureau brings some of those earlier shadows creeping back in. With them, another reminder about just how reckless all of this is.

"Are your friends going to miss you tonight?" I ask, reaching for a new topic.

Kenna arches a brow at the change in direction, and shifts again in her seat.

Closer. She's definitely closer this time. A pulse of low, burning heat moves through me and I shift my position as well, drawn to her like a magnet.

"No. They'll be fine. What about *your* friend?"

There's an edge in her voice, something I'd almost think was jealousy if I didn't know better.

"Friend?" I ask, knowing full well what she means.

"The blond."

Ah. There it is. Clear this time, her brittle jealousy reaches in and tugs at the base of my lizard brain.

Good. It's good that she's jealous. And even better that she shifts closer again, fire kindling in her emerald eyes. I mirror her movement.

We're within arm's reach now.

"What blond?"

Kenna rolls her eyes. "The one you were all over outside the hotel. Right before you saw me."

"Careful, ember," I warn. "Or I might think you care."

Like I hoped they would, the words rile Kenna's temper, a vibrant spark that shines in her eyes and has her sitting up straighter in her seat.

"Answer the question, Blair."

Again with that name. Ignoring the way it chafes, I lean closer to her, almost close enough to brush the shell of her ear with my lips.

"An old friend."

"You looked pretty close to be just friends."

"Is that so?"

Instead of answering right away, Kenna crosses her arms over her chest and settles back into her seat. She narrows her eyes, looks me up and down, and a small smirk curves her lips before she speaks.

"You're enjoying this, aren't you?"

I stare right back, returning her appraisal with every bit as much insolence. "Yes, I think I am."

Kenna would be well within her rights to call me out as the bastard I am for that remark, but it only riles her further, has her leaning in close and hissing at me under her breath.

"Answer the damn question."

My dragon hisses his own approval in response. He likes her jealousy, apparently, and I'm hardly unaffected as a shot of heat spreads through my veins, making my palms twitch and my cock ache.

"Her name is Ari, and she's the President of the Paranormal Advancement Society," I say. "She's been advocating for paranormals for nearly as long as I have. We connect every so often to discuss how the Bureau can help support her organization's interests."

"And that includes drinks in a hotel bar late on a Saturday night?"

"Sometimes, yes. Does it matter?"

"No," Kenna says lightly, picking up her drink and taking a sip. "I suppose it doesn't. I'm just trying to figure out what I'm dealing with here."

"What do you mean by that?"

"What I mean," Kenna says, setting her drink down, "is I'd like to know if I'm about to become a part of some sort of roster, or something. If I'm just another notch in that belt of yours."

About to become. So she's thought about this. Maybe even knew full well what she wanted and what she was doing when she accepted my invitation for drinks.

"And it would matter to you, if you were?"

Her eyes flash, and her next words have a bite to them that stirs something dark and possessive in the bottom of my soul. "I don't do well with sharing."

"Neither do I."

Beneath the table, Kenna's hand lands on my thigh, nails digging into me. "Good."

My body responds immediately to that proprietary touch. Fire, pure fire spreading from where her nails press into me, all the way to my half-hard cock and the ache between my shoulder blades where my wings want to break free.

If I could get her out of this bar I could shift, gather her up in my claws, and take her somewhere far from here.

Somewhere safe and hidden where I could keep her tucked away.

Kenna, though, isn't finished.

"What is this?" she asks in a hushed voice. "You... me... all of this. What is it?"

"Hell if I know."

The words are out of my mouth before I can think better of them, and Kenna's eyes flicker a little at the honesty.

I... can't read her right now. Not like I've always been able to. My ember's always been an open book for me—eyes wide and hopeful, or narrowed with temper, or glazed with desire—but right now she's blank, calculating, thinking over what I just said in a way that leaves me with no idea how she's going to react.

"It's obviously a shit idea for us to be... anything," Kenna says casually. *Too* casually, but I don't call her on it. "At least anything more than..."

She trails off, but I'm not about to let her off that easily. I'm a reckless idiot for it, but I want to hear her say it. I want to hear that Kenna wants me, too.

"More than what, ember?"

She scoots closer to me on the bench seat, leans sideways to rest her elbow on the table and her chin in her hand, looking up at me through her dark, thick lashes.

"More than a good fuck, Blair."

Everything about those words sounds wrong. The sentiment. The name.

But when she's looking at me like that... when she shifts until her thigh is pressed up against mine, they lose some of their sting.

"And is that what you want, Kenna?"

If she says no, this can be it. We can go our separate ways. I can stay away from her. I'm sure I can stay away from her.

Gods, it would be better for both of us if she has enough sense to say no. Because if she doesn't…

"Why not?" she says lightly, and again, her features arrange themselves in some configuration I can't decipher. "That's all this is, right?"

16

Kenna

"That's all this is, right?"

The words hang between us. A challenge, a gauntlet thrown.

Since we walked into this bar, since the moment I saw him on the other side of the street, some part of this has felt inevitable. Whatever ties already bind us have been straining, taut, pulled to a breaking point.

What's he going to say? What do I *want* him to say?

"Ember," he says, low and graveled.

I can't help it—the nickname sends a dark, tantalizing thrill through me.

Just a little ember, aren't you? Ready to spark a flame and burn me to ash.

"Answer the question, Blair."

Beneath the table, his hand finds my knee, squeezing

gently. The touch sends another pulse of arousal shooting straight up between my legs in an urgent, warm heat that makes me squirm a little where I'm sitting.

"I want you, Kenna."

It's not an answer, not really. Not any more than him telling me he took me because he wanted to.

A stronger woman probably wouldn't accept it. But here, now, with a dragon's golden gaze pinning me in place, no part of me is tempted to do anything but agree.

Because that's what Blair is. Temptation, pure and irresistible. Power and sex and some strange alchemy that's drawn me in from the beginning. And even though I might be able to look down this road and see where it ends, right now I'm not strong enough to choose a different path.

"Then have me."

The hand on my leg slides higher until he's cupping me over the seam of my jeans. Whether he can feel the warmth of me, the damp heat that's already building for him, I'm not sure. But when his eyes meet mine, they're burning from the inside out.

"Come back to my place?" The offer slips out before I can think better of it.

Blair's touch stills. "You're sure about that, ember? That's what you want?"

The deep timbre of his voice reaches in and strokes at the high walls I'm using to keep myself fortified against him.

A good fuck. Once. To get it out of my system.

Blair is the definition of unavailable. My boss's boss's boss. Completely unable or unwilling to acknowledge there's anything between us but simmering lust. Closed off, guarded, a predator sharp and dangerous enough for me to know I should stay far, far away.

"It's what I want."

Blair's eyes flare with heat, and he gives me a single decisive nod before setting his nearly full drink on the table, and fishing his wallet out of his back pocket. Dropping a hundred down between our drinks, he slides out of the booth, taking my hand and pulling me along with him.

"Hey!" I protest.

Blair looks down at me with a devilish smirk on his face. It's so much more devastating than the brooding, mysterious tough guy thing he's usually got going on, that whatever else I was about to say burns to ash in my mind.

"Problem?"

I stand, tugging at my shirt to straighten it, and Blair's eyes drop immediately to the cleavage I very deliberately have on display tonight.

"No," I murmur, leaning into him. "No problem."

He growls low in his throat, puts a hand on the center of my back, and leads me out of the bar. When the cool night air breaks over my too-hot skin, it raises a wave of pleasurable goosebumps up and down my exposed arms.

"So, are we taking a cab? Or do I get the pleasure of being wrapped up in those claws of yours again?"

One of these times, I'm going to push too far, tease him a little too much, but now is not that time. Well, at least I don't think it is, and if the way Blair rounds on me with that smirk of his growing even wider is any sign, he's more amused than annoyed.

"I do drive, you know."

I look him up and down. "You're alright for that? Weren't you already drinking tonight with—"

"Ari doesn't drink," he cuts in. "So I wasn't, either. And I barely had two sips of my whiskey." He pauses and thinks for a moment, and his smirk fades. "What about you? Maybe we shouldn't—"

"I'm fine." I barely touched my own drink in the bar, and the buzz from earlier has already faded.

"Kenna," his voice is low, a warning. "I want you sober for this. I won't take anything less than a clear-headed, enthusiastic yes from you."

The words make my breath stutter in my chest.

There's a whole fucking lot of men out there who wouldn't give a damn if I'd had one drink or three or seven. I met enough of them in my partying days, and know just how quickly those lines can blur. To have it laid out so simply, so clearly, with no room for argument or shades of hazy gray makes me even more certain of what I'm about to do.

Truly, the bar is in hell for men sometimes, but something tells me Blair means every word he says. Whatever this is, whatever we are to each other, he's not going to take anything I don't give freely and willingly.

And fuck, do I want to give it.

"One cocktail at the first bar I went to tonight," I tell him, reaching up to run a hand along one of his lapels. "And I had just as much of my drink in there as you did yours."

He catches my wrist in his hand, pulling it away from his jacket before brushing a kiss across the backs of my knuckles. "Alright then ember, let's go."

The drive from downtown to the Victorian passes in record time. We don't talk much, and Blair seems focused on getting to my place as quickly as possible without breaking any traffic laws, keeping a hand on my knee the whole time. When we park a half-block away, I unbuckle my seatbelt and reach for my door handle, only for the dragon beside me to squeeze my knee a little harder and grunt his disapproval.

"What?" I ask, arching a brow at him.

"Let me get that for you."

I roll my eyes. "Not necessary."

Before he can give me any more grief, I open the door and let myself out. It's even cooler now than it was when we left the bar, and I shiver a little as the night air brushes against my skin.

"I'm just up the street," I tell him as he gets out of the car and joins me on the sidewalk.

There's a crackling, static energy between us as we walk together to the house. We're not even touching, but the warmth of him beside me and the weighted possibility of everything waiting for us inside almost makes it feel like we are.

We reach the steps up to the wide front porch, he puts his hand in the center of my back, and all that static energy gathers and grows. Warm and anticipatory, it has me fighting the urge to arch into his touch.

As I pull my keys from my purse and reach for the door, Blair is right there. He crowds in behind me, running his hands over the curve of my waist in a way that's distracting enough for me to fumble with the lock. He doesn't seem to care, though, as he leans in to graze his lips along the back of my neck and chuckles against my skin.

I let out an irritated breath as I finally get the key in the lock and open the door, letting us both inside.

Blair freezes just inside the entryway. I glance over my shoulder at him from where I'm locking the door behind us, and his brow is lowered, gaze dark.

"It smells like other males in here."

I snort. "Yeah. I'm sure it does. My bear shifter and vampire roommates are both dudes."

A small growl slips past his lips.

"Cut it out," I snap at him. "The bear shifter is very, very into his nymph girlfriend and the vampire's got a rotation of incredibly hot, single men he keeps on speed dial."

Blair lets out a huff of a breath, and I turn to face him fully.

"Rule number one of this being… well, this being what it is. You don't get to be all snarly and possessive."

Before I can register that he's moving, Blair herds me back against the door, planting his hands on either side of my body.

"Did I agree to that?"

"Um, yeah?" I ask, breath catching in my throat. "You did. I mean, I know you're old, Blair, but it was less than an hour ago."

He brings a hand up to lightly bracket my throat, thumb pressing into the little divot where he can almost certainly feel my racing pulse. "You threw out your terms, ember. I don't remember saying anything about mine."

"You said—"

"I said I wanted you." That hand moves upward to cup my chin, tipping my face toward his. "And if I remember correctly, you were the one who said all you wanted was a good—"

"Implied agreement." My skin is humming where he's touching me, words coming out in a breathy gasp.

What's he even saying right now? That he wants… more?

My thoughts are hazy and my brain feels syrupy and slow when he's this close to me. With all the oxygen in the air taken up by the nearness and the heat of him, there doesn't seem to be any room left for logic or reason or common sense.

Blair clicks his tongue in disapproval. "Kenna, if you ever make a deal with a dragon, you really should ensure it's ironclad."

I open my mouth, but I don't get the chance to argue before he kisses me.

17

Blair

Kenna falls to pieces the moment I have my lips on hers.

Her moan tastes like the sweetest surrender as I stroke into her mouth—teasing her, testing her, seeing if she's going to call me out on my bullshit.

She doesn't, but her hands shoot up into my hair and she tugs, *hard.* The edge of delicious pain has me growling against her lips, a sound that only grows deeper and more ragged when I inhale and catch the other scents in the house.

Males. Two of them. And despite what she told me, I want to have her covered in me by the time I leave. When those males come back from wherever they are tonight, I want them to scent me here and know I've left my mark on her.

"Stop being so fucking snarly," Kenna grumbles against my lips.

I reach a hand down and swat her ass over her jeans.

Kenna yelps into my mouth. I do it again, and she arches her back into it. It drives me out of my fucking mind, and I press into her harder, letting her feel the weight of me, the push of my cock against her…

Gods, I'm not like this. Not with anyone but her.

Everything about Kenna makes me mindless, hungry, ready to kiss all that sass from her mouth or take her over my knee and redden her ass until she's moaning too loud to give me any more lip.

She's a flame, vibrant and alive, and I'm in the mood to burn.

Using both hands this time, I grab two big handfuls of that lush, full ass and haul her up against me. She comes to me easy, wrapping her legs around my waist and grinding her sweet, hot cunt against the erection begging to be released from behind my zipper.

The contact makes the muscles in my back ache. What I'd give to be somewhere I could half-shift and let my dragon's fire course through my veins. This house is quaint, cozy, much too close and confined to let my wings spread wide.

Just the thought of it, the idea of Kenna reaching up to put her hands on my wings when we're fucking… I'll teach her how to do it just right, how to stroke along the seam where wing meets shoulder so she makes me come hard enough to forget my own name.

I force the thought out of my mind.

Later. There will be time for that later.

Because I already know I'm not going to settle for just one night with my ember. No matter what she wants to tell me about this being nothing more than a good fuck, there's something else brewing between us that absolutely won't be satiated in the course of a few hours.

A dark, whispered warning at the back of my mind tells me it might not even be satiated in a few days with her, or a few months. It might take the rest of my existence to get the taste of my little living flame off my lips and the temptation she sparks in me out of my blood.

"Where's your room?" I ask her, low and husky, gripping her ass even tighter.

"Upstairs," Kenna pants, and her needy, breathless tone is entirely too satisfying. "Third door on the right."

She clings tighter to me as I climb the set of narrow stairs to the second floor, drawing another growl from my lips when she dips her head to scrape her teeth against the side of my throat.

When I reach the door she indicated, I throw it wide and walk us inside before kicking it shut. I'm still wholly focused on the woman in my arms as I step into the room, but when I glance up, I'm distracted immediately.

The room is every bit as vibrant as my ember.

Bright colors and wild patterns and something new to see everywhere I look. Almost more than even my dragon's greedy eyes can process. From the plush pillows on her bed, to the dark emerald armchair in the corner, to the display of bright, shiny jewelry and baubles on her painted dresser, it's like stepping into an explosion of color and life.

One entire wall is filled with artwork. Some of it's framed and arranged into what looks to be a carefully curated gallery wall. Other sections are made of tacked up sketches and prints, all gathered around a vintage roll-top desk with a tablet computer sitting on it.

Kenna's artwork. Like everything else in this space, it's colorful and whimsical, bold and eye-catching.

Setting her down gently, I turn in a slow circle, taking it all in.

"I like... color," Kenna says, and when I cut my gaze back to her, she shrugs self-consciously. "It's a lot, I know, but it's —"

"It's wonderful."

"Really?" she asks, snorting a small laugh. "I didn't think it would be your style."

"I'm a dragon, ember. And that means I appreciate beautiful things." Reaching out, I catch one of her curls between my fingers. "Like this fiery hair of yours." I let the strand drop and run my thumb over the crest of her cheekbone. "Or all the colors of your face. This delicious pink and the emeralds in your eyes."

Kenna's breath catches, and she leans into the touch.

"I'm a greedy creature," I tell her, taking a step forward and herding her toward the bed. When we reach it, I slide my suit coat off my shoulders and drape it over the footboard. "I have an eye for treasure and an even greater appreciation for when it's right in front of me."

The backs of her knees hit the bed, and she sinks slowly onto it. Her eyes stay fixed on mine as she shifts herself to lie back against the pile of pillows, and I follow her inch for inch until I'm hovering above her.

Kenna makes a needy little sound in the back of her throat and winds her arms up around my neck, trying to draw me down on top of her. I chuckle and relent, pressing her into the mattress with the length of my body. Having her beneath me, arching up and shifting to get used to the weight and the feel of me, all those soft curves of hers melting into me, is almost enough to make me forget I'm not quite done teasing her.

"It's like I've found a new hoard to plunder," I murmur, brushing my lips over hers. "A treasure just waiting to be taken."

Finally claiming her mouth again, I swallow her groan of pleasure. Kenna responds just like I knew she would, with her hands tangled into my hair and her lips parting immediately to let me stroke into the heat of her mouth.

She's delicious, all sweet spice and citrus and a hundred

other things I'd like to drown in.

Her thighs part, making space for me between, and by the way she bucks her hips into mine, I know she can feel the press of my cock behind my zipper.

Too many clothes. Far too many clothes between us right now. Shifting up onto my knees, I revel in the irate noise she makes when I pull away. I reach up to unbutton my shirt, only to have my eyes catch on something in the open drawer of her bedside table. Something that looks a lot like...

"What's this?" I ask, reaching over with wicked satisfaction coursing through me. My fingers close around firm silicone shaped exactly like a certain part of male dragon shifter anatomy. "Something you've been practicing with?"

When she sees what I'm holding, a furious blush rises on Kenna's cheeks. "Stop! That's not—"

"Have you enjoyed using it?"

She doesn't answer right away, keeps reaching and grasping to take the toy back, but I'm not done playing with her.

"Tell me, ember. Tell me how much you like having this dragon cock in you."

Kenna whimpers, and the sound of it goes straight to my own cock.

"I like it," she admits.

"Did you buy it before you met me, or after?"

She buries her face in her hands, clearly mortified, but I don't let her retreat. I pull her wrists gently away and tip her chin up so she has to look at me. There's embarrassment in her eyes, but also a sparkle of something else, something that sends a pulse of deep, dark desire pounding through me.

"After."

Gods above. The sound of that little whisper does entirely indecent and unhinged things to me.

"And who do you think about when you're using it?"

This time, Kenna doesn't hesitate. "I think about you."

Despite her confession, she reaches up again to try to take the dildo from my hand, and another wicked idea strikes me.

"Now ember, don't be selfish," I admonish, lifting it higher out of her grasp. "It's greedy not to share your toys with others. Aren't you going to let me play, too?"

Her eyes go wide and round, glazed over with pleasure and need and just a bit of uncertainty, but after a few long moments she lets out a shaky breath and nods.

"I... I can share," she says, voice raspy with desire.

"On your knees. Hands on the headboard."

She stares at me for a long moment, and I watch the conflicting desires war with each other in the tiny expressions on her face. Excitement, need, lingering embarrassment over how much she wants this.

"Ember," I say in warning. "Hands on the headboard."

This time she complies, biting her lip to stifle whatever sass I'm sure she was about to give. As she situates herself at the head of the bed and reaches for the headboard, I click my tongue in disapproval and grab her by the hips, tugging her back so she has to bend all the way over to reach. She gasps sharply at my rough handling, but doesn't make a move to change position or protest.

Leaning over her, pressing my chest to her back, I reach around her waist and unfasten the snap of her jeans. Kenna's breathing speeds up and hitches slightly as I work her pants and panties over the curve of her ass and down her legs.

When they're dealt with, I lean back over her and tug at the hem of her shirt. "On, or off?"

"Off," she whispers, and lifts her hands up from the headboard so I can strip it from her along with her bra and toss both of them aside.

I press my palm between her shoulder blades. "Hands back where they were, Kenna."

A little shudder moves through her at the command, but she complies more easily this time. As she does, I realize a slight miscalculation on my part. By positioning her like this I've robbed myself of the chance to really see her, savor her, look my greedy fill of her.

Later, I remind myself, there will be time for that later.

The mental admonishment doesn't soothe my beast in the slightest, avaricious thing that he is. He'd have all of her now, fuck delaying any kind of gratification when it comes to our ember.

Still, both he and I can admire the tantalizing sight she presents just like this.

The soft, full swell of her ass and the glistening pink slit of her cunt. The graceful slope of her back and her tumble of auburn curls, wild and messy from my hands.

I run my fingertips lightly over the lush curve of her hips, reveling in another gasp, this time of pleasure and need.

"Blair," she whines. "Touch me."

Though I still don't like that name on her lips, I oblige, stroking along her seam and spreading the pooled wetness I find there. Soaked. My ember is soaked for me. Feeling how ready and eager her body is, I sink one finger deep and can't hold in my groan at the tight, hot grasp of her cunt.

I work her slowly at first, testing her, stretching her, learning the feel of her and letting the little sounds she's making and the way she moves her body against my hand tell me everything I need to know about how she likes to be touched. She's begging without saying a word, restless and eager enough to have me leaning over her, letting her take a bit more of my weight.

"You think you can take this dragon cock, ember?" I ask, plunging in a second finger to join the first. "When you're so tight and perfect?"

A strangled sound works its way out of Kenna's lips and her hips buck against my hand. "I can take it."

Gods above. I'd like to put that boast to the test, and not just with the toy, though I suppose it's a good place to start. Drawing my hand away and chuckling at the irate noise Kenna makes, I bring the dildo up to her entrance and tease her with it.

I'm about to say something else, taunt her a little more, when the faint sounds of a door closing downstairs followed by a couple of muffled voices make us both freeze.

"Shit," Kenna whispers. "Someone must have come back early."

I keep teasing her, dipping just the tapered tip inside, and she has to bite her lip to keep from crying out.

"Do you want to stop?"

She shakes her head immediately. "No. I don't want to stop."

"Then you'll have to be quiet," I murmur. "Unless you want the entire house to hear you."

I plunge the toy in, and Kenna only manages to contain her moan by slapping a hand over her mouth.

"Headboard," I remind her, and the strained whine she lets out as she complies sends another shot of heat straight to my cock.

Grinding the toy into her, I resent the hunk of silicone with every fiber of my being. It should be my cock making her moan and writhe, my flesh filling her rather than this poor, inanimate substitute.

But... with the question of what we are, of what any of this is, still so undecided, perhaps it's best if I kept what little distance I feel capable of keeping.

Not that it feels like there's any distance at all between us as Kenna continues to pant and squirm, biting down on her full bottom lip to keep from crying out. Feeling her hold herself back, and watching her cheeks flush with pleasure, I make it my new mission to crack and break that restraint.

With my free hand, I reach around her hip and between her thighs to find her clit, swollen and tender to the touch as Kenna stifles a low cry in her throat. Drawing back the pressure a little, I slide two fingers against her, letting her own dampness slick over her and ease the way.

We find a rhythm, a push and pull some instinctual part of me knows would carry perfectly over to our bodies fully entwined, my own cock sunk into her instead of this godsdamned toy.

I make myself push the image away, to appreciate this moment and concentrate on the task of bringing my ember to her pleasure. I focus wholly on her, working her higher, hotter, out of her damn mind as it gets more and more difficult for her to hold back.

Her cunt is stretched so prettily around the dildo, and her hips are bucking, her whole body straining toward…

Kenna comes with a sharp cry, which cuts off as she drops her hands from the headboard and buries her face in the pillow. I pull the toy out of her and plunge my fingers in, greedy to feel the pulsing of her body and the power of her release. The pillow muffles some of her moans, but not all of them, and a deranged, selfish part of me hopes that whoever's out there can hear her.

Let them know who's giving Kenna her pleasure.

Her knees go out from under her and she flops belly-down onto the mattress. Pulling my hand away from her still-pulsing cunt, it's all I can do not to shove my own pants off and climb on top of her.

I'd put my knees on both sides of her thighs, press my cock into her wet, swollen entrance and feel the tight grip of her body drawing me in. I'd make her come at least twice more before I spilled myself into her, leaving her scenting of me, marked by me...

Not tonight. I'm not going to indulge in all of those dark, enticing fantasies tonight.

Instead of fucking her like I want to, I shift to stretch out on the mattress beside her. I run my hand in long, languorous strokes down her back and over her shoulder, pressing into the muscles that have gone pliant and lax. Continuing downward, I brush along the length of her spine to play with the two little dimples just above her ass.

Every part of Kenna is soft and round and smooth. It makes me want to reach for her, crush all of that softness to me, but I resist, not knowing how much more I should allow myself to take from her right now.

All of this, everything between us, still feels... dangerous. For her, for me, for the potential it has to throw both our lives into chaos.

A good fuck.

It's all Kenna said she wanted. Nothing more, nothing less. And like the reckless bastard I am, I couldn't let it go. I couldn't settle for those terms, and I'm not about to let myself take what she offered until I have time to figure this out. Until we're both in agreement about what this is, and what it isn't.

I can't think around her. Not when she's near me at the Bureau, or in the middle of the woods, and certainly not right now when she's naked and sated beside me, the dampness of her still coating my fingers.

I need time. Space. Reason.

And I won't get any of it tonight. Not as long as I'm here.

Letting out another little moan, Kenna reaches a hand over and palms my cock through my pants. The blaze it sends through me almost makes me take all that internal resolve back, but I regretfully wrap my fingers around her wrist and draw her hand away.

"You got what you wanted, ember," I tell her, and her eyebrows snap together in confusion. "I can wait for what I want."

Her green eyes blaze. "Absolutely not. If you think you're leaving here without letting me—"

When she reaches for my zipper again, I catch her hand before she can touch me.

"Blair," she protests. It comes out in a whine that makes an answering growl threaten in the back of my throat.

"Not tonight." I lean over and kiss a path up her spine, stopping to bite lightly at her shoulder.

She lets out an exasperated breath and glares at me.

Rolling off the bed, I pick up my jacket and shrug it back on. Kenna grabs the blanket next to her and pulls it over her body as she sits up.

A shame, that. But seeing her fully is just one more pleasure that can wait for now.

"Good night, ember," I tell her, and her grumbled curses follow me all the way out her door.

18

Kenna

The walk of shame is too real the next morning.

I'm the last one of my roommates awake on this fine Sunday, and when I come slinking into the kitchen drawn by the scent of Bruno's award-worthy French toast, a round of applause breaks out.

"Bravo," Wes calls from his seat at the kitchen table.

There's an unfamiliar man with a vivid vampire bite on his throat sitting next to Wes. He seems a bit confused, but claps along like a good sport.

"*Stop*," I moan, sinking down into an empty chair and immediately grabbing a plate.

From where she's standing next to Bruno at the stove, Fran props a hip against the counter and grins at me. "Have fun last night?"

I stuff a bite of French toast into my mouth so I don't have to answer her.

Unfortunately, Bruno takes that as his cue to chime in. "If the sounds I heard coming from your room—"

"Stop," I say again, swallowing and reaching for a cup of coffee. "Does this belong to anyone?"

"That would be mine," Lexa says, plucking it from my hand. "And for real, Kenna. I saw your man leaving last night, and damn."

"Not my man," I protest, standing up to get my own cup of coffee.

Fran reaches around Bruno to grab a creamer and tosses it my way. "Shifter, then? Or demon?"

"He's not a vampire," Wes says. "I would have been able to smell that."

"No sniffing house guests," I mutter, sitting back down with my coffee.

"Whatever he is, he was hot as fucking hell." Lexa lets out a dreamy sigh. "And older? What is he, like forty?"

More like five hundred. That was one detail Nora let slip about him, but I'm not about to share that with everyone and give them any more information than they're already inferring on their own.

I drop my forehead to the tabletop. "Enough."

Someone slides into the chair next to me. I tilt my head to look and find Fran studying me with a little crease of concern between her brows.

"We can tone it down," she says, glancing around at the band of heathens I call roommates. "Is everything okay?"

Sighing, I sit up. "Everything's fine. Just dealing with the consequences of my own idiocy."

A quick montage of images from last night flickers through my mind. Blair, with his golden eyes looking back at me in the dim of the bar. Blair, stripping his jacket off in my bedroom. Blair, leaving with that damned arrogant smile on his lips, knowing full well he could have had me any way he wanted.

Fran opens her mouth to speak again, but I cut her off before she can.

"Let me plead the fifth on this one?"

She nods and gives me a wry smile. "Fair enough. No more cross-examination."

The rest of breakfast passes uneventfully. I get up and leave the kitchen after I'm finished eating, letting everyone else stay to re-hash last night and talk about their Sunday plans.

Any other day I'd be perfectly content to sit and chat, but today I'm feeling restless.

Back in my room, I get dressed and pull on my coat. I only have a half-formed destination in mind, but I need to get out of this house for a while.

"Be back later," I call as I unlock the front door, and a chorus of voices from the kitchen sends me off.

Heathens they may be, but they're *my* heathens, even when they're annoying the shit out of me.

It's raining a little as I walk to the bus stop, and I pull my hood up over my head. Sitting down on the bus a few minutes later, I pop one headphone in my ear and watch the neighborhood streets pass by the window, not really seeing any of it.

No, my mind is still completely occupied reliving my night with Blair. The way his hands and body felt against mine, the way he tasted, all the things he said to me.

Oh, my god. The things he said last night.

It was humiliating, mortifying, and I should be mad as all hell he treated me like that, *embarrassed* me like that... and that damned dildo. I should have never bought it in the first place, but the things he did to me with it...

My stomach tightens with warm, squirmy heat.

God help me, I liked it.

Why did I like it?

Wracking my brain, I try to imagine any of my previous boyfriends or sexual partners treating me like that. For a few, I would have punched them straight in the face before letting them pull that shit. With a few others, it would have just been awkward as hell. And for absolutely none of them can I imagine responding the way I did with Blair—submitting to his demands, enjoying the way he teased and taunted me, the control he took over my body…

I don't even *like* him. He's arrogant and brutish and cold.

Except for when he's burning, and bringing me right into the blaze with him.

God, I'm so screwed.

I think I'd feel better about it if he'd gotten off, too. If he'd made a move to fuck me, I would have let him without a second thought. If he'd used my body for his own pleasure rather than focusing only on making me come, maybe I could be more mad about him leaving. Maybe I wouldn't have one singular, restless, uncomfortable question that I can't shake.

What does he want from me?

He apparently doesn't want a hook-up, and he doesn't see me as his mate. He obviously knows how completely batshit it is for him to be involved with a Bureau employee as Director, so… what? What else is there? What the hell is he thinking and why is he making all of this more confusing than it needs to be?

All those thoughts rattle around in my brain for the rest of my bus ride, and I'm no closer to any kind of answer as I step off onto the sidewalk.

I don't usually bother coming downtown on my days off, but the bus ride felt worth it today to be somewhere I could be surrounded by people and yet completely alone. It's one of my favorite feelings in the world, being a part of all that movement and life, without feeling the pressure to engage with it.

I stroll through Pike Place Market, enjoying the noise and the crowd and everything to see and smell. Fresh flowers and piles of produce. Fish on ice and delicious smells wafting over from the food stalls. Plenty of little trinkets and art and jewelry I pass by, but leave without buying since I'm saving all my brand new adult money.

Leaving the market, I walk a few blocks to my next destination, still enjoying the wonderful anonymity and having some uninterrupted time to think.

Pulling open the door to the Seattle Public Library, I step inside and inhale the familiar scent of books. The space is open and bright and modern, and it's one of my favorite places to tuck myself away for a little while.

I pass through the busier main lobby, take an elevator up a few floors, and find a quiet table by a wall of windows to set up.

Just being out and about in Seattle isn't my only objective today.

I'm preparing a proposal for Kerri Vaughn, one of the best-selling monster romance authors in the business. She's starting an all-new series of monster romcoms next year, and she reached out to me a while back about doing the covers for them. For a dozen of them.

I've worked with a few smaller authors, but this contract would blow every other commission I've done out of the water. She loved the first samples I sent over, and if the concept art I'm working on now fits her vision, she's going to give me the green light to move forward with the entire project. Along with a big, fat advance on my work.

God, I want this job.

Getting a contract with Kerri would open so many doors.

In addition to the paycheck, the exposure I'll get almost guarantees me more clients. The possibility that I might be moving closer to making illustration an actual career puts a bubble of mixed excitement and nerves into the bottom of my stomach.

I've got my digital sketchpad with me today, and I take out my stylus and get to work. My plan is to do some touch-ups on the proposal images I'm sending to Kerri.

Only, that's not what happens.

My hands itch and my impulse control flies out the window when I open up a blank page. Before I know it, I'm sketching the graceful arc of two enormous wings, obsidian black talons, two eyes with flames kindling in their depths. I'm filling in golden scales and wickedly curved horns, a wide mouth full of razor-sharp teeth.

I work like I'm in a trance, drawing from memory and my own fantasies, until I've got the beginnings of a golden dragon framed by ink-black pines and a million stars keeping watch above.

Goddamn it. That damned dragon has wormed his way into my subconscious.

Even while I'm mentally cursing his name, the drawing is coming together beautifully. I spend the next hour refining and filling in the details, and when I take a breath to zoom out and get some perspective on whatever madness I've been working on, I can't deny what I'm looking at.

It's good. Really good. And the visual reminder of how Blair looked on the night he took me, how simultaneously afraid and in awe I was, the way I couldn't take my eyes off him, makes my heart start to ache and a fizzy, anticipatory heat spread from the center of my chest outwards.

I'm still staring at the drawing when the motion of two people approaching makes my head snap up. I find a pair of young women standing there—a blond and a brunette, maybe around twenty—looking at me like they recognize me.

"Can I help you?" I ask, quickly clicking the lock button on my tablet and sitting up straighter in my seat.

"Are you Kenna Byrne?" the blond asks, shifting nervously.

I nod. "Uh, yeah, that's me. Sorry, have we met?"

"No," the brunette answers quickly. "We just recognized you from Twitter."

My stomach drops. "What do you mean?"

The blond pulls her phone from her pocket, scrolls through it for a moment, and then flashes the screen toward me.

"It's you, right?" she asks, getting excited now. "With that dragon? I mean, how freaking crazy..."

I don't hear the rest of what she says over the buzz of panic in my ears.

Right there, on the Seattle Whisper's official account—a gossip site dedicated to all things salacious going on in the city—is a pinned post about the dragon incident last Friday night.

A pinned post with 'Kenna Byrne' in the headline and the profile picture from my Twitter account as the featured image.

What the actual fuck?

"I have to go," I say, cutting off the blond who's still talking.

The two girls nod in unison and scurry away, and my heart is beating fast and fluttery in my chest as I shove my tablet back into my bag. I make a beeline toward the stairs, pulling my phone from my bag and opening up Twitter.

I have a thousand new followers.

Quickly setting my profile to private and making a mental note to go through later and block all the weirdos, I open up the Whisper's feed and find the article.

"Hey! It's you!" someone calls out as I reach the library's

front doors and head out onto the street.

I don't stop for a moment, but pull my hood up over my head to hide my face as best I can. Dodging people on the sidewalk, I scan the article as I walk. One line near the beginning immediately jumps out at me.

Byrne was identified by a confidential source, one who has provided proof he was on a date with her at the time of the kidnapping.

"Fucking wolf-boy," I mutter as I reach my bus stop.

My hood is still high around my face, but I keep my eyes fixed downward, not making eye contact with anyone.

How many of them have seen this? How many people know who I am?

As I continue reading, there's nothing in the article that identifies Blair. Which I suppose makes sense. It's not like Dylan would have any reason to know or guess he was the one who took me.

The article has more photos and a couple of video clips that I scroll right past, not interested in seeing myself being picked off like a field mouse in a hawk's grasp, and a sick feeling seeps into my stomach as another paragraph catches my eye.

Byrne was identified as being an employee of the Paranormal Citizens Relations Bureau, leading to speculation that this may have been some sort of workplace spat or office romance gone wrong.

Even though there's no mention of Blair in the article, seeing the Bureau brought into it is... bad. Really bad. Not only for what it means for my employment, but because this is the last thing the Bureau needs. Thinking back to what Blair said about outside pressures affecting the Bureau's work, and knowing what a circus it was after everything that went down with Daniel Sorenson last fall, the dread in my stomach grows heavier and heavier with each passing moment.

By the time I make it onto the bus and into my seat, all that dread is a lead weight. I spend the ride home with my head down in my phone, reading hot take after hot take on Twitter about me, the dragon, peoples' wild theories about what happened.

It's a welcome relief when I make it to my stop, and an even more welcome relief to hurry up the Victorian's porch stairs and have the front door closed behind me.

"Kenna?" Fran calls out as I step inside "Is that you?"

Before I can answer, she comes into the entryway from the kitchen, and whatever she sees on my face has her cursing softly.

She steps forward to wrap me up in a hug. "What happened?"

Wordlessly, I pull my phone from my pocket and open up Twitter. Fran's eyes narrow as she reads, then widen as she realizes what she's looking at.

"That was you? Last Friday? Being kidnapped?"

I nod silently, and she curses again.

"Come on," she says, grabbing my hand. "House family meeting. Now."

19

Kenna

By the time I get off the bus down the street from the Bureau the next morning, I'm feeling a little steadier than I was yesterday.

Part of it is from the warm embrace of all my roomies supporting me last night, listening and commiserating and letting me vent.

Still, with as much as I did share, I stopped short of admitting who exactly the dragon is and how I know him. Whether they've connected any dots or assumed that the man who approached me on Saturday is one in the same with the dragon who kidnapped me the week before, I'm not sure. And even if they did suspect, they were kind enough not to ask about it as they did their damnedest to cheer me up.

I wouldn't exactly call myself *cheerful* this morning, but I feel ready to face whatever's coming as I open the Bureau's front doors and walk inside.

And, as it turns out, that happens to be having the attention of pretty much every being I pass fixed squarely on me.

I keep my head as high as I can as I get in the elevator. Even with the deafening silence of the ride up to the fifth floor, I don't break.

It's not until I get to my desk and see my boss already waiting there for me that I feel the first crack in my composure.

"Hey Yvette," I say cautiously as I approach, wondering for the second time in less than two weeks if I'm about to lose my new job.

"Hi Kenna. Would you join me in the conference room for a few minutes?"

I nod and set my stuff down on my desk. I don't look up, but I can feel the weight of all my coworkers' stares on me. Following Yvette to the small conference room near the communications department, that weight only gets heavier and more suffocating with each step.

"You're not in trouble," Yvette says as soon as the door closes behind us and we sit down. "But HR is going to be joining us for a chat."

As if on cue, the door opens and Yolanda, the HR rep I met on my first day, steps into the room. Like Yvette, she's wearing a guarded expression as she takes a seat on the other side of the table.

"Ms. Byrne—"

"'Kenna' is fine," I quickly correct, and she nods.

"Kenna. We wanted to speak with you about the news that came out online yesterday. Regarding the recent dragon kidnapping downtown."

"Uh, yeah," I say. "What about it?"

"Was the dragon who took you a Bureau employee?"

My mind blanks at the question. They… don't know? I mean, I didn't think it was super common knowledge what kind of paranormal creature Blair is, but the fact that they don't know seems… unbelievable.

What would happen if I outed him now? And do I even owe him any kind of protection?

Looking back and forth between Yvette and Yolanda, they both seem entirely sincere. They really have no idea.

Without knowing why I do, I shake my head. "No. It wasn't anyone who works here."

And just like that, I've lied to my boss and to HR. I've put my ass on the line. For Blair.

"I've already spoken to the police," I continue. "It was just… a misunderstanding. It's settled."

Why am I protecting him? Blair's words from that day in his office echo in my mind, when he asked me why I didn't say anything to the police. *It would have been well within your rights to.* Even then, he was putting it in my hands, leaving it up to me to decide what I wanted to do.

And I guess I'm making the same choice now.

"Am I getting fired over this?"

"No," Yolanda says quickly. "You weren't at fault in any of this. We just wanted to ensure there's no ongoing issue at the Bureau or any violation of our employee code of conduct that needs further investigation."

The comment puts a slight sheen of sweat on the back of my neck. I'm pretty sure *everything* between me and Blair has been a violation of the code of conduct. Swallowing over the lump of nerves in my throat, I look back and forth between the two of them.

"So… what's going to happen?"

Yvette's face is creased with concern as she answers. "I think it would be best if you took some time outside the comms department this week. Just until this blows over. Having you in on meetings and discussions about how this is being handled on the Bureau's end could be seen as a conflict of interest. Both within the Bureau and if any news outlets got wind of it."

My stomach drops to somewhere near the floor. "Are you sending me home?"

I can't afford to take leave without getting a paycheck, and I don't have any vacation time banked yet. Rent in the Victorian isn't all that much, but I've got student loans to pay, a cell phone bill, groceries… I'm pulled out of my panic spiral by Yvette rushing to reassure me.

"No, of course not. I've asked around, and they're looking for some help down in Records this week."

Great. I'm being exiled from my job after less than a month, sent down to the basement to push papers. It could be worse, though, and I just nod silently again.

With that settled, we stand to leave the conference room. Yolanda goes first, and I'm just about to do the same when Yvette calls out after me.

"Kenna, is there anything else you want to tell me?"

There's a slight edge to her voice, something suspicious that makes me stop short when it hits me.

She was there.

On my first day at the Bureau, Yvette was just a couple of steps away from me when Blair was making his speech. She saw the way he stared at me, just like all my other coworkers saw.

And now she's giving me another chance to say something, to confide in her, to tell the truth.

Only… I can't.

Whatever's happening between Blair and me, that's where I want it to stay. I want to keep the rest of the world out. The idea of saying something and having all of this blow up in our faces when it still feels so precarious, when I know I've just barely started to scratch the surface with him, makes me feel desperate to keep it a secret.

This is *ours* to figure out. And if I need to be the one to take it on the chin to keep it that way, so be it.

"No," I say softly, protecting Blair once again. "There isn't."

20

Blair

My stomach is in knots as I ease open the door to the basement filing room in the Records department.

Kenna is leaning over a table, flipping through a stack of folders, but her eyes snap up immediately to meet mine when I step into the room.

"You shouldn't be here."

I fight back a flinch at the venom in her tone, even as I'm well aware I deserve it.

"Ember," I start, and she cuts me off.

"Don't 'ember,' me. What do you want, Blair?"

Despite the tension in the room, some base, lizard part of me savors her fire this morning. Burning brightly, not cowed for a moment or holding anything back now that we're at work and I'm back to being her boss's boss's boss. That spark of hers is still blazing despite what must be a mountain of stress she's dealing with.

"I want you to know that none of the information in the media has come from me," I tell her.

She lets out a short, harsh laugh. "Yeah, I already know that. It was the wolf shifter I was on a date with that night."

The mention of that male sends a flash of irritated heat over my skin. My body sways unconsciously toward hers with the instinct to either protect or comfort her. Hell, maybe both.

Kenna narrows her eyes at me. "Stop it. I already told you that you don't get to be so—"

"Ember," I say, more sharply than I mean to, but I don't want her to finish that sentence.

Crossing the room to stand in front of her, I watch as Kenna's lips press into a thin line and she regards me with suspicion. Which... fine. I don't blame her for being suspicious, but nor can I shake the gnawing guilt in the bottom of my stomach. All of this is happening because of my actions, and she's the one who's being forced to deal with the fallout.

"I'm not happy about any of this, either."

"Yeah, well," she says, bitterness creeping into her voice. "I'm the one who's dealing with it. So forgive me if I don't have a lot of energy to deal with your emotions, too."

"You don't need to be the only one dealing with it."

Kenna looks at me warily, eyes narrowing as she studies my expression. "What do you mean by that?"

"If you'd like to... make a statement. Either to the police or to the media about what happened. That's entirely up to you, and I wouldn't begrudge you if you did."

She frowns. "That would be bad though, wouldn't it? For the Bureau? And for you, I guess, if I brought your name into it."

I grimace. "It wouldn't be great. But that's no reason for you not to handle this how you want to."

"Would I lose my job if I said something?"

"No," I say emphatically, shaking my head. "You wouldn't."

Another long pause before she answers. "But *you* might."

"It's a possibility."

"And you'd just… let me tank your career? You wouldn't try to stop me or, I don't know, kidnap me again to keep me from talking?"

The laugh I let out is brittle and humorless. "No, Kenna, I wouldn't. You'd be more than justified in bringing the whole damn world down on my head if you wanted to."

Kenna considers that, and I wait to see what she's going to say next before I offer any further comment.

I don't know why she's protecting me. I sure as hell don't deserve it.

From the moment I first saw her, I haven't deserved it. I've been an arrogant ass to her, and she's repaid me with more generosity than I have any right to receive.

Kenna shakes her head slowly. "I took this job for a reason. I mean, because I need a paycheck, obviously. But also because of all the great work happening here."

Something in my chest loosens and tightens all at once. Some of the tension I've been carrying fades away, but a pulse of grief and regret rises right up to fill the space. *All the great work happening here.* I'd like to believe that's true, but it's been hard to find that certainty these past few months.

Kenna meets my eyes again, and there's a sad sort of resolve written clearly on her face that puts an echoing pulse of guilt in the center of my chest.

"I don't know why I'm doing this, whatever *this* is," she says softly as she gestures between us. "I don't know why

I'm… I'm…"

So many different ways she could finish that sentence. She doesn't know why she hasn't told me to get the hell out of her life. She doesn't know why she's protecting me. She doesn't know why she's giving me a single moment of her time or consideration.

Any answer would be right, and all are exactly what I deserve.

"What do you want to happen?" I ask her. "With us. Do you want to just call it now and walk away?"

Even as I say the words, every single instinct in me rebels against the idea. Walk away from Kenna? Let the spark of whatever's burning between us go out before I've gotten the chance to really know her, to feel all of that fire burning in her?

"That's not what I want," she whispers.

She lets out a harsh, shuddering breath, and before I can think better of it, I've got my arms around her. Kenna goes rigid in my hold for a moment before relaxing into the embrace.

It feels… right. Holding her like this. Feeling the beat of her heart and the rise and fall of her breath.

The compulsion that grabbed me by the throat when I first saw her rises in me again. The confounding instinct that would have me keep her, hold her, hide her away somewhere she'd be safe. It blanks out everything else, everything that makes me certain I should be the one to relent and let her go.

If I were a better man, I'd listen to that voice of reason.

"Come to my place tonight?" I ask her. "We need to talk, but this isn't the time or place to do so."

Kenna nods where she's got her head resting against my chest, and though it nearly kills me, I let her go and take a step back.

"I'm sorry about all of this," I tell her, glancing around the filing room. "If you'd like, I can speak with Yvette and—"

"No. I think the less we have to do with each other at work would be best, don't you?"

She's right. I know she's right. Yet the idea I can't even do this small favor for her grates against my conscience. Pushing the feeling down, I nod.

When I don't make a move to leave, Kenna gestures toward the door.

"You should probably go."

I know I should, but I stay rooted to the spot, torn by indecision.

Without giving myself time to second guess, I lean in and catch her mouth for a brief kiss. Kenna's breath hitches, and though it takes her a moment, she presses into me and moans softly against my mouth.

Gods above, I could get lost in that sound, lost in the taste and the feel of her, but luckily my ember's got better sense than I do.

"Go," she whispers as she pulls back, eyes still closed and long lashes laying against her cheeks. "Please."

With one finger under her chin, I tilt her face up toward mine. "Look at me."

Her green eyes flick open.

They're like emeralds and springtime and new, unfurling leaves. A million pure, untarnished things I don't deserve.

"You're not alone in this, Kenna."

She nods, but the doubt doesn't leave her eyes. With nothing else I can say to convince her, and knowing I've already overstayed my welcome, I hold her gaze for a heartbeat longer before turning and heading out the door.

21

Kenna

The lobby of Blair's building oozes money and class. Marble floors, expensive-looking artwork on the walls, an ornate fountain bubbling in the center of the space. A freaking *doorman* for crying out loud, one who eyes me with a bit of suspicion as the exterior door swings shut behind me.

"I'm here to see Mr. Blair. Ewan Blair."

Though the doorman's eyes flicker a little at hearing me use Blair's first name, he nods and looks down at the tablet in his hands.

"Name?"

"Kenna Byrne."

With another nod, he escorts me to the elevator, keys in a code on the touch pad next to the sliding doors, and they open immediately. I step inside and thank him as the doors close.

Inside the elevator, the silence is deafening.

I'm going to Blair's penthouse. Ewan Blair. Director of the Paranormal Citizens Relations Bureau and 500-year-old dragon Ewan Blair.

This is probably a terrible idea.

No. Scratch that. This is *definitely* a terrible idea.

But after yesterday and today, I'm completely wrung through and turned inside out. I don't know how I'm feeling or what's the right thing to do, and no matter how this turns out, the one thing I do know is that I need to speak to Blair.

And, terrible idea or not, I don't have much more time to think about it as the elevator glides to a smooth stop at the penthouse and the doors open into a large foyer.

The floor is laid in dark brown wood and the walls are painted a rich sapphire blue with inlaid trim and paneling. There are light fixtures of gleaming gold, and paintings on the walls with splashes of vibrant color. It's so different from what I expected—more marble and neutral colors and cool, sleek finishes—that I simply stand frozen for a few long moments, taking it all in.

"Kenna." Blair's deep voice snaps me out of it, and I turn to find him entering the room from an arched doorway framed in more dark, intricately carved wood.

"Hi," I breathe, drinking him in.

He's wearing a pair of jeans and a deep maroon sweater. Not exactly casual, but way more relaxed than the suits I've seen him in so far.

"I'm glad you came." His voice is still low, warm and inviting as he comes to stand in front of me. Close enough to touch.

"Yeah, I... you said you wanted to talk?"

Blair nods. "Would you care for a drink first?"

I accept the offer and follow him through the archway and into his kitchen. There's more dark wood in here, with cabinetry to match rather than the white, modern chef's dream of a kitchen I might have expected. Blair must catch some of the surprise in my expression, because he turns to me with an arched brow.

"Not what you thought it would be?"

Laughing a little, I sink onto one of the stools at the wide island in the middle of the kitchen. "Not exactly."

"I told you on Saturday," he reminds me as he pulls a few things from the fridge and from a built-in bar area at the side of the room. "I like color and beauty."

Blair works at the counter, adding a few ingredients into a glass and muddling before pouring over with liquor. I watch him as he works with his sleeves pushed back to showcase the thick, corded muscles of his forearms and his eyes narrowed in concentration.

It feels… intimate. Seeing him like this. Being allowed into this space that belongs to him.

When he hands me the drink a couple minutes later and I take a tentative sip, flavor bursts brightly across my tongue.

I hum appreciatively in the back of my throat. "What is this?"

Blair chuckles. "I'm not sure if it has a name. Something of my own creation with bourbon and ginger and orange bitters."

"Well, it's good to know that if things don't work out for you at the Bureau, you have a pretty solid back-up career as a bartender."

A second too late, I realize what I just said. And… shit. With the reality of what he would be facing if I decide to talk to the police or the media… what a stupid joke to make.

Blair, however, doesn't seem offended as he chuckles again.

"Come on," he says, picking up his own glass and

gesturing to another doorway off the kitchen.

I follow him down a short hall, and into a large, high-ceilinged room. It's not a living room, exactly, but something I might almost call a study, or maybe a library with the full wall of built-in bookcases at the back of the room.

Like the rest of the penthouse, it's decorated with dark, rich colors and pops of gold. There's a fireplace set into the wall across from the bookshelves, and another wall which features an expanse of windows looking out over downtown Seattle.

In the center of the space, a trio of wide, comfortable-looking sofas in rich brown leather frame the fireplace. When Blair sinks down on one I follow right behind him, sitting just an arm's length away. He raises a brow but doesn't comment as he takes a long sip of his drink and sets it on the wide wooden coffee table in front of us.

I do the same, pulling my legs up to tuck beneath me and resting an elbow on the back of the couch with my head in my hand like I've got all the time in the world.

In reality, I'm brimming with about a thousand and one questions, but he still owes me more than I owe him, so I'm more than content to wait him out.

He shifts a little closer, reaches a hand out to touch me like he can't help himself, but I shake my head.

"Nope. You said you wanted to talk. So talk."

I'm pinned in place for a few long moments by the weight of his heated stare, but he eventually relents.

"How was your day today?"

Snorting a laugh, I pick up my drink and take another sip before answering. "Really? That's what you want to start with?"

Blair's lips quirk up in a small, sardonic smile. "Why is it that every time I try to make normal conversation, you follow it up with sass?"

I open my mouth, then close it again. He's… not wrong. And fine, if he wants to know, he can know.

"My day sucked," I tell him, feeling no need to sugarcoat. "Pushing papers wasn't exactly what I had in mind when I took a job with the Bureau."

He frowns. "I meant what I said. I can still talk to—"

"Don't. It would just make things worse."

Silence falls between us, and I swirl my drink idly, listening to the soft clink of ice cubes. I only look up when I feel Blair's fingertips brushing lightly over my arm where I've still got it resting on the back of the couch.

"I know you said you didn't want any more apologies," he says softly. "But I really am sorry for all of this."

"Are you?"

His golden eyes narrow a little as he nods. "For kidnapping you, and for everything you're dealing with in the media fallout, of course I'm sorry."

"And for the rest of it?"

The question slips out without my meaning it to, but I can't make myself regret asking it. Especially not when a flare of heat darkens Blair's gaze, and he leans closer.

"No. I'm not sorry for the rest of it."

It would be so easy to close the distance between us, to forget about everything else I meant to say and the rest of the answers I meant to get tonight and just kiss him, lose myself in him, give in to the temptation.

With a remarkable amount of self-restraint, I shift a few inches back. Blair does, too, following my lead.

"I keep thinking…" I say, an unexpected laugh bubbling up in my throat. "How all of this would be so much easier if I hated you. If I really was still angry about the whole kidnapping thing and wanted to make you pay for it."

A flash of surprise on Blair's face, but it's quickly covered by another frown. "Why don't you?"

What a question. I let out a long breath, thinking.

"Maybe because I know you weren't actually trying to hurt me that night. And because of the Bureau, too. I had a front-row seat to everything that happened last fall through Nora, and I know another press scandal is the last thing any of us need."

"That doesn't mean you have to be a martyr and—"

I can't help it, I laugh. "A martyr? We're talking about working in the basement for a week and having to deal with some mean tweets, not me being burned at the stake, Blair."

His frown only deepens, but I press on.

"And because despite everything, I can't stop myself from coming back again and again," I murmur. "I think I know why I do, but I can't quite figure out your reason."

It's not a question, exactly, but the words hang in the air between us.

Why?

Why does Blair want me? Why has it been like this since the first time he saw me? Why hasn't he been able to leave me alone?

"For the same reason as you, ember." He slides closer on the sofa and takes my drink from my hands to set it aside. "Because there's something here. Something burning and bright I can't look away from."

I watch—frozen and spellbound—as he lifts his hand slowly and curls it around my jaw.

"Do you wish you could?" I ask in a whisper. "Turn away, I mean. Walk away from all of this."

Just as slowly, he shakes his head.

Unable to keep still, I brush off his hand and stand to walk over to the wall of windows at the side of the room. The sun is setting, and the sky is lit with yellows and golds and pinks.

Though I don't hear him approach, the back of my neck prickles and a wave of warmth washes over me just before Blair speaks.

"I'm drawn to you, Kenna," he says as I turn to face him. "I don't know why, but it's been that way since the moment I saw you."

I wish he wouldn't say it like that. Like this *means* something, this wild, undeniable heat between us that's been there since the beginning.

"That first day at the Bureau you made it pretty clear that there isn't any kind of… bond between us."

"Yes," he says softly. "I did say that."

"So, we're not mates. Does that mean we can't be anything?"

Blair hesitates, eyes flicking back and forth across my face before he answers. "I can't promise you anything… more than this."

He doesn't spell it out, but I know perfectly well what he means.

There's no real future for us.

Not only because of who he is—the Director of the Bureau, an important, powerful person who would bring a whole lot of trouble down on his head if our relationship was public—but because of *what* he is.

Blair's ancient. He's over 500 years old, and will probably live a thousand more. What's my own life compared to that? I'll be cold in my grave while he's still in the prime of his life.

So this, whatever *this* is, it's temporary. It can't last. It'll burn bright and burn out, and now it's up to me to decide whether I want to run away or let it consume me completely.

God, I know where this ends, don't I?

A small, whispered warning in the back of my brain reminds me just how much of a mistake this probably is. It's cold sanity in the burning madness of this whole situation, a harsh reality check that reminds me exactly where it's going to leave me—miserable and heartbroken and filled with regret.

And, god help me, I'm not going to listen to that warning.

Because even though I can see so clearly how it will end, there's no part of me that wants to miss out on what it'll be like before it does. Even though I can see the ashes and burnt hopes waiting, I also know I'll never experience anything quite like this—I'll never experience anyone quite like *him*—for as long as I live.

I want Blair like I've never wanted anyone. I'm a fucking idiot for it, but when has that ever stopped me from making a massive, glorious mistake?

"What if we didn't think about that?" I ask him. "What if we just... enjoyed this? For what it is. For however long it lasts."

Blair hesitates. Maybe he'll say no. Maybe he knows just as well as I do what a catastrophe this will be, and maybe he's got a better sense of self-preservation.

All those possibilities, however, evaporate to nothing with his low, graveled reply.

"Alright, ember." His hand curls around the back of my neck and he draws me closer. "We can do that."

Staring into his golden eyes, I feel that tug again. The one in the center of my chest. The one that doesn't mean anything at all. Or, if it does, it just means I'm a fool.

No matter what it is or what it isn't, it's not enough to stop me from what I do next.

Blair's lips part in surprise when I surge up and kiss him, and his hand on my neck shoots upward and tangles into my hair. He wraps my curls around his fingers and uses his hold to tip my head back even further so he can plunder me just the way he wants.

He tastes like smoke and spice, like heat and surrender, like a thousand things I should know better than to want.

With no apparent effort whatsoever, Blair cups my ass in both his big hands and lifts me up against him.

It takes me by surprise, and I let out a little yelp against his lips as he walks from the study and down another, longer hallway to a set of double doors in more dark wood. Tossing them open, he strides inside and sets me down on the floor next to a huge bed, but keeps me pinned to him, hands caressing every inch of my body he can reach.

I'm beyond ravenous at this point. I'm starved for him, for any little bit of him I can get my teeth on, and I bite down lightly on the side of his neck.

"Do you prefer to fuck half-shifted, or like this?" I ask between scrapes of my teeth. "I'm fine with either, so don't hold back on my account."

A tremor runs through Blair's broad frame, and the breath he lets out is tinged with a growl.

"You already know the kind of toys I use to get off," I taunt him. "And the last two guys I dated were a gargoyle and a demi-fae, so—"

"Ember," he cuts me off. "You are not going to talk about the other males you've fucked. Unless you'd like a detailed account of my own sexual history, and I think we both know you don't."

The jealousy that courses through me is hot and incandescent, and Blair chuckles like he can see it written clearly on my face. Which, knowing him, he probably can.

"I didn't think so," he taunts right back. "And I'd like to stretch my wings and sink my claws in a bit while I'm fucking you, Kenna."

The image that puts in my mind makes me feel even more feral.

"Then why are you still wearing so many clothes?"

Blair takes a step back and holds out his arms. "By all means, ember, feel free to rectify that situation however you see fit."

The edge of challenge in his words is enough to have me lunging for him, pulling his sweater up over his head and tearing at his belt with clumsy, eager fingers. Blair, the bastard that he is, doesn't give me any help, preferring to watch with half-hooded eyes and a sharp smirk set on his lips until my hands catch on the waistband of his boxer-briefs, the last stitch of clothing he has on.

When I pause, a low rumble of laughter echoes in his chest.

"Waiting for an invitation?"

God, he's an ass. An arrogant, provoking, sexy as sin ass.

I reach my hand into his boxers and grasp his cock. Giving him a hard stroke, he flexes his hips forward into my grip and lets out a ragged curse.

I didn't get a good look at his, well, *goods* when he was half-shifted in the forest by Nora's house, but even in his fully human form he's... large. Thick and long and already hard for me, I stroke him again, and again, and he fucks into my grasp.

"Kenna," he breathes. "Enough teasing."

"No," I sass, leaning up to catch his bottom lip between my teeth.

With a firm, urgent grip on my wrist, he pulls my hand away before roughly shoving his boxers off. As he does, I take a half-step back to get a better look at him and... holy hell. All broad shoulders, firm muscles, and acres of taut skin dusted with dark, springy hair. As I watch, another tremor runs through him. All those muscles bunch and twitch in anticipation of what's coming next.

An answering shot of arousal floods my core with heat.

"You might want to stand back for this."

I shake my head and reach up, flattening my hands on the broad expanse of his chest. "No, I don't think I do."

I want to feel him. The power of him. The magick of him. The fire burning beneath his skin.

With a ripple of muscle and skin, Blair changes right before my eyes. Scales materialize on his chest and shoulders and lower, curving along his sides and toward the center of his hips. Two enormous, deep gold wings spread from the center of his back with a sharp snap as they expand to their full, impressive span. His features grow sharper, eyes glow an even more vivid gold, and when I dare to glance down at where all those scales around his hips coalesce, I can't help the sharp breath I inhale.

The toy I bought wasn't all that far off the mark.

Blair's cock is thickest at the base, where his golden scales fade into deep, dusky pink skin. Long and thick, the length of him narrows as it reaches the tapered head, which flares slightly. He's already impossibly hard, cock jutting out and away from his body, but when I reach for him, he catches my wrist in his grasp.

I slide my eyes slowly back up to meet his gaze, taking my time to study every hard ridge of muscle.

Blair could have been sculpted out of marble with how perfect his body is. It's true even when he's in his human form, but like this, all that power is on even more prominent display.

"You're wearing too many clothes, ember."

"Nope," I say, crossing my arms over my chest. "Not when you look like that, and not when the lights are still on. I'm absolutely not—"

Blair pulls me to him, silencing my protest with another burning kiss. My hands trace the scales on his shoulders, his biceps, and they're soft and smooth beneath my fingers, hotter than his human skin and rippling with every shift of corded muscle.

He pulls back from the kiss and looks down at me with wicked amusement dancing in his eyes.

"I was born in the 1500s. The Renaissance. And do you know what our ideal of beauty was back then?"

Before I can respond, he walks me backward a few steps, then turns me in his arms so we're both looking into his full-length mirror.

"Bountiful bodies," he murmurs, playing with the hem of my tank top. "Luscious, delicious curves."

He meets my eyes in the mirror, and when I don't say anything or stop him, he lifts the shirt up. The way the silky material skims along my over-sensitive skin, and the unbroken hold his golden eyes have on mine makes me shiver with pleasure as I watch him undress me.

"You're perfect, ember," he says as he pulls it over my head and tosses it aside.

His hands land on the clasp of my bra next, opening it with deft fingers and gently pulling it off me. With my breasts out for his appraisal, he makes a low, approving sound in the back of his throat before finally breaking eye contact to watch himself reach up and take them in his hands.

"Gods, Kenna. You truly don't know how exquisite you are?"

When he says it like that... maybe I do.

With the way he caresses me—his long, elegant fingers taking my nipples and teasing them, rolling them into stiff, flushed peaks—I feel every bit as exquisite as he says I am. I arch into his touch, and he leans down to brush his fangs over my shoulder, dragging them lightly over my skin.

With one hand still at my breasts, he slowly slides the zipper on the back of my skirt down with the other. I make it easy for him this time, shimmying a little until it pools at my feet and then kicking it aside.

"Kenna," Blair groans.

I look up to see his eyes fixed on the lace underwear I'm wearing, and on the thigh-high stockings I put on this morning. The ones a tiny, naughty part of me hoped he would have the chance to see.

He wraps one arm around my waist, hand splaying over the soft curve of my stomach, and pulls me back a few inches so the entire length of my body presses against him. The hard ridge of his cock juts into my lower back and the heat of him seeps all the way through me.

My eyes drop to the big hand resting on my midriff, and Blair follows my gaze.

"Do you believe me, ember? Do you believe how unimaginably beautiful I find you?"

I'd usually shy away from being touched like this, held like this, seen like this with all the lights still on and exposed so completely in his mirror.

"Yes," I whisper.

Blair reaches up to grasp my jaw, tipping my head back so he can claim my mouth with a tender ferocity that steals my breath. The hand on my stomach dips lower, brushing beneath the waistband of my panties, tangling in the curls beneath.

Blair groans again. His wings flare wide behind him, and the way the lamplight hits his scales makes him look like a living flame. He moves restlessly against me as he shifts his hand further down between my thighs.

His groan turns into a rasping growl as he sinks one long finger into me. With as soaked for him as I already am, it meets no resistance, and he slips a second in to join the first, angling the heel of his palm just right so it hits my clit as I start to move with him.

It only lasts a few moments, though, before he's pulling away. I cry out in protest, but he just chuckles and tugs on the waistband of my panties, lowering them over the curve of my ass.

"Off. Now."

I obey that deep, compelling command without question, but just as I'm about to reach for the tops of my stockings, Blair stops me.

"Absolutely not. Those stay on."

Without waiting for me to reply, Blair lunges forward and scoops me up, carrying me bridal-style to the bed. Tossing me into the center of it, he climbs in behind me and settles on his back, his wings spread gracefully beneath him. I reach out to touch, but don't get the chance before he grabs me around the waist and lifts me on top of him.

My knees land on either side of his head, but I rear back a little and let out a squeak of protest when I realize what he intends to do.

"Problem?" Blair rumbles from between my thighs, shooting me a wicked smirk.

"I just—I'm not—I haven't done this before," I somehow manage to blurt out. "At least not like... this."

Blair palms my ass, encouraging me forward. "You're not going to deny me this sweet cunt, Kenna. Not when I've been thinking about it for days."

Another sound rasps out of my throat, something between a groan of pleasure and one of embarrassment. Still, I relax into his touch and angle my hips forward. It puts me right on top of Blair's hot, seeking mouth, and a ripple of wild pleasure moves through me.

"Hands on the headboard," he murmurs against the soft skin of my inner thigh, evoking all-too-vivid memories of him giving me that same command in my bedroom. "If you need something to help you balance. Otherwise you move however feels right. Take the pleasure you need from me."

Just like he promised, his claws unsheathe from the tips of

his fingers and press lightly into the swell of my ass. Not hard enough to break the skin, but just enough to cause a delicious little sting of pain that has me rocking forward, bracing myself against the carved wooden headboard of his enormous bed and lowering myself onto his lips.

Blair is right there to meet me. His tongue—longer and more pointed than a human man's—traces a slow, decadent swipe up the very center of me, teasing around my soaked entrance for a moment before laving against my clit.

And… fuck, just… fuck. The feel of him is incredible.

Hot and determined, focused entirely on me and my pleasure, Blair keeps a firm grip on my ass as he urges me to sink even further down onto his face. When I relax into that silent command, the feral, pleased growl he lets out sounds more dragon than man.

It ratchets up my pleasure even higher. The idea that I've got an ancient, powerful being between my thighs, putting all that predator's focus to work unraveling me completely, makes me cry out as a wave of pure pleasure washes over me.

I let myself go.

Not caring that I've never done this, not caring what I might look like, not caring that I might do something wrong or demand too much from him, I simply let myself *move.*

If Blair's rough growl of approval is any indication, he doesn't mind my enthusiasm in the slightest.

He chases every snap of my hips, keeps me anchored as I build higher and hotter toward my peak. His lips and tongue and teeth give me no mercy. Wrapping around my clit. Dipping into me and making me see stars. Rasping against my hot, over-sensitive flesh.

Blair seems to sense my approaching peak before I do, holding me tighter, working me in firm, steady, unrelenting strokes of his tongue against my clit. Again and again, repeating the same motion and pressure in a practiced technique that would take most human men multiple lifetimes to learn.

It only takes me a few more moments of that determined, dragon focus to shatter completely.

I let go of the headboard as I come, slumping forward over myself and burying my hand in Blair's hair as my hoarse cry echoes through the room around us.

22

Blair

As soon as I have the taste of Kenna Byrne on my lips, any lingering self-control burns to ash.

There's only her. There's only Kenna and her sweet cries and all her fire unleashed. For me. Just for me.

When her climax breaks over her, it feels like inevitability. Of course we were going to end up here, like this. There was never any other choice for us.

Because it was there, right there in her eyes and the soft words she offered. A temptation too sweet for me to deny. *What if we just… enjoyed this? For what it is.*

Was there anything I could do but accept?

As Kenna comes apart on top of me, as she writhes and cries out in ecstasy, I draw every last drop of pleasure from her I can. There's no time for mercy, not now, not when time already feels so short between us.

For however long it lasts.

When she spoke the words, I know Kenna was thinking of the disparity between our lifespans and the utter impossibility of us being together given the position I hold, and those are concerns, certainly. But some part of me knows that's not the only reason this thing between us can't burn so hot for long.

She deserves more than this, more than me and the battered, broken thing rattling around in my chest where a heart should be. She deserves someone who can love her in the light, who can promise her their heart and soul.

Tonight, though, it hardly matters.

Not when I've got my willing, wanting ember still pressed against my mouth, coming down from her orgasm and flushed with pleasure.

Her body slumps in sated bliss, and I shift her so she's laying just to the side of me. While she's still boneless and panting, I make quick work of shimmying off her impossibly erotic thigh-high stockings, running a hand over the smooth swell of her thighs. At least until Kenna stiffens and makes a little squeak of protest when she realizes where she's laying.

"Your wing," she gasps, shifting to move off of me.

I keep her in place with a hand on her shoulder and a low chuckle in the back of my throat. "You're not hurting me."

Laying on my wings is not the most natural position to be in. In fact, some dim instinct in the back of my brain is still protesting the feel of them pinned beneath me, but I choose to ignore it. It was more than worth it to have this beautiful woman riding my face like she was born to do it.

Kenna gives me a look which tells me she doesn't quite believe me, but she reaches out to stroke along the smooth expanse of thick, pliable skin.

And… gods. The feel of her soft fingers on me, warm and curious, sends an answering shot of arousal straight down to my hard, aching cock.

"Beautiful," she murmurs.

I pull back, startled, to meet her eyes.

Kenna laughs. She's flushed and rumpled, some kind of vision straight out of a Botticelli painting, looking back at me with soft wonder in her gaze.

"What?" she asks. "Not what you expected me to say?"

"'Beautiful' usually isn't the first adjective people reach for when they see me shifted."

Another soft laugh, a pulse of something aching and tremulous in the center of my chest.

"Would 'fearsome' be better?" she teases. "'Terrifying?' 'Monstrous?'"

"'Beautiful' works. If that's what you'd like to call me."

Her smile falters for a moment before coming back sharper and more wicked. And when her hand moves from my wing to the scattering of golden scales over my chest, the muscles there bunch and ripple in response.

"Can I?"

"Yes, ember," I rasp. "You can touch me however you want."

Her laugh this time is more of a threat. "Alright, dragon. If you say so."

A sweeter taunt I've never heard as Kenna climbs on top of me and proceeds to explore me with lips and teeth and eager, searching fingers. Kissing along the scales over my chest, learning their patterns and texture. Catching one plated nipple between her teeth in a bite hard enough to draw a warning growl from me and another sharp laugh from her. Nipping and caressing a path down over the planes of my stomach and lower, until she settles herself between my spread thighs.

Kenna glances up at me, and the emeralds in her eyes

sparkle in merciless provocation. When her soft, firm grip encircles my length, it's all I can do to hold myself back from surging up and grabbing her, flipping her over, rutting her into the mattress.

And when her mouth closes hot and tormenting over the head of my cock, an inferno erupts beneath my skin.

Kenna gives every bit as good as she got, eyes flicking up to watch herself take me apart with every lick and suck and rasp of her teeth. But when she draws me deep, pulling me all the way to the back of her throat and I feel her low moan of satisfaction break against my skin, I've had enough.

The need to be inside her is a clawing, burning thing, consuming me from the inside out. I'm not capable of being gentle with her as I lunge off the bed, but my ember doesn't seem to mind. She pulls her mouth off my cock with a gasp of surprise and meets me half-way, crashing into me in a tangle of lips and limbs and need.

Another heartbeat later and I've got her pinned on her back. My wings snap to their full width, and her breath catches again as I notch myself between her thighs.

"Tell me yes, ember."

Her eyes have already answered, but her gasped reply is a thread of sanity in the firestorm between us.

"Condom?"

"I'm dormant. Medication. To make sure I can't get anyone pregnant. You?"

"I take the pill," she whispers, moving her hips against me.

My cock slips just inside her hot, soaked cunt, and I reach for any scraps of restraint I still possess.

"Tell me yes, Kenna."

Even as I demand her surrender, I revel in this last moment on the precipice. Having her spread beneath me willing and wanting and glorious, holding onto the last few seconds of who I am before. Before having Kenna, before whatever I'll be after I've known the pleasure of losing myself in her.

"Yes." The word is whispered, but holds an iron-steady certainty. "Yes, *please*."

I thrust into her in one smooth stroke and she cries out, hips and body arching up to meet mine.

A harsh curse rips from my throat at the incredible sensation of being sheathed in her, surrounded by her heat and her scent, consumed by the impossible fire coursing through my veins.

Kenna has her eyes squeezed shut in pleasure, and I'm not having that. Not for a single second.

"Ember," I groan, grabbing her chin. "Eyes on me."

They flutter open, and the depths of glazed bliss in them make me groan again.

"You look at me when I'm inside you. Understand?"

She nods, and I grunt my approval.

"Give me your hand."

Kenna complies immediately, and I grasp her wrist and bring her fingers up to the curve of my wing. Settling them just where I want them, I lean in low and rasp into her ear.

"Stroke me, ember. Just there."

She does, and stars explode behind eyes I suddenly can't keep from closing. Her hand stills a moment later, and I force them back open with a growl rising to my lips.

"You look at me while you're fucking me. Understand?" Her eyes sparkle with wicked provocation, giving every bit of my own arrogance back to me as she strokes my wing again.

Fuck. The things her command does to me. Sharp and unyielding, threaded with a possessiveness the beast in me wants to bow to immediately.

Pulling almost all the way out of her, I thrust back in with enough force to draw another moan from her, a tightening of her hand on my wing, and then we're both moving. Easy and instinctual, like the glide of flight or the dance of two bodies who have known each other for far, far longer than a couple of weeks.

I'm mindless for her, consumed by her, and Kenna is every bit as ravenous. Meeting me thrust for thrust, massaging into my wing, testing out all the sensitive places to figure out which ones make me crazed.

Though, it would seem I've been remiss in returning the favor.

Using her other hand, Kenna grabs one of my wrists where I'm bracing myself on the mattress on either side of her. She pulls my hand down between her thighs, making her meaning more than clear.

"Stroke me, dragon. Just—"

"I've got it," I growl, even as I fight back a wave of unexpected laughter. "Do you ever stop sassing?"

Gods. Laughing at a time like this.

"No." She leans up to catch my bottom lip between her teeth in a quick, vicious bite. "I don't."

I kiss all the rest of that sass into oblivion as I pick up my pace, driving into her so she can feel all of me, and focusing on bringing her to pleasure first.

I'm sure I'd never hear the end of it if I didn't.

Though truly, making my ember come for me is no chore. Even as my body tenses with the strain of holding back my release, even as I want nothing more than to thrust deep and spill myself in her, I need to see her fall apart first. I want to hear all that sass turn into screams. I want her eyes on me, letting me see every bit of fire she's feeling.

To the endless gratification of my ego and the relief of my damningly thin restraint, she's racing toward that peak only a few short minutes later. Tightening beneath me, cries growing more insistent, hand on my wing going alternately lax and grasping as her focus centers in on her own pleasure.

"That's it," I grate out, leaning down over her collarbone so I can drag my fangs over her hot, damp skin and taste the sweet spice of her. "Come for me, ember. I want to feel you."

As soon as she's crying out and writhing beneath me, I let myself go. Wings spread wide, body slamming into hers, her hot cunt grasps every inch of me, her body arches to meet mine, and pleasure grips the bottom of my spine like a fist.

It explodes into a kaleidoscope of flame and color and sensation. I let out a hoarse shout, spilling into her as the entirety of my being comes apart at the seams. Fractured, shattered, pulsing with pleasure as wave after wave breaks over me. As my climax ebbs, it rearranges itself into something new, something raw and battered and sated.

Something that feels like hers.

23

Kenna

Blair spills into me with a hoarse shout that echoes through my bones and a snap of his massive, gorgeous wings above us. Head thrown back in pleasure, muscles straining, lamplight glinting off his scales, he looks like some sort of god or creature of myth. A being powerful and primal, awe-inspiring and a little bit terrifying as he brands me from the inside out.

He collapses onto me with enough foresight to brace his elbows on the mattress so he doesn't crush me completely, but I'm beyond caring if he does. I'm still breathing hard, thrumming with the aftershocks of the best damn orgasm I've ever had as I throw my arms around his neck and pull him even closer.

Maybe I shouldn't. Maybe it's too presumptuous, too intimate, too much like he's my boyfriend or my partner and not just the lover I've taken for however long he'll have me. Blair doesn't seem to mind, though, as he rolls to his side and enfolds me in his arms.

Crushed against the length of his body, I bury my face in his neck and let out a groan at the feel of him still pulsing in me, spilling warmth into my core. His muscles are straining, taut with the force of his release. It's a delicious contrast to my own loose limbs and melting pleasure as I fit all the soft curves of my body into the hard planes of his.

A small, idiotic voice in the back of my mind whispers how good this feels, how right. Wrapped up in him, filled by him, held even closer as one of his massive wings descends to cradle around my back.

I do my very best to ignore that voice.

A good fuck is what I wanted, and an absolutely mind-blowing fuck is what I got.

Nothing more.

Blair recovers the ability for speech first, and the low curse he lets out rumbles through his chest. "Fuck, ember. I didn't know you were going to kill me."

I laugh, biting down lightly on the nearest bit of exposed skin I can reach, and the muscles of his pec leap under the small sting.

God, why can't I stop trying to get my teeth on him?

"You seem alive enough to me."

"Barely," he grumbles, sliding out of me.

I'm still so sensitive that the movement pulls a strangled whimper from my lips, and Blair leans in to swallow the sound in a quick kiss before pulling away and sitting up.

"Stay here," he tells me, getting out of bed and crossing the room to an adjoining door.

I watch him shamelessly as he goes, greedily drinking in the sight of his firm ass and the ripple of scales on his back, the impressive sweep of his golden wings.

A dragon. I just fucked a dragon.

My head is still spinning with that thought when he reemerges a couple of minutes later. He's carrying a towel and a damp cloth, and even though I try to protest, he clucks his tongue in disapproval before kneeling next to my bent knees on the mattress. I frown at him, keeping them stubbornly together.

"I can do that."

It feels like... too much. Him cleaning me up. Tending to me like that. It feels too caring and too intimate and not like something a fuck buddy's supposed to do for you.

"Let me," Blair insists.

The deep, rumbling command makes my muscles twitch with the immediate instinct to obey, but I just frown more deeply and shake my head.

"Kenna," he says. A warning.

I roll my eyes. "Ewan."

As soon as I use his first name, he goes entirely still.

"Why the change?" he asks, voice husky with unexpected emotion.

"I don't have to use it." I shrug awkwardly where I'm still laying on my back, wondering how badly I just fucked up. "I just figured it's kind of weird to keep calling you Blair, you know, now that we've had sex and I—"

I don't get to finish my sentence before Blair—*Ewan*—lunges up and presses me back into the mattress. My legs fall open for him immediately, and my whole body arches into the rough tenderness of his kiss.

"Say it again," he rasps against my lips.

"Ewan."

He shudders as he starts sliding his way down my body. "Once more, ember."

I don't just give him one more. I say it over and over as he kisses a trail down my neck and stops to tease my nipples into tight, stiff peaks. I cry it out as he dips lower still and gives me a sharp nip just above my navel. I say it a little hesitantly as he eases between my thighs, acutely aware that I didn't let him clean me up and I'm still sticky with him and me combined.

Ewan, though, doesn't seem to mind.

"I enjoy making a mess of you, ember," he murmurs against the skin of my inner thigh. "And I enjoy tasting myself on you."

He proves he's not lying about that a moment later as he swipes his tongue up the center of me. The noises he's making against me are wet, satisfied, borderline obscene, but his enthusiasm and hunger are contagious. If he doesn't mind, who am I to complain?

Ewan makes a whole fucking production of cleaning me up with lips and teeth and tongue on my pussy, the insides of my thighs, the stiff peak of my clit as he catches it between his lips and sucks. Just as I feel the first tremors of my approaching orgasm, though, he pulls away.

With a deep groan, he lifts himself off me and grabs me by the hips. He flips me over before climbing back up the bed and hovering the entire length of his big, scale-scattered body over me. One arm bands under my belly, bringing my hips up and back against him. His knees press into the mattress between my thighs, spreading wider to open me up for him. Leaning in, he runs his teeth along the side of my neck, just below my ear, and his stiff cock presses into the swell of my ass.

"I'm going to fuck you again, Kenna. Tell me if that's not something you want."

Is that even a question at this point?

Instead of answering, I arch into him, thrust my hips back in a blatant invitation, but Ewan's not satisfied.

"Tell me yes."

"Yes. Fucking *yes*, Ewan, I—" My words cut off on a

breathless moan as he thrusts forward.

The tapered tip of his cock presses into me, and just like last time, it's so, so much better than the toy he used on me. Bigger, warmer, stretching me to an edge of delicious pressure and fullness as he eases inside. He murmurs to me as he sinks deeper, telling me how beautifully I take him, how perfectly I fit him, a steady stream of praise and filth that makes me burn even hotter.

When he's bottomed out inside me, he pauses. I look back over my shoulder and find him staring down at where he's buried in me, hands on my ass, keeping me spread open for him so he can get a good, long look.

I should feel more uncomfortable right now. Having all that focused, fire-bright energy fixed squarely on me should make me want to squirm and hide. It should make me self-conscious, wondering what I look like to him and what he thinks of me, but all I feel is heat searing me from the inside out, burning up all my doubts.

Ewan sits back on his heels and reaches an arm around my midsection to bring me with him. Lifting me like I weigh nothing at all, he presses my back to his chest, still planted firmly inside me.

"Look at yourself, ember," he groans. "Just look at how beautiful you are."

One big hand cups my chin, tugging lightly so I have no choice but to obey his command.

And fuck, he's not wrong.

My soft body is framed by the hard contours of his—full thighs draped over his muscled ones, rounded belly encircled by his corded forearm, pussy spread wide to accommodate the massive girth of his cock—and the contrast is so fucking delicious I let out a small, helpless whimper.

Held like this, it's hard for me to get any kind of leverage to move on him, but that seems to be exactly the point. With his powerful hips moving under me and his arm tightening around me, Ewan takes complete control. He moves me how he wants, works me with slow, torturous deliberateness that makes me ache and whine for more.

"Tell me what you need," he rasps against my ear, the low rumble of his voice reverberating through every place we're touching.

"More!" The word comes out on a half-sob. "I need more. Please."

"Say it again, and I'll give it to you. Say my name, ember."

"Please, Ewan! Please, I need—"

The last of my begging cuts off on a strangled cry as he lifts my whole body then brings me back down, thrusting his hips up to meet me. Stroke after stroke, he picks up the pace, bouncing me on his cock. He reaches down with his other hand to stroke my clit and there's no teasing, no slow build. There's nothing but his punishing pace and single-minded determination to make me come.

Merciless. He's being absolutely merciless right now and I fucking love it.

I revel in the power of him, the strength, throw my head back and expose my throat to him so he can drag his lips and fangs over my skin.

My climax hits hard and vicious, ripping through me with a force that draws a low scream from my chest. Ewan's rhythm falters as I spasm around him, and his whole body vibrates with the low, satisfied groan he lets out as he joins me. He floods me with heat, keeps me wrapped up in his arms and wings as we both come down from our peaks together.

This time, I let him clean me up, too dreamy and dazed to do more than let out a half-hearted protest when he nudges my knees apart.

We're both quiet for a while after that. The weight of the pleasure we just shared and our physical exhaustion make us heavy and slow as we settle back into the mountain of pillows and the soft, downy comforter on his bed.

That little detail makes me smile as I fight the heaviness of my eyelids. Ewan Blair likes soft things. Despite whatever hardened exterior he might show to the world, here, in his most personal space, he's chosen to make it soft and plush and cozy.

Even with as sated and comfortable as I am, I realize after a few minutes I should probably get going. Staying the night definitely doesn't fall under fuck buddy territory, and even though he hasn't said anything or implied I should go, it's probably best to let the dragon get his rest in peace.

It makes a strange, pinched feeling settle in the center of my chest to think about leaving, but I force it out immediately. He couldn't have been more clear tonight about what we are and what we're not.

Beside me, Ewan's eyes are closed, and his breathing has evened out. That makes me smile, too, knowing just how much I exhausted this powerful creature of magick and myth.

Sliding out from under the covers and tip-toeing to where my clothes are lying rumpled on the floor, I'm stopped in my tracks by Ewan calling after me.

"Kenna Byrne," he says, voice rough and thick with sleep. "Get back in this bed."

I turn to face him with my hands on my hips. "I need to head home."

"No, you don't."

"We're having a sleepover?"

He just grunts and holds the covers up in a silent command. And truly, who am I to argue?

Sliding back into bed, I turn onto my side. He's there a moment later, curling his big, warm body in behind me, pressing his chest to my back, his half-hard cock into the swell of my ass. One of his wings drapes over us both, encasing us in quiet darkness.

"I'll bring you back to your place in the morning so you can get ready for work," he grumbles as he wraps an arm around my waist, already sliding back into sleep. "And then give you a ride—"

"You're not seriously suggesting we carpool to the Bureau."

"Downtown," he finishes. "I can drop you off a couple of blocks away so we don't raise any eyebrows."

I hum low in my throat, imagining for a moment what it would be like to stride through the Bureau's front door holding Ewan's hand. Absurd. Absolutely absurd.

"Fine," I relent, snuggling closer into him and drawing another low rumble of pleasure from his chest. "Works for me."

A few minutes later his breathing evens back out. As mine slows down to match it, I try not to concentrate on how nice this feels. Here, safe, laying with him tucked away from the world.

It's nice. That's it. Warm, cozy, nice. He's tired and fuck-drunk and wanted to be polite. It's late, and it doesn't mean anything more that he asked me to say.

His words from earlier ring through my head again. *I can't offer you anything… more than this.*

Apparently *this* also includes some post-sex snuggles, and that's fine. All of this is fine. For now. What happens tomorrow or next week or a month from now doesn't matter. I've accepted that, and there's no use in being anything but honest with myself about it.

Still, I can't make myself regret anything that happened. Even as sleep pulls me under, and even as some part of me worries that for as long as I live I might never get enough of this, enough of him, that no one else might ever compare, there's no part of me that would take it back.

Whatever's waiting for me in the ashes, for now I'm content to burn.

24

Blair

Kenna's door closes behind her as she hops out of my car a few blocks away from the Bureau. Even though she gives me a small smile and a jaunty wave as she turns and starts heading up the street, some part of me still recoils in shame, leaving her like this.

The windows of my Mercedes are tinted dark enough that if anyone tried to peer in they couldn't see me. It protects me, while exposing her, and every instinct I have screams at me it's wrong, shameful, dishonorable to her.

Gods above, what am I doing?

By all technicalities we're on the same page. We know what this is and what it isn't. There are no promises between us, no expectations. Nothing but the indulgence of the heat we both feel, the inexplicable conflagration that's sprung up between us.

I should have let her go last night. I should have pretended

I was asleep, let her get dressed and creep out of my bedroom like she was fully prepared to do when I stopped her.

But the idea of that felt even worse than this does.

Thinking of her leaving, letting her go like what we'd shared meant nothing, it wasn't something I could stomach.

Even now, when I watch her disappear around the corner with the hood of her jacket pulled up to protect from the light drizzle of morning rain, I still feel the imprint of her skin on mine. I can still smell her, too. The sharp spice of her scent lingers in the car and on my clothing as I pull back out onto the street and drive the short distance to the Bureau.

I grabbed a bottle of spray that's supposed to neutralize scent and brought it with me, but even as I give myself a few quick sprays in the parking garage before heading inside, I'm not sure it's doing much to mask her scent.

No, Kenna Byrne seems to be infused into my skin and bones, clinging to the fabric of my being as I grab my briefcase from the backseat and head inside.

It's fortunate that not all paranormals have as keen senses of smell as shifters, vampires, and a few other creatures, but I'm not taking any chances as I give everyone I pass a wide berth and head quickly up to my office.

I've just hung up my coat and settled in behind my desk when my office door opens with my first meeting of the morning.

Cleo stops just inside the room, nostrils flaring, and I bite back a curse.

"Good morning," I say, looking back down at the pile of papers on my desk.

She crosses the room, arching a skeptical brow as she sits down. "I would ask you about it, but I'm trusting that it's still —"

"Handled," I finish for her with a decisive nod. "Yes, it is."

"Great. Glad to hear it."

Ready to put the topic behind us, I lean back in my chair and nod toward the door. "Is Ophelia on her way up?"

Cleo cracks a smile. "Yes, she is. She was chomping at the bit when I called her last night."

With the visit from HHS still looming and no indication it's going to go well, I gave Cleo the green light to bring Ophelia in for a chat, and she's stopping by the Bureau this morning to be briefed on her next assignment. It's sensitive, risky, and there are very few people on the Bureau's payroll I would trust to handle it with as much skill and discretion as Ophelia will.

Another soft knock on the door just a few seconds later announces her arrival.

Ophelia steps into the room. Like Cleo, she's got a tall, lean build, but that's where the similarities end. Ophelia has light brown eyes to Cleo's deep red, and dark brown hair to Cleo's blond. Her face is almost deceptively soft, heart-shaped and lovely in a way that masks the sharp instincts beneath.

"Director Blair," she says, striding to my desk and offering me her hand. "Nice to see you again."

After shaking it, I gesture to the empty chair next to Cleo. "Likewise. Please, take a seat."

Ophelia's posture is straight and confident as she sits, tone even and steady, ready to get to business. "I hear you've got an assignment for me."

"We're tracking some news out of Boston," Cleo jumps in. "Vampires. A few rogues, apparently, causing some trouble in the city."

"Really?" Ophelia arches a brow. "That seems… hard to believe."

She's aware, as we all are, that there's little to no chance this is just random attacks by bad actors. The vampire covens in Boston are old, organized, keeping a grip on that city with a ruthless order that would rival any human crime family.

"Exactly," I say. "It's hard to believe anything like this would be happening without the coven leaders knowing."

Ophelia makes a noise of agreement in the back of her throat, but before I can continue, Cleo beats me to the punch.

"What I'm about to say doesn't leave this office," she warns, and Ophelia nods solemnly.

Theirs is a strange dynamic, one I can't quite wrap my head around. Sisterly, but also threaded through with years of a complicated history I only know bits and pieces of. It's not for me to know, I suppose, and Ophelia's been an asset to this organization ever since Cleo joined us four years ago. They've always gotten along in a professional capacity, so I keep myself out of it.

"We have reason to believe it may be a deliberate effort to stir up trouble ahead of the elections this fall," Cleo says, information the two of us have already discussed at length.

"What makes you believe that?" Ophelia asks.

"Some very opaque intel from a few of my contacts back East," Cleo says with a huff of irritated breath. "One in particular you might still be in touch with."

Ophelia's face contorts into a grimace. "Cassandra?"

"Bingo."

"Great," Ophelia drawls. "Can't wait to see her again."

Apparently the only one in the dark about why this particular source might be a problem, I clear my throat. "Care to elaborate?"

They both turn to look, like they've forgotten I'm there, and Ophelia answers.

"Someone I used to be... friendly with. When I was living in Boston during college."

Cleo chuckles. "Someone we used to party with, more like."

They share another look, and I cut in. "And she's got some sort of connection to the Boston covens?"

"Yes," Ophelia answers. "With one of the most prominent. I'll start with her and see where I can get with any information about who might be behind this, and why."

"Good," I tell her with a satisfied nod. "And on that note, we've got another contract operative in Boston I would like you to partner with on this. He should be arriving any—"

A knock at the door finishes that thought for me.

"Come in," I call out, standing from my seat.

Ruthie opens the door, and a tall, blond vampire follows her into the room. His blood-red eyes land on me for a moment before he inhales sharply. His gaze cuts to Ophelia, eyes widening almost imperceptibly when he sees her sitting there.

"What an unexpected delight," Casimir says, recovering from his surprise with his usual careless elegance.

Ophelia's entire body goes rigid. Woodenly, she turns in her chair to face him, all the color draining from her.

"It's been far, far too long, Ophelia. It's good to see you again."

Based on her expression, I'm not sure Ophelia shares that sentiment. Her next words come out with uncharacteristic venom as she turns to face Cleo.

"You want me to work with *him*?"

Cas smiles, though it's not the easy, teasing expression he usually wears. There's something sharper behind it, and a flash of irritation in his deep red eyes.

"The two of you know each other already?" I ask, stating the obvious, but not sure how else to break the sudden tension in the room.

"We're acquainted," Cas says with a deep chuckle.

I'm surprised to see Ophelia looking so unnerved, an

actual flush climbing her cheeks. In all the years I've worked with her, she's been nothing but cool, composed, even cocky at times. Never flustered like this. When I glance at Cleo in confusion, she's staring daggers at me.

"Thanks for the heads up on that," she mutters.

"We only spoke last night," Cas says smoothly, walking to stand with a hip propped against the corner of my desk. There's no spare chair for him to sit in, but he chooses to stand right next to Ophelia, looking down at her with a glint of challenge in his eyes. "What do you say, Ophelia? It could be fun, the two of us partnering up to take down the bastards who are orchestrating all of this chaos."

By the way her face scrunches up in distaste, I sincerely doubt Ophelia agrees, but she quickly rearranges her features back into neutrality before she answers.

"Sure, maybe we'll be able to keep in touch while I'm out there, but I work best alone." He opens his mouth to reply, but Ophelia's not finished. "Cleo? Should I speak with the payroll department like usual to get them my info?"

Cleo nods, shoots me a quick look that clearly says 'don't ask', then stands and gestures toward the door. "Yeah, let me walk you down there."

I stand as well, shake Ophelia's hand, and promise to be in touch with all the details we have on the case. The two of them leave, and Cas sinks into the chair Ophelia vacated with uncharacteristic heaviness.

"There is a history between me and sweet Ophelia," he says with a dramatic sigh.

Sitting, I snort a laugh. "You don't say."

He opens his mouth like he's about to elaborate, but I stop him with a raised hand. "Is what you're about to say something that would prevent the two of you from working civilly together? Or something that would put either of you in danger?"

Cas shakes his head.

"And is it something Ophelia would rather I not know?"

A sardonic smile turns up the corner of his mouth. "Yes. It likely is."

"Then I don't need to know. If there are any issues once the two of you are out in Boston, then we can discuss it."

Perhaps I should be more cautious here, but the two of them are the best operatives on the Bureau's payroll. I want them both on this case, and fully expect them to be able to figure it the hell out. Neither one has ever needed any hand-holding on the assignments they've taken, and interfering here will probably do more harm than good.

Cas stays silent for a few long moments before he speaks again. "You think she is the right person for this work?"

"I do."

"Then I will endeavor to help her, whether she wishes my assistance or not."

"Cas," I say in warning. "I don't want you to strong-arm her. If she wants you to back off—"

I'm interrupted by his low, amused chuckle. "If one of us is going to strong-arm the other, our history suggests it would not be sweet Ophelia on the receiving end."

Now *that* interests me more than I would care to admit, but I'm not about to press him for details. Instead, I shuffle through a few of the papers on my desk.

"We can speak with human resources about payment before you leave—"

Cas waves his hand carelessly, interrupting me again. "You know I do not take payment for these matters."

I'm aware. The vampire is richer than sin, probably more than either Elias or I with the centuries he's spent dealing in artifacts and secrets and gods know what else. It's how I met him in the first place, when he tracked me down to retrieve a very large and very expensive emerald from my hoard. An emerald that just so happened to be attached to a coronet belonging to one of Britain's most ancient dukedoms.

It wasn't my fault the heir to said dukedom had bargained it away in an attempt to recoup his massive gambling debts before it wound up in my hoard. And even though Cas went away empty-handed from the exchange, we'd stayed in touch and become friends over the next few decades.

He's been in and out of both Elias's and my lives in the centuries since. He'll occasionally disappear for years or decades at a time, only to show back up as soon as we'd written him off for dead.

The past half-century, however, has mellowed him. He purchased a large home in Boston and seemed to actually settle for the first time in his existence, though for the life of me, I can't figure out the reason for it.

"I know," I tell him. "And you also know I'll always offer."

The help he's given me since the Bureau was little more than a dream for myself and a few other founding paranormals has been invaluable. Information on high-ranking government officials. Small pieces of secret, damning leverage we could employ to force hands when we needed to. And even now, he's always willing to lend a hand to the Bureau when it's needed.

Cas stands, rolling his shoulders. "You'll have more information about this assignment for me?"

I nod. "Yes, in the next couple of days, actually. If you're sticking around Seattle?"

His devilish smile returns. "I am. I fully intend to terrorize Elias and his delectable little mate for a few days. The kraken still hasn't learned what a mistake he's made by offering me free admittance into his home."

Snorting another laugh, I shake my head. Cas has full access to my penthouse as well, but I don't blame him for wanting to spend time with Elias and Nora. Their place is a true home, one that's felt full and bright and warm ever since they moved in together.

"Tell Nora I said hi."

"You can't tell her yourself?"

Hesitating, I try to think how to answer him and cover my ass at the same time. I've been avoiding Nora and Elias since Kenna and I have been... well, whatever we are. I'm not sure how to face them, or how to answer any of their more than fair questions about just what the hell I'm doing with Nora's best friend.

"Just send my regards."

"Send them yourself," Cas insists. "Join us for dinner this weekend. Unless there's a reason you'll be tied up here in the city? Something that might have to do with the way you smell like you've been dipped in a vat of orange juice and... ginger?"

Cas leans in and takes a good, long whiff of me. Red eyes dancing, he opens his mouth to speak again, and I hold a hand up in warning.

"Not the time."

"Fine," he concedes. "Then I'll look forward to stopping by before I head back to Boston."

As soon as I'm alone in my office, a strange heaviness settles itself into my chest. A weariness, maybe, some kind of exhaustion that seeps down to my bones.

This whole business in Boston makes me uneasy, and I can't put my finger on exactly why. Maybe because I'm not convinced it will make a damned difference, even if it works out the way it's supposed to. The ghosts of the same old battles to fight coming back to haunt me again and the recognition of the futility of it all, even as I know I can't step back from the fight.

Or perhaps it's the visit from HHS next week hanging over me like a headsman's ax. With all the chaos here in Seattle this past year—both of my own making and otherwise—part of me wouldn't even be surprised if they tried to fire me outright.

I've got other ammunition I could deploy if that came to pass, other favors to call and levers of power to pull, but thinking about it now just makes me feel tired.

And, all of that aside, there's an accompanying pulse of pain in my chest right next to that exhaustion. Sharp need and cloying guilt twisted together in a vice around my heart.

The image of Kenna's face comes to mind, dappled in morning sunlight, eyes closed and full lips parted slightly as she slept. She was sprawled across my chest when I woke this morning, and I had the pleasure of watching her sleep for a few long, precious minutes. Kenna was relaxed, utterly peaceful, and I felt as if I could have stayed there watching her for hours.

But, like it always will with us, life and reality came crashing back in. And now all I have is the remnants of her scent on me as I turn back to the unending pile of responsibility on my desk.

I settle in and get back to work, all my frustrations and exhaustion and that needling ache in my chest hanging over me like a dark cloud.

25

Kenna

"Kenna," Ewan growls. "Enough teasing."

He's sitting on the padded bench at the foot of his bed, wings spread behind him. I'm kneeling on the rug, kissing up and down his thighs, nipping at his contracted abs, touching him everywhere but where he really wants it.

And god, is it a fucking power trip.

I told him he couldn't touch me, and so far he's held himself back.

But by the way his wings are flared, his muscles are straining, and his cock is standing at full attention, I'm not sure how much longer that restraint is going to last. Until then, though, I'm going to enjoy every single moment of driving him out of his mind.

I hum low in the back of my throat and lean in… just to stop a couple of inches short.

"Ember," his voice is a harsh, graveled warning.

Taking the stiff length of him in hand, I peer up through my eyelashes. A jolt of wicked excitement moves through me at the tortured, frustrated look on his face.

"Yes?"

Like he really can't help himself, one big hand sinks into my hair and nudges me forward. "Enough."

"No. Not nearly enough."

Even as I sass him, I give him a little mercy. Flicking my tongue out, I lick just under the head of his cock, along the sensitive ridge of flesh I know will make him wild.

That hand in my hair tightens, and I pull back. Ewan opens his mouth to protest again, and I cut him off with a sharp smirk and more sass I know will rile him up even further.

"So eager," I murmur, raising higher on my knees. "Five hundred years old and you haven't learned to be patient?"

Ewan's wings flare again, his body shifts restlessly as I reposition myself between his thighs, and though he lets out an impatient huff of breath, he doesn't offer any retort.

Good dragon. He's learning he can't always get his way with me, and it's enough to make me want to reward him a little.

Cupping the sides of my breasts, I lean in and nestle his cock between them, savoring the broken groan that rasps from his throat. He reaches up to cover my hands with his, and I let mine drop away so he can squeeze me tighter as he thrusts.

Good, but missing something.

"This would work better with a bit of lube."

A strangled, impatient noise rumbles in his chest, but he seems to agree as he nods toward his nightstand. "Right side of the bed. Top drawer."

It only takes me a few seconds to find it, and when I return to kneel in front of him and glance down at the bottle, I let out a short laugh.

God, he even has expensive lube. In a sleek black tube with a brand name I don't recognize, I pour some into my palm and inhale the sharp, spicy scent of it. My eyes widen as it immediately starts to warm and tingle against my skin.

Ewan smirks down at me. "Enjoying that?"

"Yes." I reach out to curl my fist around his cock. "But I think you will even more."

I'm absolutely right about that as he thrusts into my grip a few times, letting out another frustrated groan before holding out his hand in a silent command. I hand him the bottle and arch my chest up for him as he squeezes a generous portion on my breasts and massages it into me.

The tingling warmth and the firm pressure of his hand makes my skin flush. Ewan chuckles with satisfaction as he reaches down to roll a nipple between his fingers and spread the warmth there, too.

"So pretty and pink for me," he murmurs, moving his hands to the sides of my breasts and resting his cock between them. "So soft and perfect, ember."

He starts to move, sliding himself between my tits, and I hold my mouth open, tonguing him on each upstroke. I watch him, too, and feel another surge of power. Face contorted with pleasure, a low growl building in his throat, seeing how much I affect him sends a shot of hot, liquid arousal coursing through my veins and straight down to my pussy.

I brace my hands on his thighs, digging my nails into the golden scales there as he thrusts harder. His movements get a little erratic, uneven, and just before he's about to come all over me, he stops with a harsh curse and his hands fall away from the sides of my breasts.

"Well damn," I tease. "That was just getting interesting."

"As appealing as the idea of coming all over your tits is, ember, I want to be inside you. Now."

The impatient command in his words sends another shot of heat through me as he reaches down and pulls me into his lap.

Straddled across his hips, I grind myself into him, spreading the slick arousal from my pussy along the length of his cock. He's probably already lubed up enough, but if a job's worth doing, it's worth doing right. And the added benefit of spreading the warm, tingling lube against my pussy is just another perk.

Ewan meets me stroke for stroke, sinking the tips of his claws in a little where he's got his hands on my ass. He keeps me held firmly against him, running his thick length over and over my clit until he reaches the end of his patience.

"Enough," he says again, and by the edge in his voice, I can tell he's close. Too fucking close.

He's not the only one. I'm about two good strokes away from coming without him in me, and that feels pretty fucking unacceptable right now.

Bracing one hand on his shoulder, I wrap the other around his cock and notch him at my entrance. Shifting impatiently, I start to slide him inside, but the angle is more difficult than when he's been on top of me or behind me, and I let out a tight, impatient whine.

"Could use some help here," I pant, rocking my hips into him.

Whether he picks up on my rising desperation to have him in me, or on the slight wince of pain in my expression as he stretches me toward my limit, something about the words gentles Ewan. His grip on my hips loosens, fingers soft and coaxing rather than sharp-tipped and insistent.

"Easy, ember," he rumbles, stilling me and slowing us down.

I wish he wouldn't.

Talking to me like this, soothing me like this, showing this kind of restraint and taking it easy on me. It feels too much like... well, I don't know what the fuck it feels like, but I know it's not what I want. Not from him. Not right now.

I angle my hips a bit differently, breathe in and out to get myself to relax, and he slips another couple of inches inside.

The curse Ewan lets out is muffled against my shoulder as his lips find my skin, and his fingers press harder into my hips.

"You're going to fucking kill me."

"Good," I rasp.

If I'm going to fall apart, then so should he.

Rocking again and feeling myself soften around him, the sharp drag of his fangs on my shoulder makes me relax even more. It's what I want—the hard edges of him, not the soft.

It's an award-winning effort on my part, but I eventually get him all the way inside. I'm breathing hard, grinding myself down on his scaled pelvis and reveling in the way the rippled feel of him rubs against my clit. I do it again, and again, until he pricks me a little harder with his claws, drawing my attention.

Ewan's head is still dipped down, eyes fixed on where we're joined, but when he senses me looking he drags his gaze up to mine. Our eyes meet, and I freeze. I'm caught, completely transfixed by the golden flames swirling there, pinning me in place. It makes me feel seen in a way I don't want to be—exposed, cracked open, every part of me laid bare for him to examine—and it's almost enough to make me want to climb off him and run away.

Almost. Because what he says next breaks the spell and reminds me exactly why I'm here.

"I said *enough*, ember. If you're not going to fuck me properly, then I have no problem taking you to the floor and rutting you there."

A flash of heat breaks over my skin. There it is.

That's the dragon I need.

Using hands and knees and my whole body for leverage, I raise up until he's almost all the way out of me before sinking back down fast and brutal and drawing strangled, broken noises from us both.

Ewan moves with me, rocking his hips up to meet mine, digging his claws in so deep I wouldn't be surprised if I had a set of bruises there tomorrow, dragging his fangs nearly hard enough against my skin to draw blood.

I revel in all of it. The edge of pain, the furious way we push each other higher, harder, until we shatter together in a mess of sweat and shaking and straining muscles. Tenderness feels like too much, but this? This feels fucking incredible.

As we come down, Ewan keeps his arms around me and drags me with him up onto the mattress. He's breathing as hard as I am, brow damp with sweat and a low groan in his throat as he rolls onto his side.

"I'm too damn old for this."

I huff a breathless laugh, pushing up onto an elbow to look over at him. If he were an ordinary human man he'd look like he was about forty, but in this half-shifted form he looks ageless, mythical. If I didn't already know how old he was, I wouldn't even be able to guess.

Instead of thinking about it too hard, I just give him a condescending pat on the shoulder.

"That's alright. I can grade on a curve. 'A' for effort."

A growl rolls low in his throat and he tugs me down against his chest. Before he can do anything about that bit of sass, though, his phone rings where he's left it lying on the dresser.

Ewan's body stiffens, and a moment later he's gently

shifting me off him.

"I should take this."

Nodding mutely, I watch him pad naked across the room and pick it up before stepping out into the hallway and closing the door behind him. Whatever he's talking about, I guess it's not for my ears.

Bureau business, probably, and the small intrusion sends a shot of unease through me.

I lay back on the mattress and let out a long sigh. My body is sated, exhausted, tingly from the remaining lube on my skin and in my pussy, but my mind is… unsettled.

Unable to shake the feeling, I roll off the bed—groaning a little at the delicious soreness in my muscles—and cross to stand in front of the floor-to-ceiling windows at the side of Ewan's room. I'm still completely naked, but this side of the building looks out on an unobstructed view. Any prying eyes are at least ten stories below, I'm pretty sure the windows are tinted anyways, and it feels a little surreal to be up this high and so far away from it all.

I stand there in silence, watching the city so far below, and try not to feel uneasy about whatever call Ewan just had to take. Or about those couple of weird moments while we were fucking.

How do I even tell him not to do that?

Uh, sorry, Ewan, but would it be possible to avoid looking at me like that while you've got your cock in me? Like you like *me. Like this is more than a good fuck?*

God.

Maybe it's just a dragon thing. Maybe he doesn't even know he's doing it. He's… intense, when he's shifted. All of those instincts, I guess, the beast in him coming out to play. It probably doesn't have anything at all to do with me.

I'm still thinking about it when I feel the warmth of him at my back. I didn't even hear him come into the room.

Ewan wraps his arms around me from behind, resting his chin on my shoulder. "Come away with me, ember?"

The words, spoken against the shell of my ear, send a shiver all the way through me.

"What? Where?"

"Let me surprise you. Are you busy this weekend?"

I turn to face him, arching a brow. "A whole weekend away? Why? Where is this coming from?"

It's his wings this time, curling forward and brushing against my arms, that make me shiver again.

"I want to see you in the sunshine," he says, low and quiet. "Somewhere we don't have to be careful or look over our shoulders."

There it is again, that damned tenderness, mixed with a warning I'm not going to ignore.

"Does this have anything to do with the phone call you just took?"

Ewan stiffens. "Not… entirely."

"What does that mean?"

He lets out a short, tense breath. "Just a final confirmation of something happening next week."

"Something you can't tell me about?" I guess.

He doesn't answer, but I suppose that's answer enough.

"Is it something I should be worried about? You know, with everything that's been in the media?"

His rumble of discontent vibrates through me as he pulls me closer. "No. It's nothing you need to be worried about."

I make a small noise of acknowledgment in the back of my throat, but I don't answer his question about going somewhere with him, not yet. Not when he hasn't really given me a reason to.

"I'd like to get away for a couple days," he says after a few long, silent moments. "It's been… a while since I've taken any time away from Seattle. I'd like to go somewhere, and I'd like to bring you with."

His exhaustion is clear in his voice, and I don't doubt that he doesn't get a lot of vacation time. Why he'd want to spend it with me, I'm not exactly sure, but it puts a lump in the back of my throat and a pulse of nerves in my stomach to think about spending all that uninterrupted time with him.

Ewan goes quiet, and when I glance over my shoulder at him, his expression is guarded.

"You don't have to say yes."

Another line, blurring. Another step closer to him I probably shouldn't take. One more shovelful of dirt out of the grave I'm digging for myself.

But I'm not dead yet, and I want to see him in the sunlight, too.

"I'll go," I tell him. "But you're paying. Just so you know that up front. I'm broke as a damn joke right now and I don't have the spare cash for a fancy trip somewhere. If you have a problem with that, we can—"

"I don't have a problem with it."

There's a sparkle in his eyes that seems almost… pleased. Like he's enjoying the idea of paying for me, treating me… Nope, not going to go there. He can feel however he wants about it and it doesn't matter to me a damned bit.

"Good," I say, before stepping away and searching for my clothes on the bedroom floor. "I should get going."

When I glance back over at him, all that satisfaction is gone, replaced by a deep frown. He buries it when he sees me looking, covering it with a taunting smirk.

"Really? After only one round?"

Damn dragon. He's more than aware what a challenge like that does to me, but I'm not giving in.

I fish my phone out of my discarded purse and check the

time. "I'm serious. I've got a bus to catch in fifteen minutes if I want to—"

"I can give you a ride. Later."

I shake my head. 'Later' is going to turn into another round or three of orgasms, and before I know it I'll be too tired and sex-drunk to remember I don't want to sleep over tonight.

For practical reasons, but also because last time was a mistake. Going away with him this weekend is an even bigger mistake, but for my own sanity I'm going to cling on to whatever bit of distance I can until I make it.

Ewan is still watching me like he knows he has me, that predator's focus of his sharp and triumphant. I let him think he's won for a few more seconds as I cross the room to stand in front of him.

"Drive me home if you want, but I'm not staying over tonight." He opens his mouth to protest and I stop him with a finger against his lips. He bites it gently as he growls his irritation, but I'm not about to let him win this one. "Fran and I do yoga on Thursday mornings. 5 am at the gym a couple blocks from the house. So unless you want me waking your ass up before dawn tomorrow, stop it."

That's apparently enough to convince him. He agrees, and I duck into the bathroom to clean up before grabbing my clothes from his floor and putting them back on.

Ewan is dressed and sitting on the bed when I reemerge, watching me with a distant, displeased expression on his face.

"Stop pouting," I tell him as I crouch down to put my shoes on. "You'll get me all weekend."

His eyes snap up to meet mine, and though a small smile turns up the corners of his lips and he lets out a soft chuckle, the troubled expression doesn't leave his eyes.

I straighten and cross over to the bed. My immediate reaction is to ask about it, try to figure out what's got him tied up in knots and see if there's anything I can do to help, but I stop myself.

That's not why I'm here. That's not what any of this is for.

"Come on," I say, holding out a hand and nodding toward the door.

It seems to snap him out of it as accepts my offered hand.

I turn to leave the room, but he tugs me back, right into a waiting embrace. His lips land on mine, kissing me with a mixture of heat and teasing and more of that aching, dangerous tenderness, before he pulls away.

"Let's go, ember. You'll need as much rest as you can get before I exhaust you completely this weekend."

26

Blair

By the time Saturday morning rolls around, I'm more than ready for a couple days away with Kenna.

I haven't gotten more than a passing glimpse of her at the Bureau since we parted Wednesday night, and there's a dark, clawing hunger in the bottom of my belly to see her again, have her near me, bask in her scent and her presence.

It's not rational, I know, and probably another in a long line of mistakes I'm making with her, but there's no damn force on Earth that could stop me from getting in my car on Saturday morning and driving to her house. When I pull up and see my ember waiting for me, my dragon hisses his approval.

Standing on the front steps, Kenna has a duffel bag slung over her shoulder and aviator sunglasses perfectly framing her full cheeks and bouncy curls. She's wearing white denim shorts that hug her thighs and a soft green t-shirt with a scooped neckline that shows off acres of her pale, freckled skin.

When I park the car on the street out front, get out, and make my way to her, she props a hand on her hip and looks me up and down.

"What?" I ask, holding my hand out for her bag.

Satisfyingly, she hands it over without giving me any lip.

"I just… thought we might be flying."

I bark a laugh at that as I settle the bag over my shoulder and take her hand, leading her to the car. "The place we're going is a couple hundred miles away. You'd want to be pinned in my talons for that long?"

Kenna doesn't answer, but laughs and slides into the car after I open her door for her. I toss her bag in the back and circle around to the driver's side. As we pull away from her place, she shoots me a teasing look.

"Maybe I could have ridden you."

I look over at her, amused. "Ridden me?"

"Yeah. In your full dragon form. I'm sure I could just slap a saddle on you and ride you like a horse."

I swear to all the gods, the mouth on this woman.

"Nobody's ever ridden me, ember."

Well, at least not in the sense she's implying. In the other sense of the word, however…. She smirks and opens her mouth, probably to make that exact point, but I speak again before she can. "You've ridden horses before?"

Kenna nods. "Yeah. My parents have a farm back in Idaho. It's pretty much impossible to grow up out in the sticks and not end up on a horse a time or two."

The sudden image of Kenna in tight jeans, a plaid shirt, boots, and a cowboy hat makes me smile.

"Tell me more about it."

"What do you want to know?"

"Any of it." *All of it.*

By the way she's looking at me, I can tell she isn't sure where this burning need to know more about her is coming from. And instead of trying to understand it myself, I decide that teasing her a little is much more likely to get me to my goal sooner.

"Humor me?" I ask as we leave her neighborhood and head for the highway. "It's going to be a long drive, and I'd love to hear more about this rodeo career of yours."

Kenna shakes her head with a wry smile on her face before launching into a story about how she sprained her wrist once when she tried to vault up into the saddle. It's followed by another about a classmate of hers who rode a horse to their senior prom, and then another about her own prom date. A boy who apparently passed out on spiked punch before they even got the chance to dance.

There's an honesty and an openness to the things she shares, along with certain beats of sarcasm and even a slight edge of bitterness when she touches on some details about the place where she grew up. I'm intrigued by the contradiction, but don't want to pry beyond asking encouraging questions that keep her talking.

The sound of her voice, the irreverence and humor and candor in the stories she tells, all of it lulls me into a calm, mellow satisfaction as I navigate us out of the city.

I'm taking us to a lake house a few hours outside Seattle. It's surrounded by peace and quiet, trails for walking and towering pines that give it the illusion of being in a world entirely separate from the one we're leaving behind for the weekend.

The place belongs to Ari and her husband, and though they don't get away from the city to stay there as much as they would like, they're always more than generous with letting their friends make use of it. I've never gone there myself, but it was the first place that came to mind when I got the idea of taking Kenna somewhere.

Still, the same nagging sense of shame won't leave the back of my mind as I consider what we're doing. Coming all the way out here. Spending this time together where no one we know will see us.

I want to see you in the sunshine.

What an idiotic thing to say. Not because she doesn't deserve to be seen and appreciated outside dark bars and her quiet bedroom and the four walls of my condo, but because it's something I have no right to ask of her.

I'm still entirely aware of the fact my ember deserves someone better than me. But that doesn't mean any part of me would pass up having her here, now, scrolling through her phone to put something folky and acoustic up on the car's speakers as she continues to tell me about her life growing up in Idaho.

I sprinkle in a few of my own anecdotes here and there. Some of them get more raised eyebrows or curious questions, especially when I let something slip that happened in my life decades or centuries ago like it might have been last week. Mostly, though, I enjoy listening to her speak.

A couple hours into the drive, we stop to fuel up and Kenna heads inside the station. She walks out a few minutes later with a giant fountain drink in one hand and a plastic bag filled with gas station delicacies in the other.

"Absolutely rancid choice of snack, ember," I tell her as she settles into her seat beside me, gleefully opening up some neon-orange chips.

"Oh, really?" she challenges. "Fine. Then you can't have any."

I'm already reaching a hand over the center console to dive into the bag she has nestled in her lap. "Hand them over."

She makes a good show of protest before finally relenting and passing me the bag.

"Why is the Bureau in Seattle, anyway?" she asks a few minutes later, after taking a sip of her soda and handing it over so I can do the same.

A small intimacy, and one I don't really register until I hand it back to her and she sets it in the cup holder. The fizz of the drink still lingers on my lips, and when I swipe my tongue over them, I almost imagine I can taste Kenna, too.

Apparently not as tripped up by the soda sharing, Kenna continues.

"I've always wondered. Seems like it would make more sense to have it in Washington D.C."

It's a fair question.

"The way the Bureau was founded was a bit... unorthodox," I tell her, thinking how to best explain. "We never intended it to be an extension of the United States government, at least not at first."

"What did you intend it to be?"

"An organized effort to bring paranormal creatures out of the shadows. To help all of us achieve a better life than the one we'd been relegated to."

"Living in hiding?"

I nod. "In hiding, or never free to shift forms, or employing various forms of glamours and practical disguises."

"Never able to be yourself," Kenna murmurs, and I nod again. "But that still doesn't explain why it's headquartered in Seattle."

There's always been an abundance of paranormal creatures in the Pacific Northwest. There is in other parts of the country, too—Appalachia, the deep southern swamps, the far north of Alaska—but whatever stars needed to align for us to come together and found the Bureau had shone over Seattle.

I explain it to Kenna as we continue on toward the cabin, and she seems just as content to listen to me speak as I was her. She asks questions here and there, astute and thoughtful, and I answer as much as I can within the bounds of confidentiality.

"And you left Morgan-Blair Enterprises to help start the Bureau?"

"I did. Though truthfully, my heart was never in the business the way Elias's is. I always felt my purpose was elsewhere."

It's surprising, the ease with which the words come, the way it feels almost… natural, to let her in like this. We talk a little more about the Bureau and its history, where I hope it will go in the future, and the words keep coming easy and free.

It's not until Kenna leans back in her seat and asks her next question that all of that ease comes to an abrupt halt.

"Nora once let something slip about you and Elias and some adventures you might have gotten into on the high seas?" she asks with a smile in her voice. "Before you started Morgan-Blair?"

Though she's done it inadvertently, the tenor of the conversation instantly shifts with her question.

Just the mention of those days is enough to put a leaden weight into the bottom of my stomach. Memories of Lizzy, of the day I lost her, of everything that followed, rush in between the cracks in the walls I've been letting down with Kenna, reminding me exactly why it is I put them up in the first place.

Swift and violent, the storm of emotions they bring with them has me biting down hard on my jaw and clenching my hand on the steering wheel.

I'm silent for long enough that Kenna glances over at me, and whatever she sees on my face has her sucking in a surprised breath.

"Sorry," she says quickly, lines of worry appearing on her forehead. "You don't have to answer that."

Snapping myself back to the present and swallowing

around the sudden lump in my throat, I shake my head to clear my thoughts.

"It's alright," I tell her, voice coming out hoarse. "It's just not a part of my life I care to revisit."

She nods quickly. "Okay. Yeah, we definitely don't have to talk about it."

Silence falls, and for the first time since I picked her up this morning, the air between us is charged with discomfort. It's a stark contrast to our levity from just a few minutes ago, and I want nothing more than to salvage it in any way I can.

"You did nothing wrong, ember," I say quietly. "And I'm sorry for how I reacted."

Kenna looks at me again, expression soft with understanding, though also more guarded than it has been all morning. She reaches across the console and offers me her hand. I take it, wrapping my fingers around hers and resting our bound hands against my thigh.

"It's okay," she says. "Let's just keep things light this weekend?"

I nod in agreement, even as a pang of doubt and discomfort and disappointment lodges itself in the pit of my stomach. I'm struck again by the realization of just how long it's been since I've let anyone in, since I've spoken about any of it in any meaningful way.

And Kenna shouldn't be responsible for shouldering the burden of my own stunted emotional capacity.

Doing my best to set it aside, I squeeze her hand again and choose a different topic—how she decided to move from Idaho to Seattle—something casual, something easy, something light, and she picks up the cue immediately.

Her voice fills the space between us, and I let myself hold on to it like a lifeline as we continue on toward the cabin.

27

Kenna

When we reach the lake house, I'm thankful as hell to get out of the car and breathe in some fresh air.

I feel awful about what happened on the drive here. When I asked Ewan about Elias and the fact that the two of them used to be freaking *pirates* of all things—or, at least that's how it sounded when Nora let it slip—I had no idea how he would react.

He's been off ever since. Although he's making an effort to move past it, to keep things light, my stomach is still tied up in knots as we get out of the car.

We reach the cabin just before noon, and it's breathtaking. Set onto a private piece of lakeside property, it's rustic in a charming, down-to-earth way. A modern log cabin with a porch that wraps all the way around, and a huge wall of two-story windows looking over a sparkling blue lake.

As I step out and take my first deep inhale, some of the

tension from inside the car slips away. This place is peaceful, serene, and when I look back at where Ewan is taking our bags out of the trunk, his expression has lightened, too.

"Come on," he says, nodding toward the cabin's back door. "I'll show you around."

The inside is every bit as beautiful as the outside. Lots of warm wood and a fieldstone fireplace in one corner of the expansive living room. A dining space that opens up with a set of glass doors to connect to the porch overlooking the lake.

"This place belongs to my friend Ari," Ewan says from behind me as he sets our bags on the kitchen island.

I turn to face him, folding my arms over my chest. "The blond?"

He chuckles and steps toward me, loosening my arms and pulling them up to loop around his neck. "Yes. The blond. She and her husband are more than generous with sharing this place with their friends."

Ass. Ewan is an ass.

I prove it to him by leaning up and catching his bottom lip between my teeth, nipping at him hard before he clasps a hand in my hair and tips me back to deepen the kiss. We go on like that for a couple minutes, trading deep, stroking caresses and teasing nips.

I'm just about to pull him toward the hallway and explore some of the cabin's bedrooms, maybe see if we can work off the rest of the tension between us, when he leans back and smirks down at me.

"I thought we could go for a hike."

Despite my best effort, a whine of protest sneaks out of me. "Or we could... not go for a hike."

Sex probably isn't the best idea right now, and Ewan must have a better grip on his self-control than I do, because he pinches my chin between his forefinger and thumb and laughs again.

"Come on. We drove up here to enjoy the sunshine. Would be a shame to spend the entire weekend inside."

He's got a point. Damn dragon. And as much as I want to keep protesting, I can't remember the last time I actually spent time in the great outdoors.

Well, besides the night he kidnapped me.

We leave our stuff in a guest bedroom before changing into hiking clothes and heading out on the trail that starts just up the road from the cabin.

The day is beautiful. Perfect, even. The sun is shining through big, white, puffy clouds, and there are towering trees and vibrant green ferns lining the path. It's everything I could have imagined if I had to pick a perfect day to be outside.

Despite the lingering tension from our conversation earlier, we both attempt to just enjoy this gift of a day. We talk about everything and nothing as we walk. Places we like to eat in Seattle. TV and movies we enjoy. We argue about music and whether it's appropriate to wear socks to bed. Laughing and talking, trading small touches and brief kisses, it's all too easy to pretend this is any normal day with any normal—albeit extremely handsome—guy I'm dating.

The feeling only grows when we make it back to the cabin late in the afternoon and Ewan grabs my hand and tugs me toward the dock at the edge of the lake.

"Swimsuit?" I protest. "If you haven't noticed, I'm not wearing one."

He grins at me. "Neither am I."

I don't even have time to react to that before he's stripping off his clothes. Fully naked, he half-shifts before running and diving off the edge of the dock, giving me a good long look at his taut, scale-accented ass as he does. His body makes a graceful arc as he dives, disappearing beneath the water for a few moments before he resurfaces and shakes droplets from his dark hair.

Sun-kissed and dripping wet, grinning at me with a bit of wicked teasing in the curve of his lips, I've never seen him like this. His shoulders are loose, and all the tension has disappeared from his face, like he has nothing to worry about but being here in the sunshine with me.

He seems... younger, somehow. Lighter and brighter than he's been since I met him.

It's enough to tempt me into taking a few tentative steps out onto the dock.

"Going to join me, ember?"

That teasing in his eyes turns into something else, something dark and hungry as he runs his gaze along the length of my body, still covered in a tank top and shorts.

I glance up and down the shore. There are only a handful of other cabins on the lake, and there don't seem to be any other people around or anyone out boating... but skinny dipping? In the middle of the day?

When I look back at Ewan, he's still got that challenging smile on his lips, amber eyes glinting in the summer sun.

Fuck it.

Not feeling bold enough to do any kind of sexy strip tease, I tug off my clothes, leaving everything in a haphazard pile on the dock.

My cannonball is much less graceful than his dive, and before I can break the surface again, Ewan is there. He reaches for me in the water, pulling me into the solid wall of his body.

"Very nice, ember," he says, brushing his lips over mine. "Ten out of ten on form."

"Yeah, yeah," I grumble, kissing him right back. "We can't all be graceful dragons with aerodynamic wings."

"They do come in handy."

To prove it, he spreads them wide and leans back in the water, letting them keep us afloat as he settles me into his chest and closes his eyes to bask in the sun. I do the same, savoring the warmth and the cool kiss of the water, the peace of birds calling in the distance and the knowledge that I have nothing else to do today and nothing else to worry about, not right this second.

No, right now it's just... us. Bared to each other. Alone under a bright summer sky, tucked away from the world for however long this reprieve from reality might last.

The sun is setting over the lake after dinner as we step out onto the cabin's wrap-around porch. We choose a spot with some comfortable, padded patio furniture and a beautiful view of the water. There's a fire pit built right into the deck, and I sit down while Ewan gathers some logs and a torch from an outdoor storage shed.

"Damn," I murmur as he gets to work lighting it up.

Ewan, currently in his fully human form, looks back over his shoulder. "What?"

"I was hoping I'd get to see you light it with dragon fire. You do have dragon fire, don't you?"

His deep chuckle draws a smile to my face as I watch him finish stoking up the fire. When he's done, he comes back over to the couch and takes a seat on the attached lounger at the end of it, grabbing a soft blanket he brought out earlier. With a meaningful look and a pat to the space between his legs, my smile grows into a grin as I join him.

A warm, satisfied noise breaks from his chest as I settle between his thighs. With the blanket he drapes over us, the fire at my front, and the warmth of him behind me, I'm beyond cozy right now.

"I do have dragon fire," he says. "Though I doubt I'd be able to tamp it down small enough to light a fire like that."

"Oh really?" I ask, glancing over my shoulder at him. "You're just the big, bad dragon who'd burn this whole place down?"

"Yes," he says with deliberate, graveled char in his voice as he leans in to press his teeth lightly against the side of my throat.

I shiver. "Stop that."

"Stop what?"

"The whole broody, dangerous, hot shifter thing. You do it at the Bureau, too."

"Do I?"

"Yes, you do. And with how perceptive you are, I'm sure you know it."

He chuckles, but doesn't correct me. "Well, I'm sorry. And I'm sorry the hot, broody shifter thing ruined your first day."

I nudge my elbow against him, and he squeezes me tighter. "You didn't ruin my first day. And besides, I was already nervous as hell about it even before you showed up."

"Why?"

"I had this whole thing about being new-Kenna." As soon as I've said it, I realize how entirely idiotic it sounds.

"New-Kenna?" Ewan asks, and when I tilt my head back to look up at him, he has one brow arched in question.

"Never mind," I mumble, cheeks burning as I face the fire. "It's stupid."

Ewan reaches forward to cup my chin in his hand, turning my face back toward him. "Tell me."

Light. We're supposed to be keeping things light. Maybe he's forgotten, but for some reason I don't feel like reminding him right now.

"I've always been kind of... a lot, you know?" I say, shrugging like it doesn't matter. "Ever since I was young. I speak without thinking, and just kind of jump into whatever seems right at the moment and hope things will turn out for the best. And honestly, they haven't always turned out for the best. When I took the job at the Bureau, it felt like a fresh start."

I tell him a little bit more about where I was before the Bureau, and how long it took me to finally graduate college. Though he asks me a couple of questions here and there, Ewan doesn't sound judgmental or disappointed. Even when I talk about the years I spent doing nothing much at all with my life other than partying and going to bars and picking up dudes, I get a satisfyingly jealous little grumble, but no judgment.

When I'm finished, I pause for a few seconds, then laugh with a memory that pops to the surface. "A heat-seeking missile, my sister likes to call me. Barreling into whatever's going to get me into the most trouble."

Ewan's arms tighten around me. "You say that like it's a bad thing."

Laughing again, I crane my neck back to look up at him. "I mean, it's not good. Or at least it hasn't been when it comes to school and a career and getting my life together."

Ewan thinks for a moment. "That may be true, but it's probably also the reason you've made the lasting friendships you have, and why you've been able to put so much passion into your art."

I shrug against him. "Maybe. It also means I've had a lot of people judging me, especially when I was younger."

"Is that part of the reason you left Idaho? You sounded a little sad earlier, when you were talking about your hometown."

I nod, surprised he picked up on that. "Yeah, that's part of it. I had a bit of a reputation by the time I graduated high school, and leaving to start over somewhere new sounded really appealing."

"A reputation?"

"Yes," I tell him, putting a bit more humor back in my voice, shaking off some of the heavier memories. "For parties and boys and all sorts of other things I shouldn't have loved so much."

"For living life," Ewan says softly. "For having a spark that wouldn't be contained."

The words are... dangerously close to being too much. Too much like tenderness. Too much like being seen and understood and vulnerable. All things I've never really shied away from in the past, being someone who so foolishly wears my heart smack dab in the middle of my sleeve, but with him? With whatever this thing between us is? Warning bells are ringing inside my ears.

"And you've done well for yourself," Ewan continues when I don't answer. "You should be proud of everything you've accomplished. And never feel you need to fit into someone else's mold."

I don't know how to answer him. I don't know if I *can* answer him.

We shouldn't be doing this.

I have to remember why it's better that way, better for both of us. Better for whenever this ends. If I don't give so much of myself away, there won't be nearly as many broken pieces to pick up when it's over.

Still, with the soft crackle of the fire and the sound of waves breaking on the shore, with the last streaks of daylight peeking from the horizon where the sun has set, painting the sky in a watercolor of pinks and blues and lavenders, it's hard to listen to all of those warnings.

Especially when Ewan speaks again.

"Besides, you already know how I feel about all that fire of yours." His tone is hushed, words gentle and reassuring, and they pull down one more brick in that wall I'm so damned determined to keep between us.

"Sorry," I say softly, leaning into him as he pulls the blanket up over me, curling me deeper into his warmth.

"Sorry for what?"

"We were supposed to keep things light."

Ewan goes silent, tensing a little behind me. A minute passes, then two, and I'm not about to be the one to break that silence.

"Because of how I reacted earlier," he says finally, and it's not a question. It's not even directed at me, really, but more a thoughtful murmur to himself. "When you asked me about my days as a pirate."

My days as a pirate. What a strange concept. I've always been able to see it in Elias, he's just got that kind of vibe. But for serious, guarded, stoic Ewan, it's never quite made sense.

"We don't have to talk about it," I say, not wanting to draw the same reaction from him I did in the car—jaw tight, body completely tense and on edge. Pain, so much pain in his eyes.

"Do you want me to talk about it?"

The question catches me off-guard. "What do you mean?"

"I mean," he says slowly, like he's choosing his words carefully. "If you don't want to... deal with all of that from me. Emotional baggage, grief. You don't have to."

Something tight and aching pinches in my chest at the words. He's right, I know he's right. I should take him up on the offer to step away from this cliff, keep myself from tumbling headlong into whatever's waiting over the edge.

We don't owe each other anything more than sex and friendship and casual fun. Lightness.

Still, I can't shake the memory of that pain in his eyes. And I can't stop myself from wanting to help him with whatever he's carrying that's so damn heavy.

"You can tell me."

Ewan lets out a long, tense breath before he speaks.

"You were right," he says, voice low and soft. "About

what Nora told you. About the fact that Elias and I spent a few decades of our life at sea. And not on the right side of the Royal Navy."

My imagination spins with the idea, picturing billowing sails, swashbuckling crews, and buried treasure.

"The way all of it ended… It's not something I like to look back on."

A lump settles in my throat at the exhaustion and grief in his voice, but I stay absolutely silent, waiting for whatever he's about to say.

"During that time in my life, I met a woman… one who I recognized as my mate. Her name was Lizzy."

The world tilts, then stops spinning entirely. I'm not sure I'm still breathing when I whisper my next question.

"What happened to her?"

"She died. Over two centuries ago."

A wave of devastating understanding breaks over me. So that's what Nora meant when she talked about him dealing with baggage and loss when it came to having a mate.

Other parts of everything that's happened between Ewan and I begin to make sense, too. How even though he's been drawn to me from the beginning, it's not because he ever thought I was his mate.

Of course I'm not.

He's already found his mate.

And lost her.

My stomach turns over and my chest tightens painfully at the thought of how much something like that must have destroyed him. How even now, hundreds of years later, he's still dealing with the grief of losing her.

Ewan takes a deep, shaky breath before he speaks again. "She joined Elias and I on a journey from France to England, just a short trip, and I fully intended on leaving the ship once we made it back. She and I were going to start a life away from the sea.

"Before we could, though, our ship was attacked. I shifted to fight off the two ships that attacked us, and so did Elias, and though we saved our ship and most of our crew, we couldn't save her."

He falls silent for a few moments, and when I steal a glance over my shoulder at him, he's staring into the fire. The shifting light of the flames plays over his face, highlighting the tension and sorrow etched in his features, and the weight in my chest grows even heavier.

"I've carried that guilt and grief with me ever since."

I grasp his hand where it's resting against my thigh, squeezing it tight in a gesture of comfort I honestly don't know is worth anything at all. Ewan startles a little at the touch, but tightens his grip on my hand a moment later, lifting our joined hands to kiss mine briefly before resting them back where they were.

"Tell me about her?" I ask softly, not knowing if it's the right thing to do. "What was she like?

Ewan looks down at me with inscrutable gold in his gaze. I almost think he'll say no, close down, shut me out completely. But whatever he sees on my face has all that icy reserve fading a moment later. His expression softens, eyes going distant in memory.

"She was… a force to be reckoned with."

Ewan goes on to tell me about a woman with black hair and a teasing smile and an adventurer's spirit who he fell for hard and fast. One who was bold and fearless enough to hop aboard a ship crewed by monsters and sail off into a new life with the dragon she thought was her mate.

She sounds incredible.

Fierce, brave, beautiful. The kind of woman who might have songs or poems written about her. As he speaks, my artist's brain runs away from me, mentally sketching her at the prow of a ship framed by sea spray and the wild waves of the open ocean.

It's no wonder he loved her so deeply. A love deep enough even centuries haven't dimmed it.

"So the two of you were... bonded?" I ask him when he falls silent.

Ewan shakes his head slowly. "We weren't. She died before we could be."

"I'm sorry." I'm not sure there's anything else I can or should say right now. "For all of it. I can't imagine going through something like that."

"Thank you," he murmurs. "If truth be told, time does strange things to grief and memory."

He goes quiet again, but the look on his face is thoughtful, considering, and I simply take the silence to study him. The firm cut of his chin and jaw, the gold of his eyes—softer than I've ever seen it—the faint lines of age and exhaustion framing it all.

"It's different now," he says finally. "I'm not even sure when it started to change, but it hurts less than it once did. Aches instead of stabs, holds a smaller, quieter place in my mind instead of the all-consuming nature it once had."

I nod, though truthfully it's hard for me to fully comprehend what he means.

That kind of love, that depth of loss, it's not something I've ever experienced.

Still, it doesn't stop me from wanting to be close to him, to offer him whatever kind of comfort I can, even if I don't completely understand how he's feeling. I lean back into him and pull the blanket higher over us to block out the deepening evening chill.

We stay that way for a long time, not saying much of anything else, while the fire burns low and the stars shine brightly above.

And later, when we go inside, when we get ready for bed and head into the guest bedroom, I lay down while Ewan stands at the window, staring out into the darkness.

I fall asleep watching him there, wondering where his thoughts have gone, what distant years and lands and seas they're traveling.

28

Blair

By the time I crawl into bed, Kenna is already sleeping. Although her breathing is even and deep, lines of worry and tension still bracket her forehead and mouth.

I ache to reach over and put my arms around her, to pull her to me and hold her close like I did the last night we spent together. I want to feel the warmth and the softness of her. I want to feel her breathing and hear the little noises she makes in her sleep. I want to feel her shift and grumble against me when I gather her into my embrace.

I want to savor all the life in her.

At the same time, I'm not sure I have any right to touch her.

Not right now. Not when, even though I've never felt closer to her, it's never been so achingly clear why all of this has been doomed from the start.

What I wouldn't give in this moment to be a mortal man. To be able to offer her all the things she needs and deserves.

The weight of the compassion and understanding in her eyes and her words when we sat before the fire still sits on me like the warmest blanket. The absolute humbling of being seen and heard and known in a way I haven't been for centuries.

I've never resented more who and what I am, how much it limits what I can give her.

Mating bonds are wondrous things. Magick and inexplicable, drawing two souls together for reasons only the gods can know.

Or at least that's what we creatures like to tell ourselves.

Because the alternative would be maddening.

Not a gift, but a curse. Something that might make a creature happy for a time, even deliriously so. But at what cost? To lose one loved so deeply, to face a too-long lifetime alone once they're gone.

And then to be left to pick up the pieces, to live centuries in the darkness of grief, only to find a ray of sunshine that was never meant to be mine.

If I were a more selfish creature, maybe I'd try to keep Kenna anyway. To hoard her exactly like the dragon in me demands. To take her days and her nights and all the years of her life. To savor her fire and her sweetness for as long as I can.

I might do just that if I wasn't fully aware how unfair it would be to her. How unimaginably cruel, to choose a partner who'll live the entirety of her full, vibrant life while I stay exactly as I am. Not growing old with her, not changing with her, not moving through the seasons of our lives together.

And that's saying nothing of the fact I'd only be setting myself up for the absolute devastation of loving her and losing her. Of living the rest of my dragon-long existence alone with the ghosts of the two women I've cared about most in this life.

Perhaps that makes me a selfish creature, too, but I can't fathom the idea of it.

As it stands, I can still cling to a last grasp of distance. I can still keep some walls in place. I can still make myself do what I know I have to. Soon. Because this has already gone too far, and even though it just might kill me, I know it has to end before any more damage is done.

But I'll be damned if I can end it tonight.

Knowing just how reckless and stupid and selfish it is, I shift over on the bed and pull her to me. Kenna stirs a little, eyes fluttering open for a moment to meet mine. Her green gaze is soft, still laced through with that painful, wonderful understanding, like she sees all of me and hasn't chosen to look away.

Her body melts into mine without a word. Kenna tucks herself into my side, a soft hand on my chest and her head nestled into the crook between my neck and shoulder. She exhales, and her body relaxes, her breathing slows, and after another minute or two she's a heavy, wonderful weight against my side.

Sleep doesn't find me for a long time. Not until the clock has crept well past three in the morning. Not until my eyes are so heavy I can't keep them open anymore. Not until I lose my fight to cling to every last moment with her I can.

29

Kenna

It's been four days since Ewan dropped me off after our weekend together, and I haven't spoken to him since.

The last I saw of him, he walked me to my door, set my bag down on the wide front porch and drew me close with an arm slung around my waist.

"Thank you for this weekend, ember," he said as he lowered his mouth to mine. "Thank you for everything."

The way he said it, the slow tenderness of his kiss, and the tarnished gold of his gaze as he pulled away, made a cloying panic rise in the back of my throat. It felt like... goodbye.

Not that he had the courage to end it outright, and the uncertainty of it all has made me feel vaguely nauseous ever since.

Still, I haven't texted him. I'm not going to text him. Or call him. Or march my ass up to his office and ask him what the hell he's thinking.

Despite everything that's happened between us, and despite how world-tilting our night at the cabin felt, I've still got a little dignity. If he wants to pretend like we never shared those moments or slow-fade this whole thing into oblivion, I'm not going to beg him to reconsider.

Well, probably.

Ask me tomorrow and I might have a different answer.

I've kept myself as busy as I can finishing up the last of my proposal images and sending them off to Kerri Vaughn, and keeping my head down in the office. I've finally been sprung from the Records department, but things haven't stopped being awkward with my coworkers since the story came out in the Whisper.

And tonight, at least, I'm glad I've got something to do to distract myself. Walking up to an apartment building just outside the center of downtown Seattle, I let myself into the vestibule and ring the buzzer. A few seconds later, Holly's voice crackles over the intercom.

"Buzzing you up."

When I reach her door a couple minutes later, she swings it open, takes a good, hard look at me, then calls over her shoulder at Nora, who's standing near the kitchen counter with a corkscrew in hand.

"Wine, stat."

Well, damn. So much for putting on a brave face.

Nora pours three liberal glasses of Chardonnay and we settle into familiar spots in Holly's living room. As soon as we're seated, the weight of my two best friends' gazes settles on me.

Too bad for them, though, because I'm not in the mood to talk.

At least not about Ewan. I have absolutely no idea how to

unravel everything going on between us. I have no idea how to explain it or justify why I, in my infinite recklessness, have taken things so far with someone I should have stayed far, far away from.

Holly opens her mouth, but I cut her off before she can speak.

"Let's not start with me," I tell her, raising my glass. "At least not until I've made it through one of these."

My friends might be a bit nosy, but they also know when to listen and give space. I've never appreciated it more than I do right now, as they both nod in agreement.

"I… have some news," Nora says tentatively, and my appreciation doubles to have a new topic of conversation.

"Oh?" Holly asks. "Spill."

"Elias and I are… mated. Officially."

Both Holly and I gawk at her for a couple of seconds, but I recover the ability to speak first.

"Girl, what the hell? When did this happen and why weren't we invited to the party?"

Nora flushes. "Just last weekend. And it wasn't, uh, really an occasion to share with others."

"Nice," I drawl. "So I take it this wasn't a fancy wedding with flowers and a white dress?"

Nora's face goes even more crimson. "No, it wasn't. It was more like a… kidnapping, of sorts. A kraken-napping. I don't know. There was a rowboat involved."

"Oh, hell yes," I say, pumping a fist in the air. "Any more details you want to share?"

"Absolutely not."

Beside me, Holly stifles a giggle behind her hand. She won't come right out and ask for details like I will, but I know she's just as psyched Nora's in a very happy, stable, sexually satisfying relationship with a genuinely good guy. After what she's been through, she deserves it.

"We're going to plan a wedding, too," Nora assures us. "Maybe sometime next spring or summer. This just felt more important. It was something we both wanted to do."

She reaches into her coat pocket and pulls out a ring. Slipping it on, she holds it up for us to see. It's a huge, glimmering sapphire surrounded by a halo of diamonds set into a platinum band, and for the second time in five minutes, both Holly and I are speechless.

"I didn't want to ruin the surprise," Nora says, flushing with pure happiness this time. "But Elias gave this to me. After... well, after everything. Seems kind of silly, I guess, considering we're already bound for life, but he insisted."

"Not silly at all," Holly says, reaching forward to take Nora's hand and look at the ring. "I'm so happy for you, Nora."

"I am, too," I tell her. "Congratulations!"

I mean it, I truly do. Nora and Elias deserve to be happy, and I'll never be anything but ecstatic for the both of them for finding each other.

Still, sitting here, seeing the absolute joy in her expression, something tight and painful constricts in the center of my chest. I do my best to ignore it, swallow it down, and shake my head to clear those feelings.

The conversation drifts into talking about wedding venues in Seattle, how likely we think it is that Elias will shell out to fly everyone somewhere for a swanky destination ceremony—very likely, if Nora's blush is any indication—and more good natured discussion about bridesmaids' dresses and bachelorette parties and just how freaking happy both Holly and I are for Nora and Elias.

Before long, however, the conversation lulls, and two pairs of expectant eyes turn my way.

Damn. I guess avoidant time is up.

"So," Nora says, leaning forward and resting her elbows on her knees, her chin in her hands, smiling gently. "Any dragon news to share?"

I wonder what Elias has told her, or, maybe even more important, what Ewan has told *him*. I can't imagine Ewan's been forthcoming about our… situationship with many people, but if what Nora told me is true, he and Elias are best friends, so maybe he's confided in him.

I shrug, pretending to be indifferent. "Not really."

"Not really?" Holly asks, incredulous. "What I saw downtown a couple weeks ago looked like a lot more than 'not really.'"

That catches Nora's attention. "Downtown?"

"Yeah," Holly says. "I was out bar hopping with Kenna and the rest of the Victorian crew and we ran right into—"

"Anyway. There really isn't much more to say about it." Nora and Holly are both probably aware what a big, bald-faced lie that is, but they don't call me on it. I shrug, forcing casualness. "Let's talk about something else?"

They exchange a brief look, but mercifully let it drop.

We get onto other subjects—a winter backpacking trip Holly is planning for later this year, some renovations Nora and Elias are doing in their house.

It's just simple, normal conversation, but the entire time I feel like I'm sitting a couple inches to the left of my body. It's like I'm looking on as a spectator, watching the scene play out and nodding, agreeing, adding a comment here and there, but not really present at all.

I'm sure my friends can feel it, but whatever they're thinking, they don't voice it, and I'm grateful all over again. Maybe it makes me a shit friend for holding it all back from them, but like it has so many times, this thing with Ewan still feels like *ours*. Some part of me is afraid of what will happen if I crack it open and let anyone else inside.

Later, after we say goodbye and I catch the bus back to the Victorian, I have to face even more of the people I care about and rely on. They greet me and ask me how I'm doing, and I tell them I'm fine before disappearing into my room.

I'm probably a shit for that, too, but there's only one person I want to talk to right now, and he's not here.

I suppose I could call him, ask him if I can come over, but tonight I'm just so, so tired. And afraid. Because the next time I talk to him, I'm pretty sure I'm not going to like what I hear.

Hiding some more, I get ready for bed and crawl under the covers, feeling the ax of the end hanging over my head.

30

Blair

When I show up to work on Friday, there's a vampire sitting in my office.

Even though I did, in fact, tell him he was welcome to stop by to learn more about his assignment with Ophelia before he returns to Boston, I still grumble a little as I take my seat and face him.

"Cheerful this morning," he says, that teasing Transylvanian lilt back in his voice today.

Ignoring him and shifting a few things around on my desk, I find the file folder I'm looking for and slap it down in front of him.

"Here," I say, with no preamble or ceremony. "Everything we know so far about what's going on in Boston. Ophelia has the same information."

Cas barely spares the file a second look before setting it

aside and inhaling deeply. "More of that delicious spice today?"

I ignore him. "Any questions about the assignment?"

Leaning back in his chair, Cas gives me a slow, provoking smile. I do the same—minus the smile—mimicking his posture until we both look like a couple of arrogant assholes locked in a stalemate.

"I do have other work today," I deadpan. "So unless there's something you'd like to—"

His smile falters. "You're really not going to talk about your human? I may give you hell for it, but after the happiness Elias has found, I would never—"

"This is different. This isn't like Elias and Nora."

The words fall sour and discordant into the space between us.

This is different.

Images from last weekend flash through my mind.

Kenna, naked in the summer sun, pale skin scattered with all of those freckles of hers as she fearlessly joined me in the lake. Kenna, gilded by firelight, offering soft reassurance and kindness as I poured my damn heart out to her. Kenna, a furrow of worry set between her eyebrows as she watched me drive away, leaving her alone on her front porch.

All of those memories are laced with sour, accusing shame. I haven't called her. I haven't even sent a damn text.

I don't know what to say or what to do. I don't know how to let her go.

But I know I have to. This past weekend has made that perfectly clear. I can't offer her any kind of future, can't give her all the things she deserves from this life, and it would make me the lowest of creatures to indulge the baser urges that would have me keep her with me anyway.

Lost in that spiral of dark thoughts, it takes me a moment

to realize just how long I've been silently brooding. When I do, I find Cas watching me with a puzzled, slightly worried look on his face.

"You claim this woman is not your mate?"

"You know my history," I say shortly. "So you know why that would be impossible."

"Stranger things have happened, my friend," Casimir murmurs. "There's never been any stories of a dragon taking a second mate after losing their first?"

Hell if I know. By the time I was born almost five hundred years ago, most of the dragons were gone. My parents had both passed on by the time I was barely more than a youth, and they weren't mates themselves, so I doubt they would have known much about it.

It's never come up with the other handful of dragons I've met, most of them near the end of their long, solitary lives in their distant corners of the world. Or with any other shifter friends of mine.

Nor do I have any evidence—anecdotal or otherwise—that would suggest it's possible to be blessed with not one, but two fated mates in a lifetime.

No, the common wisdom and belief has always been that there's one, just one, for any creature who might be destined to find their other half. And in all the years I've watched fate offer her blessings and curses to unsuspecting beings, I've never known her to be generous enough to hand out such fortune twice.

Whatever he sees on my face, Cas inclines his head in a brief show of deference.

"Forgive me for any presumptions. I do not know what it is like for shifters and their mates. Vampires take our bloodbound partners by choice, not fate, so perhaps I should not speak on that which I do not understand."

A blessing, that. Choice. Free will. The ability to take your life into your own hands rather than leave it to the whims of fickle fate.

"No apologies necessary," I say, and clear my throat, hoping he gets the message that we need to move on. "So, about Boston."

He takes the hint. "Ah, yes. My work with lovely Ophelia. When are we to begin?"

"She's already on her way east. Driving, not flying, so you should have a couple of days before she's in the city."

"Driving all the way across the country?"

"Yes. She... well, you know what? I'll let her tell you about it if she wants to."

Ophelia lives out of a converted van, and even though I offered plane tickets and a short-term rental courtesy of the Bureau, she insisted on taking the van since she didn't know how long she'd be on the east coast. And after Cleo's justified admonishment about springing Cas's involvement on her, I'm going to let this detail stay private.

I had no idea Cas and Ophelia had a history, and I don't know how much she wants him to know about her whereabouts while she's in the city. They're both damn good operatives and I'm sure they'll figure it out.

Or they'll be at each other's throats the entire time they're in Boston.

Whatever the outcome, it's nothing I've got the bandwidth to worry about today.

One corner of Cas's mouth quirks up in a wry half-smile, showing a fang. "I very much doubt she will want to. But nevertheless, I look forward to our time together."

With that, he scoops up the folder and gives me a nod of farewell, promising to check in once work is underway in Boston. When the door shuts behind him, I let out a long breath and rub idly at the faint pulses of pain kicking up behind my temples.

The headache has been lingering there all week, since I dropped Kenna off on Sunday afternoon. It ebbs and flows, but serves as a constant, low-level reminder about my failings with her and my need to decide what happens next for us. Soon.

And, as fate would have it, it's not my last headache for the day.

It's late in the afternoon when Ruthie knocks on my door again. She steps inside, and her usually cheerful face is drawn with irritation when she announces who's waiting to come in and speak with me.

"Send him in," I tell her, and she disappears for a moment before my visitor walks through the door and takes a seat on the other side of my desk.

Andrew Harrison is a hard man. Somewhere in his mid-to-late fifties with a broad build and neatly trimmed salt and pepper hair that speaks to the decades he spent with the armed forces, I'm not exactly sure how this former military man made his way to HHS as one of the highest ranking Deputy Secretaries. Despite that, it's been clear since the first time I interacted with him that he runs his career the same way he might have once run a unit of soldiers. Strict, unyielding, married to procedure and protocol, with little room for indulgence or understanding.

Sitting across from me, his posture is ramrod straight, and there's a knowing look in his dark brown eyes that I don't particularly care for. Keen, cunning in a way humans rarely are, a way that feels uncanny and sends a pulse of warning up my spine.

Whatever he's here to accomplish, there's not going to be any room for compromise or negotiation.

He's been skulking around the Bureau all week after an initial meeting on Monday, speaking to my department heads and having his staff comb through records. It's all within his right to do, and as much as I've tried to be civil throughout the process, it's been difficult not to lose my patience with the way he's been needlessly critical and abrasive in his dealings with Bureau employees.

"I've about wrapped up my investigation here," he says. "And I'm not sure Secretary Thompson is going to be happy about what I've found."

Gina Thompson has never had a problem with the Bureau. She's been one of our loudest champions since the Bureau's inception. Still, she had to sign off on Harrison's little fishing expedition out here in Seattle, and the bastard is just smug enough to raise a few alarm bells in the back of my mind.

"And what did you find?" I ask.

"You know I'm not at liberty to say. Not until my findings are summarized and handed over to the Secretary for a decision on next steps for oversight and correctional measures."

Oversight and correctional measures. More bullshit. I know this organization inside and out, and I know that we're running a clean operation.

Another, darker impulse wants to ask him if I'll also have to wait for this report to 'leak' to the House Paranormal Oversight Committee, so we'll have to deal with all their bluster and posturing, too. I hold my tongue, though, with just enough self-restraint left in me to swallow the words.

Once upon a time, I might not have. Whether it's time and experience that's taught me discretion can be the better part of valor, or the soul-deep weariness I feel knowing that no matter how I might challenge him, I can't pull rank here, I stay silent.

Like so many choices I've been making lately, that one too sits uneasily.

My instincts are shaky and raw in a way I can't ever

remember them being. Volatile. Untrustworthy. Self-doubt is not a feeling I'm well-acquainted with, and I don't know what to do with it now that it's plaguing me.

"Then I can't imagine any further conversation is necessary," I say shortly, and stand to gesture toward the door. "I look forward to hearing Secretary Thompson's feedback on your findings."

Harrison's first tell shows itself on his face as he stands and straightens his suit jacket. It's just a twitch, but betrays a pulse of irritation, likely that he's not getting more of a rise out of me.

Good. Let it irritate him all the way back to D.C.

"Excellent," he says, mask of confidence firmly back in place. "Expect it by the end of the month."

Arrogant prick.

Not bothering with any parting pleasantries, he takes his leave. It's not until I'm finally alone in my office again that I let myself show any kind of reaction to his words.

With a rough hand through my hair and a harsh curse breaking from my mouth, I stand from my desk and cross to the windows.

Harrison's bullshit shouldn't unsettle me as much as it does. All of it will likely come to nothing. Secretary Thompson is a reasonable person, everything the Bureau's been working on has been well above-board, and the small, annoying voice of doubt in the back of my mind is likely no more than my own inner turmoil creeping into the reality of the situation.

Still... I can't deny that I've been doubting my instincts these last few months. Since before I met Kenna, maybe even since before all the ugliness with Sorenson last fall, those threads of doubt have been fraying around the edges of the certainty I used to feel about my place and purpose here. Cleo can sense it, too. In the hesitation I've shown, in my tendency to hedge where I've always been decisive.

Maybe it's the never-ending politics of the role, or the fact that after twenty-five years of building and five years of leading, it's hard to see the forest for the trees. I've been so close to the Bureau for so many years that it's damned near impossible to have any kind of objective perspective anymore.

With an irritated sigh, I return to my desk and find that it's already past the end of business hours.

Flipping on my computer, my hand twitches on the mouse in a split-second of reason before I make a monumentally stupid decision. Opening up the company chat software, I enter a name into the search bar, and it only takes a moment to find what I'm looking for.

A little green checkmark next to a name that makes my heart clench.

Again acting before I can think better of it, I type out a message.

And then I wait.

Another check mark appears, letting me know that she's seen it, followed by three bouncing dots as she types her reply. When it comes through a second later, the weight that's been sitting on my chest loosens for the first time all day.

31

Kenna

Standing on the top level of the parking garage next to the Bureau, I try not to think about how stupid this is.

It's barely after five, it's still full daylight out, and although there aren't a lot of cars parked up here on a Friday afternoon, that doesn't mean someone couldn't drive up at any point and catch us.

Still… it only took a couple of seconds after getting Ewan's message to agree to meet him up here.

Just to talk. That's all.

Since he dropped me off on Sunday and then went radio-silent, I've been feeling less and less generous about giving him the benefit of the doubt. After days without hearing from him, part of me is starting to feel like it might be best if he really is coming up here to end it. At least then I'd have some closure.

Even if the thought of that makes my stomach roil, it

would still be better than all of this uncertainty.

I'm still brooding and mulling it all over when the sound of approaching footsteps catches my attention. Assuming it's Ewan, I don't bother turning around and open my mouth to ask him what we're doing here, when an unfamiliar voice calls out.

"Kenna Byrne?"

I turn and see a man walking toward me. Something about his tone and the knowing way he's looking at me put me immediately on edge.

"Yeah?" I say, crossing my arms over my chest. "Who's asking?"

The man is in his fifties with a broad, athletic build and a serious expression on his face. He's wearing an expensive gray suit and carrying a leather messenger bag over his shoulder.

"Andrew Harrison," he says as he approaches. "HHS Deputy Secretary."

That roiling in my stomach gets even more violent. Fuck. HHS. The guy who's had everyone on edge this week hanging around the building and conducting closed-door interviews with his team.

"Alright," I say, arms still crossed. "How can I help you?"

Maybe not the best way to talk to a guy who's... what? My boss's boss's boss's boss? But something about him's still got me on edge.

"There's something I wanted to speak with you about."

He reaches down and pulls a folder out of his bag, opening it up and taking out a photograph.

I only have to look at it for a moment to realize what it is.

A dragon. A downtown sidewalk. My flash of red hair as Ewan carries me off.

Shit.

"I'd like to ask you about your recent kidnapping. This is

you, isn't it?"

Slowly, I shake my head. "I've got nothing to say about that. And it wasn't a kidnapping. It was just... a misunderstanding."

He arches a brow, clearly skeptical. "Is that so? And is that what you told the Seattle PD when they interviewed you about it?"

"Uh-huh."

He pauses for a moment, like he's waiting for me to elaborate, but I have absolutely no intention of giving him anything more. I didn't say anything to the police, and whatever he wants to know about what happened can't be good for me or Ewan or the Bureau.

"Right," he says, slowly, like he's talking to an idiot. "And this article from a local news source, the Whisper, it claims the dragon who kidnapped you was a Bureau employee."

"Not a kidnapping," I reiterate. "And it had nothing to do with the Bureau."

The half-truth slides easier off my tongue than I expected. It's not *exactly* a lie. What's been going on with Ewan and I really doesn't have anything at all to do with our work at the Bureau, and even if it did, some part of me knows I'd still lie to protect him. My instincts are screaming at me that something about this guy is off, and I want to keep Ewan's name out of it.

"Well—" Harrison starts, but I cut him off before he can get another word in.

"How did you know to find me up here, anyway?" I ask. "It's after work hours and I didn't tell anyone I was coming up here."

A small glint of satisfaction crosses his face. "You should be aware that messages sent on internal Bureau software aren't confidential, Miss Byrne."

Double shit.

If he knew I was going to be up here, then he also must have seen the message from…

"Harrison." Ewan's voice cuts through the weighted silence as he appears at the top of the stairs. "What are you doing up here?"

His eyes track from Harrison to me and back again, and my heart skips a beat. He doesn't think I had anything to do with this, does he?

"I was just filling Miss Byrne in on the proper use of Bureau technology," Harrison says in a smug, satisfied tone. "And on the fact that chat logs can be monitored."

I see the moment it registers on Ewan's face that we've been caught, that we won't be able to play this off as some kind of coincidence or accidental meeting. His eyes harden, and with a few more decisive strides, he comes to stand in front of me, putting himself between me and Harrison.

His posture is rigid, and standing this close to him I can almost feel the waves of tension and anger rolling off of him.

Triple shit.

"You need to leave," he tells Harrison. "Your business here has concluded."

"My business with *you* is concluded," Harrison says. "Kenna and I were still in the middle of a discussion."

At Harrison's use of my name, Ewan goes absolutely still, and I catch the faintest rumblings of a snarl building in his chest.

"Ewan," I whisper. "Stop it."

He needs to calm the fuck down. If Harrison hasn't realized by now there's something far, far beyond an employee-supervisor relationship going on, then *he's* the idiot.

"Leave," Ewan says again, this time with a low, inhuman growl to his voice.

Bad. Very bad. I try to take a step forward and put myself

between them, but that riles up Ewan even further as he keeps me behind him with a firm, unmovable grip on my wrist.

"Very well, Director Blair," Harrison says, still with that greasy little smile on his face. "I'll go. This will be an interesting sidebar to my conversation with Secretary Thompson."

Ewan doesn't say anything as Harrison walks away, and he doesn't let me move, either. He keeps me tucked behind him until the deputy secretary has disappeared into the stairwell at the other end of the garage.

"Ewan," I say, irritation rising. "You need to let me go now."

He obeys, but doesn't move or speak after he releases his grip on me. Stepping around him, I have to snap my fingers in his face to make his laser-focus on the door Harrison just disappeared through snap back to me.

"What the hell was that?" I ask him.

Ewan's muscles are rigid, his eyes molten gold as he stares down at me. A few long, silent seconds tick by, and the longer I look at him, the more worried I get.

There's something... unsettled about him right now. Something fragile. It's there, in the fires lighting his eyes, something that seems desperate and unbalanced.

"What's wrong?"

He shakes his head, unable to answer.

I reach up and lay a hand on his cheek. "Talk to me, Ewan."

At the contact, his eyes slide shut and a harsh breath breaks from his chest. Still, he doesn't relax, and when he opens his eyes again, that fierce light in them is still burning.

"I... I need to take you somewhere."

"Where? Your place?"

He shakes his head. "Just... away. Away from here." His

hands grasp my waist, dragging me closer to him. "Please, ember. Let me take you somewhere."

I don't know if I should trust him. Not now. Not like this. But when I meet his eyes again there's not just anger shining there, but pain, fear, a shock of desperation that makes my chest ache.

"I'll be safe?" I ask him in a whisper.

All that ragged emotion burns even more brightly. "Always. You'll always be safe with me."

I don't know if that's true.

Physically, sure. I've been certain he wouldn't hurt me since the night he kidnapped me.

But beyond that? I don't trust him for a second, not right now.

Because the way he's looking at me—with all that pain and desperation in his eyes, all the silent pleading for me to agree—it reaches in and tugs at that stubborn, painful thing in the center of my chest.

And even as I nod, even as Ewan's body starts to ripple and twitch with his coming shift, I don't doubt for one single second that I'm a million miles away from safe right now.

32

Blair

There are no rational thoughts in my half-dragon brain.

There's nothing but Kenna and Harrison and danger. The soul-deep need to get her away from here. Take her somewhere she'll be safe. Keep her tucked away forever.

No. Not forever. Just for as long as it takes for me to be certain the danger has passed.

When I shift, she's still there, staring at me with her big green eyes and a mixture of worry and shock and… fear?

Does Kenna fear me?

My dragon's head drops low, showing her we're not going to hurt her.

We'd never hurt her. Impossible. Impossible that we'd hurt her.

She draws in a long, ragged breath, and seems to remember the request I just made.

"Alright," she whispers. "Alright. You can take me somewhere safe."

As soon as we have her permission, my dragon moves, launching from the ground and scooping her up in one smooth move. She's wrapped securely in the dragon's claws, and he's mindful enough to keep her away from the sharp, brutal points. Her soft hands stroke over his scales, soothing, even as she squirms a little trying to get comfortable.

Vaguely, some human part of my consciousness still lingering in the far corners of my mind remembers the remark she made about riding me.

Would she like that? Would it be more comfortable for her than being carried like this?

Surprisingly, my dragon doesn't hate the idea. The thought of Kenna on top of me, riding me, feeling the same thrill and exhilaration I always do when I soar so high above the world and all my problems back on the ground.

Dangerous, perhaps, but maybe there would be a way to make it safer, some kind of contraption to...

No. Not right now. I don't need to be thinking about it right now. Not when the only thing that matters is getting her somewhere safe.

The first place that comes to mind is the same place we went on the night I took her from downtown. The forest clearing. Not too far from Elias and Nora's place. Private. Safe.

It doesn't feel *quite* right. The right place would be somewhere more remote. Maybe somewhere underground. A cavern or a den where I could stash her, keep her, hoard her...

I force some rationality back into my dragon's brain and he gives his thick skull a shake.

The forest clearing will have to do, and I'm thankful for the sunny day and the smooth air as we leave Seattle. The scenery bleeds from city to suburb to something even more green and less populated, and by the time we reach our destination, I've almost managed to calm the dragon down.

Almost. Not quite. Because the moment I drop her down in the clearing, that same sense of wrongness rears right back up.

She's too exposed here. This isn't right.

Watching Kenna get her landlegs back with knees that knock a little and her curls a mad riot around her face, my dragon and I both take a few long moments to simply stare at our treasure. In the late-afternoon light, she glows like a jewel. From the carnelian of her hair to the rose quartz of her cheeks to the emeralds of her eyes, she's more beautiful than an entire hoard's worth of treasure.

And safe. She's safe. She's far away from the person who threatened her. Who threatened us both.

But she's still too exposed.

With an irritated huff, my dragon takes a step toward her, and she takes a step back. He bows low, trying to communicate he's not going to hurt her, but the apprehension doesn't leave her eyes.

He steps again, and so does she. A slow dance moving across the clearing until she glances over her shoulder at the tree line behind her.

"The woods?" she asks, tilting her head in question. "You want me to go into the woods?"

The dragon huffs another breath, and she must understand it for the affirmation it's meant to be, because she nods slowly and takes a few steps closer to the cover of the trees. When she glances back over her shoulder and sees the dragon following her, she gives a puzzled little smile that melts some of the lingering fear in my heart.

Just beyond the tree line, she turns back around. The dragon seems pleased enough to see her where she is, and he crouches low to the forest floor in another show of deference and reassurance.

"Ewan?" Kenna asks softly. "Can we talk?"

I'm not able to pull out of the shift. Not now. Not when the dragon's instinct is so close to the surface.

When I don't make any move to shift back, she frowns.

"Ewan?" she tries again.

More silence. She stares at me for a few long moments, contemplating, before taking a step closer. Then another.

Neither the dragon nor I are capable of moving a single muscle as she approaches.

"You're going to stay right there, right?" she says, voice a little shaky. "You're not going to bite my whole hand off if I touch you?"

The dragon drops his head until his chin is laying against the soft moss.

"Alright," she mutters. "I guess that's about as good as it's going to get."

When she comes within arm's length, she pauses for a few final moments before extending her arm.

"I trusted you when you said you wouldn't hurt me, Ewan. Don't make me regret that."

Kenna lays her hand on my dragon's snout, and although she's still shaking slightly, she doesn't move away. Her fingers brush gently over his scales, followed by her palm flattening against him. All her breath leaves her in a long, trembling exhale as she closes her eyes and steadies herself.

When she opens them again, there's no fear, no hesitation. There's just a soft understanding, a knowing, and when she speaks, there's nothing but kindness in her voice.

"Ewan," she murmurs. "I need you to shift for me. I need to talk to you."

Doesn't she understand? I can't shift. Not now. Not when she might still be in danger. A brief pulse of frustration moves through the dragon. I do my damnedest to put myself back in control, but he's still got the reins right now.

"Ewan." Kenna's voice is stronger now. Unflinching. And when the dragon flicks his golden gaze back up to meet hers, the commanding glint in her eyes makes a rush of instinct rip through him—from the knife-sharp tips of his claws to the spiked end of his tail.

Listen. Yield. Obey.

33

Kenna

What the fuck am I doing?

I don't know where Ewan is right now. I don't know how much of his reaction this last hour has been him, and how much has been the dragon. I don't know if my impossible, infuriating, wonderful lover is anywhere in there, or if I'm making the biggest mistake of my goddamn life.

Still, as I lay my hand against the dragon's nose, I'm also more than a little bit in awe.

His scales are smooth and warm, shifting against my fingers as he breathes in and out. Those golden eyes are fixed solely on me, and the power radiating off of him feels magnetic and threatening all at once.

I don't believe he'll hurt me. Well. Mostly. And I've got to do something to try to help pull him back from wherever his mind's gone.

"Ewan." His name comes out clear and steady, and the dragon's eyes flicker in a way I almost recognize as being the man I know.

But just a couple seconds later, he gets agitated again. He tosses his big golden head and takes a few steps away from me, huffing fast, frustrated breaths through his nostrils. When I see a bit of smoke come out on one of his exhales, I glance nervously at some of the dry brush at the edge of the forest.

The Pacific Northwest does not need another damn forest fire.

"Ewan. Can you shift for me? I'd like to talk to you."

The dragon doesn't respond. He just gives his head another shake and turns away.

"Hey." I step closer, keeping my voice low. "Look at me."

Before I can take another breath, I'm face to face with Ewan's dragon again. He's turned to face me fully, golden scales catching the late afternoon sun. This close to him, I'm struck once again by just how big he is.

And how beautiful.

His breathing has calmed, and he's standing still now, watching with fire-bright eyes as I take another step.

He didn't seem to mind the last time I touched him, so I extend my hand again. This time, he leans into my touch. As soon as my fingertips brush against his scales, a deep rumble breaks from the back of his throat, and I snap my hand away.

Shit. Did he just growl at me?

Those golden eyes look almost confused as he nudges my hand. I don't pull away and when the rumble sounds again, I listen a little closer.

Not a growl. It's more like a purr. Not exactly similar to the one you'd hear from a cat, but still a noise of unmistakable pleasure.

I don't know how long we stand like that, but as his

rumble continues, I get a little bolder. I stroke along his snout, between his eyes, up over the crown of his head. He tilts down a little so I can run my hands over a couple of his curved horns, and the rumble grows even louder.

It's … kind of cute. Not exactly a word I ever thought I'd use to describe this giant, fearsome, scaled creature in front of me. I'm still way too hopped up on adrenaline to fully process what's happening, but as the minutes pass and the pleased rumbling continues, I feel my heartbeat slow down to match it.

When I'm pretty sure he's about ten seconds away from rolling over and showing me his scaled belly, I try coaxing him out of his shift one more time.

"Ewan." My voice is barely above a whisper, gentle and pleading. "Can I talk to you now?"

With a couple of slow blinks, some of the dazed pleasure drains from his golden gaze, replaced by a sharpness that makes me suck in a surprised breath.

There he is.

In the span of a few heartbeats, Ewan pulls back into a half-shift, taking deep, pained breaths as he orients himself. When his eyes meet mine, those rasps turn into a groan. Before I can react, he hauls me up against him.

As soon as I'm pressed to him, his whole body trembles with nerves or anger or relief, or maybe some combination of all three, and I swear I can feel all of those emotions echoing through me.

It *hurts,* this thing in my chest. The beat of pain and longing I can't shove to the side right now.

And I don't want to shove it down. Not when I feel so impossibly close to him. Not when some part of me knows he needs this, needs me.

"Ewan," I say, my voice coming out hoarse. "Talk to me. Tell me what you're thinking. Tell me how I can help you."

He shakes his head, swallows roughly, and pulls me even tighter. I open my mouth to speak again and he smothers the words with a kiss.

There's a moment, just one, when I know some line is being crossed that there's no coming back from.

The heat pulsing between us is pure and primal, the spark to start an inferno, a blaze that reaches in and scorches a corner of my soul I didn't even know existed.

Like it's been with Ewan since the beginning, though, no part of me can turn away. Come what may, there's nowhere in the world I could be right now but here. Right here. With him.

When I part my lips for him, he groans again. I swallow the sound, reaching up to run my hands over the scales on his shoulders and back, to tangle my fingers in his hair, to cup his jaw and hold him to me.

His hands are just as urgent as he tugs at my clothes, discarding piece after piece on the forest floor around us. I don't know how it happens as fast as it does, but when I come up for air, I'm as naked as he is. The balmy afternoon air brushes up against my skin and makes me shiver at being so exposed.

Ewan hasn't said a word, not a single damn word, and he stays silent as he puts his hands on my hips and walks me back a few steps until my bare shoulders brush up against a wide tree trunk.

Then he falls to his knees.

His wings drape elegantly behind him, and he looks up to hold my gaze as he reaches around to cup my ass and lift me, settling the backs of my thighs on his shoulders.

I scramble, trying to shift myself so I don't go tumbling onto the forest floor, but there's no need. Between the steady strength of him beneath me, the firm grip he keeps on my ass, and the smooth bark against my back, I'm not going anywhere.

When he dips down, taking a long, slow lick up the very center of me, my head lolls back into the tree. I arch into his mouth, grind myself against his face, and the growl he lets out sounds just like his dragon—pleased and primal and vibrating against my core.

Ewan works me with single-minded determination, pushing me higher, faster, barreling toward a peak. There's no slow build, no leisurely tasting. No, apparently he doesn't have the patience for that right now, and neither do I.

I want to break. I want him to take me apart piece by piece until there's nothing left but pleasure and heat, until this thing in my chest stops hurting and I can pretend it was never there at all.

I come with a hoarse, strangled cry, and Ewan doesn't give me a moment of mercy until I'm boneless and trembling, barely able to keep myself upright as the last waves of my orgasm subside. Only then does he move, maneuvering me with effortless strength until he's standing and my legs are around his waist. He keeps me pinned to him—one arm banded around my back so I don't have to lean too hard into the tree—and when the thick head of his cock notches against me, he pauses.

"Tell me yes, Kenna."

My choice. Whether or not I want to leave the line blurred or obliterate it completely.

"Yes."

He drives into me with a single hard thrust and I cry out again, body arching in unimaginable pleasure and fullness.

Ewan is just as relentless as he was when he was on his knees. Desperate, wild, slamming into me with hard, punishing strokes. There's nowhere to hide, no inch of space between us, so I just hold on to him, panting and breathless, tied up in knots as he drops a hand to my clit and rubs in firm strokes.

"I want to feel you, ember," he rasps into the tender skin just beneath my ear. "Let me feel you."

Peeling my eyes open with an effort that takes every spare bit of concentration I can muster, all the air in my lungs stutters out on a gasp.

Ewan Blair is undone completely. Stripped bare, looking at me with a wildness in his eyes that I've never seen, a desperation that wraps around my throat like a fist. He looks almost... afraid. Of whatever this is, of whatever's happening to the two of us right now.

I lay a hand against his cheek, the touch gentle enough to startle some sanity back into him, to make his wings flare wide and the punishing pace of his hips to falter.

"Only if I get to feel you, too," I whisper, and kiss him.

There are no more words after that. There's nothing but the unrelenting stroke of his hand, the fullness of him moving in me, the shared rasp of our breath, and the balm of the summer air surrounding us. And as soon as I feel the first tremors of his release, I'm right there, too. Falling apart. Just as undone as he is.

Ewan spills into me with a hoarse shout. Wave after wave of liquid heat lashes my core, feeding into the storm of my own orgasm. Unable to stay on his feet, he sinks to his knees on the forest floor, taking me with him so I'm straddled across his thighs, still hugged tightly to his chest.

It's a few long, hazy minutes before either of us speaks again. I take the time to savor this, savor him, savor these moments of connection like I already know they won't last much longer.

Because as the minutes pass and the silence stretches on, I swear I can feel the distance growing between us. And when Ewan finally speaks, I can hear it in his voice.

"I'm so sorry, Kenna," he rasps, low and distraught.

"For what?"

His eyes snap to mine and a short, disbelieving laugh breaks from his lips. "For what? For all of it. Reacting the way I did. Losing my head like that. Kidnapping you—"

"Not kidnapping," I interrupt him, stroking my hands through his hair. "I agreed to come with you."

He holds my gaze until the pleasure of my nails raking over his scalp is too much and they slide shut, another rumble of pleasure kicking up in his chest. At the sound of it, though, he seems to snap back to reality.

He gives his head a sharp shake, and I drop my hands.

"I'm sorry for what happened with Harrison," he says. "You should have never been involved with any of it."

Strange, how I haven't really even thought about Harrison for the last hour.

Well, maybe not so strange considering I was dealing with a massive golden dragon who may or may not have been about to eat me.

The reminder of what happened back at the Bureau makes my stomach clench. "Does he... does he know?"

"If he doesn't at least strongly suspect, he's an idiot."

"Suspect," I repeat slowly. "About you? Or us? Or..."

"All of it," Ewan says bitterly.

He looks beyond me, scanning the forest around us like he's seeing it for the first time. And maybe he is. I still don't know how much of him was here with me before he shifted back.

I take his chin in my hand and turn his attention back toward me. "What... what do we do now?"

As soon as I ask, something in Ewan's gaze falters, then shutters completely.

Don't do that. I want to plead with him. *Don't keep shutting me out.*

But I know it wouldn't be any use. Already that expression of his is morphing back into certainty.

"I'll handle it."

My heart sinks. Sure. I'm sure he'll handle it. Like he's been handling it when things get too heavy and he decides to pull away. Like he's been handling tough conversations by avoiding them completely.

I don't say any of that, though. How could I?

I know what this is, and what it isn't. I know who I am to him, and who I'm not.

I should probably be angrier about it, but right now all I feel is tired. All I want is to get the hell out of this forest and go home.

"Alright," I say finally, dropping my head to lean my forehead against his shoulder. "Alright."

I can't look at him. Not now. Even when he threads his hands into my hair and tries to tip my head back to meet his eyes, I stay stubbornly right where I am until he relents.

"We should head back to the city."

The way he says it makes it sound like everything is alright. Handled. Settled.

Still, when he slides out of me and helps me find my clothes so I can get dressed, when he shifts back into his dragon form and gathers me up gently in his claws, taking off and flying back toward the city, it doesn't feel like anything is settled.

It feels like the last bit of candleflame winking out. It feels like another goodbye. One that's about to be permanent.

34

Blair

I haven't been able to think straight since Friday.

Not since I lost my last thread of control and took Kenna out of the city. Not since her gentle words and the touch of her hand were the only thing that could bring me back when I felt entirely lost to my baser nature. Not since I fucked her like it was the last time I'd ever get to touch her, and felt the moment she realized it would be.

By the time Monday afternoon rolls around, I'm stretched to a breaking point.

It's been quiet so far today. No calls from Harrison or Secretary Thompson. No salacious tabloid fodder or scathing political article outing the Director of the Bureau as an unstable dragon and a kidnapper. Nothing but silence and normalcy and business as usual that only ratchets up my sense of impending dread even more.

I am, as Kenna would probably phrase it, freaking the fuck

out.

Not that I've talked about it with her. Guilt and shame have been clogging my throat since the moment I dropped her off on Friday. They've been sitting like an anvil in the center of my chest, and for the life of me, I don't know how to make it right. I don't know what to do or say to fix anything between us, or how to work up my nerve for the conversation I know we need to have.

The one where I let her go.

I almost did it on Friday when I dropped her off back at the Bureau parking garage, after I'd shifted and pulled a spare set of clothes from my car to get dressed. It was on the tip of my tongue to say it, but the weight settled on my chest and the chokehold of emotion creeping up my throat kept me mute.

At least until my phone started ringing, and a quick glance down showed a half-dozen missed calls from Cleo.

Grasping onto the one straw I could reach, I'd made an excuse to Kenna and left her there. Just left her there like the coward I am.

I could feel the weight of her eyes on me as I walked away, just as certainly as I could feel the sting of it in my chest, the pounding of guilt behind my temples, and the soul-deep ache that's been plaguing me ever since I left her.

It's constant, burning, an unending reminder of all the ways I've failed her and how completely, utterly selfish I'm still being.

I've barely been able to function these last couple of days, let alone sleep or think rationally about what I need to do next.

I'm still barely hanging on just after end of business on Monday, when the sound of my office door opening breaks through the dull static in my brain. Ruthie's been at an off-site meeting with Cleo most of the afternoon, and I'm not expecting anyone.

I'm especially not expecting a kraken with an expression like thunder on his face.

"What the hell, Blair?"

I swallow around the thickness in my throat. "What do you want, Elias?"

Not bothering to take a seat, Elias crosses to the desk and braces both his palms on it.

"What did you do to Kenna?"

A shot of ice moves through my veins. "What do you mean?"

"I mean, my mate has been worried about her for weeks. And then two days ago Nora gets a phone call, goes to see Kenna in the city, and comes back looking pale as a damn ghost over whatever the two of them talked about. Care to provide any insight into what that might be?"

"Nora spoke to Kenna? Is Kenna alright?"

Cursing harshly under his breath, Elias removes his hands from my desk and runs one of them through his unkempt black hair before finally taking a damn seat.

"I have no idea. I wasn't about to pry for more details when Nora was so upset."

"So why do you think it has anything to do with me?"

Elias's laugh has no humor in it. "Please, don't patronize me. Of course it has to do with you. Tell me what the hell happened."

Briefly, in halting sentences and scant details, I tell him about Harrison and what went down on Friday. His veiled threats to Kenna and the Bureau. What followed when I had no choice but to shift and take her somewhere, though I leave out most of the finer points about what happened when we got there.

"Fuck," Elias breathes. "I've seen your dragon when he

loses his shit. You could have killed her."

The very idea of that is so abhorrent I can't stop the low, threatening growl that slips into my next words. "Never. I would never hurt her."

In the history of my friendship with Elias, there's always been an imbalance of power between us. Perhaps because of the discrepancy in our ages, or because his own nature has always been gentler, more flexible, understanding, while I've had free rein to be a domineering prick.

But now, when I snap at him, he doesn't flinch. He just keeps studying me with an expression on his face that looks almost like pity. Or—perhaps more likely—*empathy*, but whatever it is, I don't have time for it right now.

I open my mouth to speak again, and he cuts me off.

"And it's been like that since you met her, hasn't it? That instinct."

Knowing precisely where he's headed with this, I give my head a swift shake. "None of that means anyth—"

"Oh, really?" Elias says, getting angry now. "Do you hear yourself, Blair? You can't leave this woman alone. You're drawn to her beyond reason or sense. You lose your damn mind when she's threatened or in danger. What the hell do you think that is, if not a mate bond?"

"I already had—"

"You never bonded with Lizzy," Elias says, and though his tone has lost its edge of anger, it's no less firm. "I know what she meant to you, and I know how much you still grieve her. And perhaps at one time she truly was meant to be your mate, but why would that mean Kenna isn't?"

Unable to summon a spoken reply or meet his accusing gaze, I shake my head again.

It's not… possible. It can't be possible. It shouldn't be possible.

"Ewan," he says, and it's such a shock to hear that name used by someone who isn't Kenna, I look up and meet his eyes. "Have you really not considered it?"

Again, I can't answer.

Of course I've considered it, and discarded it just as quickly. That's not the way it works, and especially not for a fates-cursed creature like me.

"Haven't you—" Elias tries again, and I cut him off with a growl.

Every single conflicting instinct and emotion that have been roiling in me for weeks flare dangerously close to the surface.

Burning desire and the need to hoard. Grief and memory and the slippery sensation of trying to make sense of this too-long life I've lived. Fierce possession and unending awe of my ember.

My own arrogance and rigid inability to be wrong.

Kenna's beautiful face and hopeful eyes when she sat down across from me, right there, in the spot Elias is sitting now.

What had she said, that very first day?

I know it happens fast, recognizing a mate, and I was wondering if that's what…

Gods almighty, what if she knew before I did?

As soon as I consciously allow space for the possibility, it settles into the center of my chest with a sense of *rightness* that chokes me even further.

Mate. My mate.

Still, I push back against the sensation, clinging to the last bit of reason or denial or whatever the hell has had me so sure from the very beginning she wasn't meant to be mine.

What if I've been wrong all this time?

The full impact of what that would mean slams into me.

Gods, what would be worse, if Kenna isn't my mate after all, or if she is and I've been keeping her at arm's length, holding myself back from her, making her think...

"Blair," Elias says. "What if Kenna really is your—"

This time, when the words come out I know they're a lie. I don't know what makes me say them, what makes it so damn hard to let myself accept the truth I should have held close and treasured since the beginning.

All I know is guilt is climbing up the back of my throat, and the walls feel like they're closing in around me, and I want this damned kraken out of my office so I can think, make a plan, come up with some way to fix this.

"She's not my mate."

35

Kenna

"She's not my mate."

All the air is sucked out of my lungs, the room, the whole damn building as Ewan's words ring out from the other side of the door.

No, not Ewan. Blair's words.

That's who's talking right now, Director Blair issuing a command.

I didn't mean to eavesdrop, but the last few days have been a living hell. I haven't been able to sleep or eat or think right. I hung around the office an hour after work with the sole intent of coming up here and trying to get some time alone with him.

Just a few minutes. Just to make the ache in my chest go away.

When I got here, Ruthie's desk was empty and the door to

Blair's office was slightly ajar.

I could hear voices from inside. Elias. Blair. Angry words being traded back and forth. All leading up to the one flat, harsh statement that makes me feel like the wind was just knocked out of me.

She's not my mate.

I knew that already. I've known it since the very first day I met him. And yet standing here, hearing him say it like that, it makes that painful lump in the center of my chest crack and shatter into a thousand pieces. I slap a hand over my mouth to stop the broken sound that rockets its way up my throat.

I'm still standing just like that when a noise from behind me has me whipping around to see who's there. Ruthie is standing near her desk, deep black eyes wide with concern.

"Kenna," she whispers, having obviously just heard what I did.

I shake my head slowly. "It's... I'm... I've gotta go."

Without waiting for her to answer, I walk away from Blair's office. Reaching the elevator, I step inside and press the button to take me to the lobby, when I hear it.

Blair's voice. Raised and coming from somewhere nearby.

"Kenna."

I'm frozen again, standing in the back of the elevator as I watch him cross the room in long, determined strides. His golden eyes are blazing, guilt and regret etched on his face, but it's not enough to make me move.

Just before he reaches me, the elevator doors slide shut. The last thing I hear before they do is a harsh curse and the sound of a plastic button cracking as he presses it to keep the doors from closing in his face. He's not fast enough, and as the elevator sinks my body loosens from its paralysis. I slump against the wall and try to control the panicked tempo of my breath.

She's not my mate.

I knew this was coming.

From the very beginning.

I just didn't expect it to hurt so much when it did.

No, I force myself to remember, crossing the lobby and heading for the front door as soon as the elevator doors open, *I can't lie to myself like that.*

I should have expected every bit of this hurt. From the moment Blair's golden gaze landed on me that first day in the Bureau. From the moment I started to get to know the man behind all those walls he likes to keep around himself. From the moment I started to trust him, feel safe with him, want him like I've never wanted…

Stop. I have to stop. I need to get away from here.

The early evening air is balmy when I make it outside. I don't even know where I'm going. All I know is I need to get away from this building.

Blair's probably following me, and I'm sure it won't take him too long to catch up with me, but I want as much time between now and then as I can manage.

I don't even know what I want to say to him.

Do I even have a right to be angry with him? I mean, he's been clear since the beginning what he can offer me and what he can't. I've always known the deal.

I can't offer you anything… more than this.

He *told* me. He told me in no uncertain terms exactly who and what I was to him, and it's not his fault I didn't listen.

But that's just who I am, isn't it? Kenna Byrne, certified fuck-up. Always taking the path guaranteed to have the most spectacular crash-ending. Forever determined to make the absolute worst choice possible in any given situation.

I'm so lost in those self-deprecating thoughts that I nearly jump out of my skin when Blair calls out from behind me.

"Kenna."

The stern command makes me falter a step, but I keep walking, keep determinedly striding down the sidewalk a block away from the Bureau until he's right beside me. He puts a hand on my shoulder and I immediately shake it off.

"Not here."

We're not doing this here. Not so close to the Bureau. Despite everything between us, it's not the Bureau I want to hurt, and a public meltdown between the Director and a low-level employee would do just that.

I keep walking, mind settled on a small park a couple blocks away as my destination. Mercifully, Blair takes the hint and doesn't say a word until we're there.

Cutting through a maze of walkways and green space, I find a quiet corner of the park that's going to offer us as much privacy as we can hope for right now.

And then there's no more time.

When I stop walking, there's no more time to think, no more time to hide, no more time to do anything but face this.

"How much of that did you hear?" Blair asks from behind me.

"Enough."

Elias's suggestion that there was a possibility Blair and I might have been meant for each other all this time. A chance that everything I've been feeling since that very first moment we locked eyes might not have been just my imagination.

Followed by Blair's immediate, flat denial.

Blair makes a noise in the back of his throat that's not quite agreement and not quite disagreement, just acknowledgment of the fact that I've spoken.

Something about the sound sparks my temper immediately.

That's it? That's all he's going to give me?

Steadying myself with another deep breath, I turn to face him with as much resolve as I can. Arms crossed over my chest to protect the soft, fragile spot right in the center of me, chin held high.

I can do this.

I can end this.

I can make it out on the other side.

Blair is still standing there, silent and stoic and studying my expression. Neither of us speaks for a few long moments, but just as I open my mouth to reply, he cuts me off.

"That wasn't what you think it was."

It takes a couple of seconds for the words to sink in, but as soon as they do, my temper doubles.

"Yeah, right," I say, and my voice comes out bitter and cold enough that it surprises both of us. "I think you were pretty damn clear about what you meant."

I don't know what I expect. More arrogance, maybe, or more excuses. More of that inscrutable dragon's certainty, his power, the way he's always been the one to decide for the both of us.

What I don't expect?

The devastation. The way Blair's head bows forward and his expression melts into pain and regret. It sends me reeling, but only until he speaks again.

"I can explain."

For a terrible, heart-wrenching moment, I almost give in. To his pain, to the immediate instinct that makes me want to soothe him, help him, hear him out.

To Blair, who's shut down every single suggestion that things between us are anything more than casual, then acted in ways that have left me feeling so confused and unsure of myself. Who's burned so hot and then left me out in the cold with no explanation whenever he doesn't feel like I'm owed one.

This has gone on too long. I know it's gone on too long. I've felt too much for him, fell too hard for him, and that's on me.

But that doesn't mean he's blameless, either.

Whatever the fuck he's feeling and whatever reasoning is going on in that dragon brain of his that's made him act the way he has, that's on him. I'm done excusing it.

"Fine," I tell him, feeling the last of my sympathy burn away. "Start explaining."

36

Blair

"Start explaining."

Where can I even begin? My mind is still racing with the implications of my conversation with Elias, the shame of Kenna having heard, and the panic that's quickly rising over the hard, flat look in her eyes.

I still don't know how to process it. I don't know how it can be possible. And as I stand here and watch my mate retreat further and further into herself, I don't know how to fix any of it.

I must be silent long enough to crack some of that ice she's shielding herself with, because a few moments later she lets out a ragged breath and turns away from me.

"Or I can just go," she snaps as she takes a couple of steps away. "If it's going to be like this. If you still can't fucking *talk* to me after everything we've—"

"Kenna," I call after her. "My ember—"

"No!" She whirls around to face me, and there are tears shining in her magnificent eyes. "Not your anything. Remember? You made that very clear from the first day we met."

"That wasn't… I made a mista—"

"Don't say it. Don't you dare." Her tears are spilling over now, running down over her full cheeks and dripping from her chin. She swipes at them angrily with the back of her hand. "You don't get to fucking do this, Ewan."

Ewan. What a luxury, to be called by that name. After so many years, it still makes my heart ache to hear it said aloud.

And when Kenna says it? It scorches my very soul.

"I'm done," Kenna continues, wiping away the last of her tears. "With you. With all of this. I'm done."

"Please," I try once more. "If you would just—"

"No."

For a few tense moments, neither of us speaks. Kenna's breathing is still shaky, her eyes are still damp, and even though every single instinct in me is screaming to reach out and touch her, hold her to me, ease away all the pain she's feeling, I hold myself back.

I have no right to touch her right now.

"This needs to be over," she finally says as she squares her shoulders and gives her fiery curls a defiant toss. "Both of us should have always known better."

My brave ember. My strong, beautiful mate.

"What are you saying?" I ask, though I already know. I just want to hear her say it. I want to know how broken things are so I can start figuring out a way to fix them.

"This," she says, gesturing back and forth between us. "All of this, it was never going to work anyway. And not just because I'm not your mate."

The words are sacrilege. *I'm not your mate.* They reach in and twist the knife deeper into the center of my chest.

But what can I say?

Wait just a second, ember. I've had a revelation that's going to fix all of this. Make it right. Just ignore the way I've been treating you for weeks, listen to me when I've never given you a reason to, stay even though you have every right to go.

All of it's worthless right now.

"I've been such a fucking idiot," she says. "Letting myself get so far into this when you've been telling me the whole time what the deal is."

Gods above, the number of mistakes I've made.

Keeping her a secret when I should have had her at my side since the very beginning. Making her life at the Bureau and in the public eye a living hell. Forcing her to shoulder burdens that should have always been mine.

Kenna's still studying me, watching my reactions to her words play out across my face. At whatever she sees, she lets out a shaky breath and drops her gaze to look at the ground.

"I guess it's pretty obvious by now," she whispers. "The fact that I don't do anything half-way. Not my fuck-ups or the things I get right. Not the way I care about people. Not the way I... I stupidly let myself fall for you."

Everything stops. The beating of my heart in my chest. The turning of the world beneath my feet. Time and space itself as her words settle themselves into the very fabric of my being. Where I already know they'll be for the rest of eternity.

"Kenna." Her name is a broken, fragile thing in my throat.

She continues like I haven't spoken. "And that's on me. I should have known better. But... I can't do this anymore. This thing with us, all this back and forth. God, this whole fucking conversation. I just... I can't."

I swallow once around the lump in my throat, and then

again. There are words there—apologies and assurances and promises—but I know what all of them will sound like right now: excuses.

Kenna has no reason to believe anything I say. No reason to trust me. Not after the way I've behaved.

Beyond that, am I truly ready to face what it would mean to have Kenna as my mate? To be the male I need to be for her, to have my own issues sorted out enough so they don't just become more she has to endure?

"I'm sorry," I finally manage to say. "I'm so sorry, Kenna, more sorry than you can know."

Kenna doesn't look convinced, and I don't blame her for that either. She's been nothing but honest and transparent with me since the beginning. She walked into my office that first day with kindness in her eyes and her heart on her sleeve, willing to recognize and accept what I couldn't. She's suffered because of me, gotten her beautiful heart broken because of me, and I haven't even begun to scratch the surface of doing what I need to win her trust.

"I'm going to leave now," she says—calm, flat, devoid of any fire or emotion. "And you're not going to follow me. You're not going to call me. You're going to stay far, far away from me. Got it?"

The dragon in me hisses his disapproval, but I ignore the prick and give Kenna a single, decisive nod.

It violates every instinct to let her walk away, but I have the horrible certainty that trying to do anything else right now would just dig the grave I'm standing in deeper.

I need time. And a plan. Before I do any more damage.

"Good," she says, and although she's still trying to maintain that detached, emotionless tone, there's a crack in it this time. Barely there, but enough to slam through me like a bolt to the heart.

"Goodbye, Ewan."

I nod again, still unable to make any words come out.

When she turns to go, I don't stop her, and when she rounds the corner and disappears out of the park, I stay right where I am.

I'm a ruin of a creature right now, not the male she deserves. Not the mate she deserves. And though I barely know where to begin, I do know one thing for certain—I'm going to be that male, that mate. I'm going to make myself worthy of Kenna Byrne if it's the last thing I ever do in my whole, miserable existence.

37

Kenna

It hurts.

Holy shit, it hurts.

Each step I take away from Blair echoes through my chest. It pulses and stabs and makes every part of me ache.

But I keep walking. One foot, then the other. One step, then another. Even though every inch of distance feels wrong and my whole body is fighting it, like my blood and bones are still tethered to him, reaching for him.

She's not my mate.

No matter what my heart and soul are telling me, I keep walking.

It's done. Over. Finished.

So why does it still hurt so goddamn much?

Because you let yourself fall for him, idiot. The answer is immediate and damning. I let myself fall for someone who was always going to be just out of reach.

I've made plenty of poor decisions in my life, but this might be my masterpiece. The giant supernova of a mistake to put all the rest of them to shame.

Maybe it's a good omen.

Maybe messing up this badly means I'm finally ready to start getting things right. Maybe it's the last big fuck-up I needed to get out of my system. The fireworks grand finale at the end of the night.

It must be, because I can't imagine anything hurting more than this.

It pounds through me like a deep-tissue bruise as I make my way back into the Bureau and grab my stuff, mercifully not running into anyone I know this long after the end of business hours.

It continues pulsing with red-hot regret as I walk to the bus stop and get on the bus, settling into a seat and resting my head against the window.

All I need to do is get home. Take a bath. Curl up in bed. Try not to think about the night Blair was there, tempting me, teasing me, making me want him to...

I stop that train of thought right there, mentally scolding myself and starting the long, long process of excising Ewan Blair from my brain. I can't let myself think about his stupid, handsome face, or the way his scales shimmered in the sunlight that day at the lake, or the way his wings always spread and arched above us when we...

Goddamn it.

There's a ringing in my ears, making it hard to think. A parade of memories all crowding in, competing for their chance to pummel my heart a little bit more. I can't process, can't deal with any of it, can barely breathe, and with that damned ringing...

I don't realize it's my phone ringing until I see the woman

in the seat across from me looking at me with a frown on her face. Fishing it out of my pocket, I look down at the caller ID and my stomach does a little flip. I should probably let it go to voicemail, being in the absolute trash can of an emotional state I am right now, but before I can think better of it, I answer the call.

"Kenna?"

I clear my throat, trying to dislodge the thick lump of emotion that's settled itself on top of my vocal cords.

"Yes," I croak. "This is Kenna."

"Great!" Kerri Vaughn's voice is bright and cheerful. "Do you have a couple of minutes to chat about the proposal images?"

The proposal images. For her book covers. The ones I've completely forgotten about with everything else going on.

I clear my throat again and sit up straighter in my seat. "Yes, I do."

There's a slight pause on the other end of the line, and I brace myself for more disappointment. It wouldn't even surprise me at this point if she told me the covers are crap, I'm worthless as an artist, and she's going with someone else.

Only that disappointment never comes.

"Well, Kenna, I've got wonderful news."

38

Blair

A week after my fallout with Kenna, I'm back at Ari's lakehouse.

I'm by myself this time, needing the peace and the solitude, the opportunity for some time to be truly alone. What it is about this place that feels right, I'm not certain, but bless Ari and her generosity, because it felt like the place I needed to be.

Perhaps because it's the first place I could truly speak of Lizzy since the day I lost her, though I can recognize that had more to do with the person who was listening than with the words themselves.

But here, now, even on my own this time, the calm and serenity of this place makes it all too easy to unlock those memories again.

It's been a hell of a long time since I've let myself sit with her ghost like this.

I've been running from her, from everything that happened and all my guilt and shame about my part in it. In the way I refused to speak her name or welcome memories of her, in the way I refused to let anyone new into my heart, in the way I've chosen to live and what I've chosen to live for.

Some parts of it I'll never regret—establishing Morgan-Blair with Elias, advocating for paranormals as long as I have, helping to build the Bureau into what it is today. But other parts? The single-minded dedication to working as hard and as long as I could, so there was no time for the memories. The lonesome years and refusal to let myself acknowledge and honor everything I lost. Those are harder to face.

The longer I sit, the clearer the memories become. Things I haven't let myself think about in centuries come flooding back.

The way Lizzy used to sing on the deck of the ship, the sea breeze billowing through her black hair. The way she would so clearly talk about our future, like it was already alive in her mind. Her effortless charm and the endless enthusiasm she had for life.

Like everything else, those memories are hazy now, and faded around the edges, but sinking into them no longer fills me with dread and regret. I've held her spectre at bay so long, hardly able to face it, that it catches me off guard how easily and gently it returns.

But... perhaps that isn't quite accurate. Lizzy has felt closer this past month than she has in centuries. Ever since... ever since I met Kenna.

And truly, it's no surprise that meeting my second mate resurrected memories of my first.

That's who Lizzy will always be, my mate. As certainly as Kenna is. Whether or not we ever bonded, I know who she was to me, and though fate had other designs for us, that simple fact will never cease to be true.

Lizzy was my mate.

I loved her, and I lost her, and now somehow I finally have to figure out how to live a life without her. An actual life.

Late in the evening, when the stars have come out and the fireflies are winking slowly off and on along the lakeshore, I finally end my vigil feeling fragile and battered, but somehow also stronger and more ready to face whatever's coming next.

"I'm sorry, Lizzy," I say to the night air, to the watching cosmos, to whoever might be listening. "For everything."

It's only the beginning, barely a start. As I head inside and get ready to sleep in the bed I shared with Kenna the last time we were here, I pull my wallet from my back pocket and look again at the card tucked inside.

A grief counselor—a paranormal grief counselor, to be more specific—one who we've referred plenty of clients to through the Bureau's support services. From what I've heard, he's a basilisk who's nearly as ancient as I am, and specializes in the type of trauma only creatures who've lived too-long lives can even begin to understand.

The thought of being seen like that, of spilling my innermost heart out to a virtual stranger, still feels like a step I'm not sure I'm ready to take. But as I lay down and stare at the empty space across from me, I know I owe it to my mate—to both of them—to try.

Another week passes, and another hard, necessary day arrives.

"What's that?" Cleo asks, sitting down across from me and gesturing to the paper on my desk.

"My resignation." Her mouth snaps open, but I hold my hand up. "My resignation, and my strong recommendation that you be named as the Bureau's next Director."

She's absolutely silent for a few long moments, eyes wide and disbelieving.

"Blair," she finally manages to say. "You can't... you're

quitting?"

"I am. At the end of the month."

Cleo lets out a long breath. "And you're putting me up for the job?"

"If you want it. I won't give you any bullshit about leading this organization or pretend it's not a damned nightmare at times, but nor will I deny that you have the chance to do real good in the role, if you want to take it."

Cleo frowns. "Then why step down?"

Why, indeed.

I consider the question for a few moments before answering.

Kenna is part of the answer, certainly. Me not being in the position I am here at the Bureau takes away a massive hurdle to our relationship. But if I'm being honest with myself, it goes a hell of a lot deeper than that.

"I've been doing this work for over thirty years," I say. "And I'm not sure I have the same energy for it I did back then. Perhaps it's time someone else got the chance to lead."

She shakes her head slowly. "I've never met anyone more dedicated to this cause."

"Even so, I don't know if the Bureau is the right place for that dedication anymore."

I think about Ari and the work she's doing with the Paranormal Advancement Society, of the dozen or more organizations that have sprung up around the country doing the same sort of work. I think about the paranormal beings running for office or lobbying for change, starting from grassroots and building community in our country and beyond.

The Bureau will always have a place in that landscape of change, but my own place within it is a lot less certain.

And maybe Cleo can see some of that written on my face,

because she lets out a long breath and slumps back in her chair.

"Fuck," she breathes, shaking her head. "You really think I'm up for it?"

"Take the time you need," I tell her. "And talk to Stephanie. Decide if it's best for the two of you. But yes, Cleo. I absolutely think you're up for the job."

Scrubbing her hand down the side of her face, her eyes snap back to mine and narrow. "Does this have anything to do with the redhead down in Communications?"

Just the mention of Kenna sends a pang of longing through my chest. "Perhaps."

One of Cleo's brows quirks up, and her mouth sets into a smirk. "I thought you said it was handled."

"It is handled," I tell her, with a bit of bite in my tone for old time's sake, and she laughs.

"Good," she says. "Glad to hear it. So what are you going to do now?"

The corners of my lips turn up in a wry smile. "Well, for starters, I need to fix the godsdamned mess I've made of my life."

"And then?"

"And then..."

Gods, I really don't know. But for the first time in a very, very long time, that uncertainty doesn't scare me. Nothing scares me except the thought that I've damaged things with my mate beyond repair.

"And then I suppose I'll enjoy a little bit of peace."

39

Blair

My last day at the Bureau comes a week and a half later. As I pack up the last of my things from the Director's office and arrange for them to be dropped off at my home, it's with a strange absence of grief over closing this chapter of my life.

Perhaps it will hit me later, but shutting the lid on the last box and taking a good, long look around the room, all I feel is certainty.

Cleo is going to make an excellent Director. She has the energy for it, and none of the same baggage I brought with me to the position. I have no doubts she'll be confirmed, if my conversation with Secretary Thompson earlier this week was any indication.

The same conversation in which Thompson assured me that nothing from Harrison's visit was going to negatively impact the Bureau or my future here.

Even that I can hardly dredge up any true annoyance for.

Harrison is a symptom of the larger attitudes and forces shaping the future of paranormal folk in this country, and I look forward to finding out what impact I can make on those forces from outside the confines of my position with the Bureau. With Cleo at the organization's helm, I don't doubt she'll give him and the rest of the naysayers in HHS hell in her own right.

But all of that can wait for now. The turning wheels and machinations of government and politics will continue on with or without me.

Today, I've got something much more important to focus on.

I haven't spoken to Kenna since that disastrous day she said goodbye. I've avoided common areas and used back entrances rather than the lobby. I've tried to give her any space and time she might need, to give myself time to get my life together so I'm in a better position to speak with her.

I have no idea if she'll even entertain a conversation with me, or tell me to go to hell, but I'm ready to take whatever she wants to throw at me.

Even if it takes me the rest of my existence, I'm going to convince my mate to take me back.

It's the single purpose pounding in my veins, the force driving me as I leave the Director's office for the last time and take the elevator down to the fifth floor. I just need to see her. Just for a moment. To look into her beautiful green eyes. To ask her if we can talk when she's done working. To begin repairing everything I've broken.

Only when I get to Kenna's desk, it's empty.

I stare at the cleaned-out cubicle for a full ten seconds, not comprehending what I'm seeing.

"Kenna quit."

Startled, I look up to find Yvette watching me through narrowed eyes.

"When?"

"Last week. Know anything about it?"

I shake my head slowly. She quit? Because of me?

Stomach turning inward on itself, I clear my throat. "Did she say where she was going? If she had another job lined up?"

"No," Yvette says flatly. "She didn't."

With that, she turns and heads back to her own cubicle, clearly done with the conversation. I'm still rooted to the spot, staring at Kenna's empty desk.

Fuck.

She's supposed to be here.

Where is she?

The reasonable, rational part of me that's been giving her space and time these last couple of weeks has gone strangely silent, and that same damned instinct pushes to the fore.

Where is she?

Before I know what I'm doing, I turn and head for the stairs, too impatient to wait for the elevator to take me back down to the ground floor. As soon as I'm through the lobby and out the front door, I pull my phone from my pocket.

I call her cell, and it rings three times before going to her voicemail. Cursing, I hang up and try again. This time, it only rings once.

Not trusting myself enough to leave a coherent voicemail, I hang up again and start typing out a text.

Ember… I start, then erase the word when I remember how badly she reacted the last time I tried to use that name with her.

Kenna, I'd like to speak to you. Can you give me a call?

I hit 'send' and wait with held breath for a few seconds.

The message comes back as undeliverable.

It's not surprising, but my stomach drops even further when I realize—Kenna's blocked my number.

As frustrated as I am, part of me admires her for the commitment to cutting me out completely. It's commitment I mean to shatter entirely the moment I find out where she is, but for now the little spark of fire from her brings a reluctant smile to my lips.

"I'm not giving up that easy, ember," I mutter to myself as I head for the parking garage. "Not by a long shot."

I hit another dead end at Kenna's house.

Knocking on the door, I'm met by one of her roommates. I recognize her immediately from the night I ran into Kenna downtown—a nymph with deep brown skin and startlingly silver hair.

"Kenna's not here," she says, crossing her arms over her chest and propping her shoulder on the door frame.

By her expression, it's clear she knows who I am. Or, at least, knows enough to know I shouldn't be here.

"What do you mean? Did she move?"

The nymph narrows her eyes at me. "And I should tell you that why?"

"Because I need to find her." The words sound ridiculous even to my ears. What right do I have to show up at Kenna's front door and demand to speak to her?

Kenna's roommate seems to share the sentiment, because she shakes her head. "Listen, buddy, if you'd seen the state Kenna was in a couple weeks ago, you'd understand why I'm not just going to give you a map to where you can find her. She left town. I'm not telling you where she went, and I'm not telling you when or if she's coming home. If she wants you to know, she'll reach out and tell you herself."

I open my mouth to keep trying, only to have the door shut in my face. Cursing, I head back down the steps and make a call I was really hoping I wouldn't have to.

I get an answer on the second ring. "Hello?"

"Nora." My voice comes out harsher and more unhinged than I intended. "I need you to tell me—"

"Not a chance," she interrupts. "You fucked up, Blair. With my best friend. Sorry, but she comes first for me, so you're shit out of luck if you think I'm going to help you find her."

If I weren't so distraught, I'd almost laugh at the easy, firm command in Nora's voice. So different from the woman I met last fall, and good for her. She has every right to tell me to fuck off.

Not that I'm happy about it. Not for a fucking second.

"I know I messed up," I tell her. "And now I'm trying to fix it. But I can't do that if I can't find her."

Nora lets out a low, disapproving hum. "And what are you going to do if you find her?"

"I'm going to tell her she's my damned mate!" The words are loud enough to earn me startled looks from a couple walking down the other side of the street, but I don't really care right now.

Nora is silent for a few seconds. "Do you really mean that?"

"Of course I mean it."

Another pause, followed by the sound of Nora letting out a long, disappointed sigh. "I'm still not going to tell you where she is."

I open my mouth to protest some more, but Nora cuts me off.

"I'm sorry, Blair. I really am. I'm sorry it took you this long to realize who she is to you, and I'm sorry for how upsetting it must be not to know where she is. But she's still my priority. She'll come home eventually, and you can talk to her then."

The dragon in me roars his frustration over coming up against the brick wall of another person who loves and values Kenna the way I always should have. Another person determined to protect her from me. Hot shame creeps up the back of my neck, pulsing right alongside my desperation and my need to find my mate.

But none of this is Kenna's fault, or Nora's, and—feeling like an absolute ass for the tone I just took with her—I apologize immediately.

"Can you at least let me know if she's alright?" I ask after I've finished eating crow.

When Nora answers, it's with more kindness and understanding than I deserve. "Yeah, Blair. She's okay. Physically, I mean, she's somewhere safe."

Somewhere safe. Even as I hate myself for it, I start mentally compiling a list of where that might be.

Where would she have gone?

"And it really took you this long to call me and ask about her?" Nora continues. "What the hell have you been doing?"

"Trying to get my life together," I answer gruffly. "For her. I wanted to be... better for her."

A few seconds of weighted silence pass before Nora answers. "Blair, I'm really sorry to say this, but you're an idiot. Have you met Kenna? She's like the patron saint of accepting people, flaws and all. Why do you think she practically adopted me when I first moved to Seattle and was such a mess?"

Despite myself, I laugh. The sound is rusty and broken, and Nora echoes it on the other end of the line.

"You don't think she's done with me for good?" I ask the question not sure if I really want to know the answer.

And Nora, honest as always, doesn't sugarcoat her reply. "I don't know. The two of you are going to have to figure that out."

With nothing much more to be said, we say our goodbyes and hang up.

I stare at the blank screen of my phone for a few seconds, half out of my mind with the idea that maybe Kenna will call or text me, give me some small sign she's not done with me completely.

She won't. I know she won't. She has no reason to. Perhaps my flaws are too much for even her accepting nature to look past.

But… no. I can't think like that. Not yet. Not when I haven't gotten the chance to try at least one more time.

Standing in the middle of Kenna's street, my mind races.

Somewhere safe. Where would that be?

The answer comes a moment later, accompanied by an inexorable tug in the center of my chest, one that has me looking toward the eastern sky.

40

Kenna

Idaho isn't as terrible as I remember it being.

Granted, I'm not eighteen anymore, and I don't have to deal with all the bullshit judgment I did back in high school, but being back in Glensbrook for the last week has been... strangely peaceful.

My parents own a small hobby farm out of town, a little place with an incredible view of the mountains. They were both tax attorneys in their working lives, but now that they're semi-retired from their tax business they've taken up raising chickens and goats and alpacas. It's kind of cute, actually, a couple of sixty-something tax nerds chasing after a herd of small, adorable livestock.

And, fortunately, they don't mind having their wayward adult daughter back to stay with them for a little while.

I quit the Bureau a few days ago. Probably a pretty fucking stupid thing to do given that beyond the advance I got from Kerri, and a couple of other commissions that have come in over the past few weeks, I don't have any other steady income on the horizon. But I'm making that a problem for future Kenna.

Being in that office building was just… too much. I know it probably makes me a damn coward to have turned tail and run, but staying another day felt intolerable.

So I'll figure it out, like I always do. Maybe I'll get a new job when I get back to the city. Or maybe I'll just move home for good and spend my life ranching alpacas.

Alright, so maybe that second option isn't the greatest, but when I'm out here under the clear blue Idaho sky and all my problems back in Seattle feel a million miles away, it doesn't seem half-bad.

I've taken dad's four-wheeler out today, up one of the back roads leading away from their farm to a stretch of wide-open grassland. I'm honestly not sure who owns it or if I'm allowed to be here, but no one's come out yelling at me for trespassing yet. It's become my favorite spot to walk out into the tall grasses and wildflowers with a blanket and just lay down to stare up at the sky like I'm some kind of destitute prairie woman whose husband died on the Oregon Trail.

Dramatic, I know, but I'm nursing an epic broken heart, so I get to be dramatic right now.

Not that I'm supposed to be thinking about Blair. As a matter of fact, I am absolutely, positively not supposed to be thinking about him. That was the whole point of quitting the Bureau and coming out here—forgetting about him.

Even though that's pretty damned impossible to do today considering he called me out of the blue a few hours ago. It's been weeks. *Weeks.* And he thinks he can just call and I'll answer? Sure, maybe it wasn't the most mature move on my part to block his number the second time he tried, but I've been making progress these last few weeks getting over him.

Well... kind of. Progress is all relative, right? And I'm not going to let what little progress I have made be destroyed just like that.

I'm here to find peace. I'm here to forget about Ewan Blair.

Closing my eyes, I let out an irritated breath at my runaway thoughts. I try to focus on the breeze whipping through the grass, the fresh summer air, the brief shadow on my face as a cloud crosses the...

Wait... there are no clouds today. It's the reason I came out here, to soak up some uninterrupted sun.

The shadow crosses my face again. I peek one eye open to look and can't believe what I'm seeing.

The silhouette of massive wings against the sky. An enormous, familiar horned head and spiked tail. Golden scales glinting in the summer sunshine.

My heart stutters, then starts galloping.

The dragon has clearly seen me as well as he starts circling lower and lower over the grassland.

I should get up and move, run, get back on the four-wheeler. There's no chance in hell I'd be able to outrun him, but it's got to be better than sitting here like a piece of damn prey just waiting to be picked off, doesn't it?

My paralyzed limbs decide for me as the dragon circles to the ground. I can't move, can barely breathe as I'm pinned in place by the otherworldly sight.

When he finally lands, the ground vibrates with the force of his massive body coming to rest just a few yards away from me.

Like the last time I was face-to-face with this mythical, magickal beast, some distant corner of my mind is aware I should be terrified. But there's something about him now, like there was then... something soft in the gold of his eyes and gentle in the dip of his head as he approaches me slowly.

Also like last time, I'm not sure who I'm dealing with right now. I'm pretty sure dragon-Blair is a separate entity from human-Blair, but just how much crossover they have, I really don't know.

"Easy," I whisper to the dragon when he's just a few feet away, and he huffs out a breath, almost like he's telling me the warning is unnecessary.

It certainly seems to be the case as he eases that gigantic head of his down and I have to lie back in the grass to avoid being crushed.

But it turns out I don't have to worry about that either, because like a giant, terrifying, scaled puppy, he comes to a stop and rests his chin on me. He's not giving me enough of his weight to be uncomfortable, but crowding in close enough that I have nowhere to look but at him, nowhere I can go without pushing him off.

He lets out another huff of breath that breaks across my face.

"Ugh," I complain, reaching up to stroke his nose. "Dragon breath."

A deep rumble echoes in his chest and he gives a little toss of his head that might almost seem like an eye roll if I didn't know better.

It's so human, so strange, that the reality of the situation slams into me all at once.

Blair found me. Or at least his dragon did. He's here. Acting like nothing happened. Like it's totally fine for him to come crashing back into my life.

"I don't forgive you," I whisper. "Blair either, if he's listening."

It's only a split second after I feel the scaled head on my chest starting to shift that I hear a familiar, char-edged voice.

"I'd prefer if you called me Ewan."

Jolting upright, I push him off me and scramble to my feet. "I don't care what you'd prefer."

Blair should look ridiculous, lying here naked under the Idaho sunshine, but he somehow doesn't. He's still in his half-shift, wings spreading wide as he pushes himself into a kneeling position in the grass.

"Hi, ember."

Damn him, and damn that stupid nickname and the things it does to the bottom of my stomach and the center of my chest.

"What are you doing here?"

I expect him to stand, crowd into me in that way he does, push his advantage. But he doesn't. He stays kneeling, looking up at me as his eyes rove across my face like he's memorizing the sight of me.

"I came to see you."

I shake my head, irritation growing. "Yeah, I guessed that. What I mean is... what the *hell* are you doing here?"

"You blocked my number."

He says it like flying across two states to talk to me when I made it clear I didn't want to hear from him is a perfectly logical choice to make.

"Did you stop to consider there might be a reason for that?"

The ghost of a smile flashes across his face. "It may have occurred to me, yes."

"And?"

"And what?"

"You still thought it was okay to fly your dragon ass all the way out here to harass me?"

Blair finally pushes to his feet, brushing some of the grass off his body. I don't mean to look, I really don't, but the flash of those scales is like a fricken fishing lure, and I'm the stupid trout who can't keep her eyes to herself.

Goddamn it, I've missed the sight of him.

Not that I should even admit that to myself, but apparently my body hasn't gotten the message I hate him now and I'm no longer interested in fucking him. My hands ache to reach out and touch, and that stubborn, cursed thing in my chest is whispering what a great idea it would be to step closer, wrap my arms around his waist, and press my cheek into the golden warmth of his chest.

Blair must be able to clock at least a little of that on my face, because the ghost of his smile is back as he replies.

"Like I said, I came to see you. We need to talk."

"Talk?"

"Yes. Talk. About what happened. About—"

"I have absolutely nothing to talk about with you."

"Em—"

"No," I interrupt him again. "It's been weeks, Blair. I've moved on."

Apparently he's not too happy with the idea of that, because a displeased grumble kicks up in his chest.

"Moved on?"

"Not with anyone else," I snap at him. "I just mean from this. From us. From the Bureau. I'm done with it."

"I'm not."

And just like that, I can't take this conversation anymore. I can't take him anymore. All this certainty. All this conviction. All these *words*. Where was any of it before?

And that's not even saying anything about the fact that all the reasons this was such a shitty idea from the beginning are still as true as ever.

"And you think you just get to decide?" I demand. "You think you can just show back up and what? I'll forgive you? Forget about everything that happened?"

"No, Kenna, I don't," he says solemnly. "I intend to spend as many months or years or decades as I need to making it up to you."

Months or years or decades. God. Why does he have to be so fucking cruel? There's no need to rub it in like this.

"Yeah," I say, feeling broken and raw and needing to lash out. "Until you decide you're done with me again."

He shakes his head slowly. "Not going to happen, ember."

"Don't fucking call me that."

His mouth snaps shut, and the flash of pain in his eyes as he gives me a quick nod almost gets to me. Almost. Because I'm not that damn weak. I'm not. I swear I'm not.

I make myself look away and run a hand through my wind-tangled hair. "How did you even find me, anyway?"

Blair is silent for long enough that I turn back to face him, and find him watching me with a soft expression on his face.

"I felt you, Kenna." He lays one hand in the center of his chest. "Right here."

My breath catches. He can't be saying what I think he's...

"You being here is so beyond invasive," I snap at him, desperately clinging to whatever bit of righteous indignation I still can . "You know that, right?"

Blair nods solemnly. "I know. Doesn't mean I'm going anywhere."

It's kind of impressive, the amount of absolute audacity this centuries-old dragon has now that he realizes he's not getting his way with me so easily anymore.

Blair's still studying me, still holding that hand over his heart, when he speaks softly again. "Do you really want me to leave, Kenna?"

I should say yes.

I need to say yes.

I dredge up every ounce of hurt and frustration and anger

that I can, clutching it tightly in my heart, right on top of that ache I've been trying to ignore. The one that maybe doesn't hurt so much now that he's here.

"I don't really care what you do." My voice sounds childish and bratty even to my own ears, but Blair just gives me another unreadable smile.

"Alright," he says in that same soft voice.

For a few long moments, we're at a stalemate. Watching each other. Waiting each other out. I'm sure as shit not going to be the one to give another inch, not when I feel like I've just given a whole damn mile without meaning to.

Mercifully, Blair's the one to break the silence. "Will you let me borrow your phone?"

I stare at him for a full five seconds, disbelieving. He's really asking me to do him a favor right now?

"Why?" I ask, already shaking my head no.

He gestures down at his sculpted, naked body. "I didn't pack anything."

"And how is my phone going to help with that?"

"I need to call in a couple of favors."

My hand twitches toward my pocket before I can think better of it.

"No," I say instead of pulling it out and giving it to him. "No, I don't think I'm going to help you. You had the bright idea of flying all the way here. You can figure it out."

Instead of the grumbling I might expect, Blair grins at me with challenge sparkling in his eyes. "Alright. I guess that's fair."

When his muscles start to bunch and ripple with his coming shift, I take a reflexive step closer and speak without thinking.

"Where are you going?"

Internally cursing myself as his grin grows even wider, I

watch his wings spread and his scales catch the afternoon light.

"Don't worry," he says just before he shifts. "You'll be seeing me soon."

With that, his body ripples again as the impossible magick of his shift turns him back into his full dragon form. He spares me another nudge with his big, warm snout and huffs a breath that sounds almost like a chuckle before he steps back, launches himself skyward, and disappears in the direction of the distant mountains.

41

Kenna

Still recovering from my encounter with Blair, I'm fairly certain the sight that greets me when I walk downstairs the next morning takes a full five years off my life.

Blair is sitting in my parents' kitchen.

With my parents.

Eating pancakes.

My brain can't process it. All the elements are familiar, but the picture they create has just short-circuited me.

He's wearing khaki shorts and a short-sleeved white button-up and looking so completely *normal* that I freeze in the doorway.

"Good morning," mom says cheerfully when she sees me standing there. "You forgot to mention you had a guest stopping by."

"D-did I?" I stutter. "Huh. How stupid of me. Blair? Would

you mind joining me outside?"

He nods, takes one last sip of his juice—orange juice. Blair drinks orange juice, my still-sparking synapses note—and turns to my mom with a wide smile as he stands up.

"Thanks for breakfast, Mrs. Byrne. It was delicious."

My mom returns his smile and giggles, actually giggles—which, first of all, gross; and, second of all, traitor—and my dad glances over the top of the newspaper he's reading, squinting at me from the other side of his glasses.

"Everything alright, carrot top?"

"Just fine, dad," I say, ignoring the huff of a laugh Blair lets out and wishing like hell a sinkhole would open up and just swallow me whole at this point.

Striding across the kitchen, I put my hand on Blair's elbow and steer him toward the door. He comes without a fight, though not before mom pipes up behind us.

"Feed the chickens while you're out there, would you?"

"Sure mom!" I call out, trying to tamp down the edge of hysteria in my voice as Blair and I exit out the side door into the yard. I don't stop dragging him forward until we're next to the coop, out of earshot of the house, and my anger is reaching its boiling point.

"What the actual hell do you think you're—"

I don't get the rest of the question out before Blair wraps his arms around me and pulls me into a bone-crunching hug. My cheek is smashed up against his chest, and he cradles my head in one big hand until I'm pressed close enough to hear the wild beating of his heart.

"I wanted to do this yesterday," he murmurs into my hair. "But I figured you'd probably be less mad about it if I wasn't naked."

I'm supposed to be mad about it, aren't I?

But… fuck, it feels good. Being back here. Where I belong.

No, I make myself remember, not where I belong. Not anymore.

Pushing away, I plant my hands on my hips and scowl up at him. I open my mouth to start berating him again, but he interrupts me by picking up the metal coffee can on top of the container where my parents keep the chicken feed.

"Wouldn't want the chickens to go hungry," he says, holding it out to me.

Scowl deepening, I take the can and open the feed box.

"I can feed them and chew you out at the same time."

"Oh," he says, watching me aggressively dip the can in and fill it up with feed. "I'm sure you can."

Walking over to the little fenced area outside the coop, I start sprinkling it inside and glare at him.

"I'll ask you again. What the hell are you doing here?"

The question doesn't phase him for a moment. "You said you didn't care what I did, so I figured it was alright to stop by."

I don't bother asking how he knew where my parents live, not when the answer is sitting squarely in the center of my chest.

As I walk around the coop, Blair stays right on my heels, apparently content to watch me.

"You're not going to leave until I hear you out, are you?"

He shakes his head. "No. Or until you tell me you don't want me here anymore."

Angrily dumping the rest of the feed into the dirt, I put the can back and start walking away from him.

"Come on," I shoot back over my shoulder.

I walk past the chicken coop, past the barn where the goats and alpacas are kept, past a couple of other small outbuildings to a stand of trees at the far edge of the property. Dad built mom a gazebo here, and in the height of summer it's covered in vining plants and hanging flower baskets spilling over with blooms. It's been one of my favorite spots to sit and read or just enjoy a few minutes of quiet and shade.

Inside the gazebo, there's a bench swing hanging right in the center. I sink down onto it, but Blair hovers just inside the archway that serves as the door, watching me.

His golden eyes are soft, posture tense, and as I sit and stare at him, I realize I've never really seen him like this. Nervous. Uncertain. It's such a contrast to his usual arrogance or reserve or burning sensuality that it catches me off guard. Not that I can let it. Swallowing past the lump in my throat, I make myself remember how mad I am at him.

"Alright. Let's get this over with. What did you come all this way to tell me?"

"I wanted to start by apologizing again for what I said at the Bureau. I was wrong, and I never should have said it."

I open my mouth to speak, but he's not done.

"And for everything that came before it. The way I treated you. The way I kept abandoning you to deal with mistakes that always should have been mine to deal with."

"Mistakes? So you're saying we never should have—"

"Gods, no, Kenna," he says, taking a quick step forward and reaching out like he's going to take my hand before he thinks better of it and stops just out of reach. "I don't regret any of the time we spent together."

"You don't? Because from where I'm sitting, it seems like we both could have saved ourselves a whole lot of time and stress by never getting involved in the first place."

I haven't even finished speaking before Blair starts shaking his head.

"Not a single second," he says solemnly. "There's not a single second with you I'd take back."

God. The way he sounds right now. Did I ever think Ewan

Blair would take that tone with me? Soft. Reverent. Almost like he… I have to shake my head to clear away the end of that thought.

"That's great," I snap. "Fantastic. But it still doesn't take away all the reasons this was never going to work out in the long run."

"All the reasons," he murmurs. "Like the fact I was so adamant from the beginning you weren't my mate."

My mate. The sound of those two words in his deep, graveled voice sends a corresponding jolt through the center of my chest.

"Yup," I say, wincing internally at the crack in my voice. "Bingo."

Blair takes a step closer and gestures to the seat next to me. "Can I sit?"

Wordlessly, I nod.

The swing sways as he settles into it. My body does, too, like I'm being tugged on an invisible string toward him. I make myself resist it, keep my back straight and eyes forward, even when I feel his big, warm hand close over mine where it's resting on the worn wood.

"I was wrong. When I said you weren't my mate."

Ten words. It takes ten words to send my entire world spinning end over end. Upside down. Completely thrown out of its orbit.

My heart is hammering in deep, aching beats when I find enough air to answer him. "You already had a mate."

Blair's fingers tighten around mine. "I did."

"I don't understand. How can that… what do you…"

I'm not sure I'm breathing as Blair lifts my hand to his lips and presses a brief kiss to the backs of my fingers before he answers.

"When I lost Lizzy, I couldn't bring her back, and I knew I

wouldn't be joining her for hundreds of years, wherever it is we go after this." His voice is low and rough, words scraped from his chest like each one is an effort. "All I could do was honor her in the only way I knew how. Locking away all the parts of myself I felt died with her."

I think about everything he told me about her—the vibrant, adventurous woman he lost—and his words don't make a lot of sense.

"You think she would have wanted you to live like that?"

Blair visibly flinches.

"I'm sorry," I say, immediately feeling like an ass. "I don't mean to pretend like I know anything about—"

"No. You're right."

We both fall silent. Blair's looking out of the gazebo, over the wide expanse of plains that bleeds into distant mountains. I'm looking at him, watching the play of his thoughts over his face, waiting with held breath.

"I didn't think... I never even considered the possibility I might have another mate out there somewhere. So when I met you, I didn't know what to do with the fact that I couldn't take my eyes off you. That I didn't want to be anywhere in the world other than near you."

I let out a short laugh, hoarse and shaky. "Other than to be an absolute menace to me. Stalking me, pretty much."

He flinches again. "I was wrong for that."

It's my turn to squeeze his hand this time, and when he looks back at me I give him a small smile. "I already said we're square," I say, thinking back to that day in his office, just after our first kiss. "As long as there's no more kidnapping."

His lips twitch up at the corners, but the regret doesn't leave his eyes.

"Even so," he murmurs. "I plan to spend the next few centuries making it up to you. Making it *all* up to you, Kenna.

Every time I left you to pay for my mistakes. Every time I made you feel anything less than cherished. I plan on making up for it all."

In the silence that follows Blair's solemn declaration, the enormity of his words washes over me. Of what he's saying. Of what it makes me.

Mate. Blair's mate.

Even as something small and trembling blooms in the center of my chest, I'm not sure what to think, what to believe. If what he's saying is true…

"I think she would have liked you, Kenna."

The words might almost feel manipulative, if it weren't for the soft sincerity in his tone, the note of longing and sorrow and fragile hope that puts a massive crack right down the middle of that wall I've constructed around my heart.

Suddenly, it's too much. All of it.

Standing, I cross the gazebo and brace myself on a post, doing everything I can to keep my breathing even and my heart from shattering completely. Even when I hear a couple of slow, soft footsteps behind me, I can't make myself turn and face him.

No, I just keep breathing, keep my eyes fixed on the horizon as I try to process what he's just told me. It's only Blair's soft voice from behind me that pulls me out of the spiral of my thoughts.

"Do you need some time?"

Do I? Would that fix any of this? Maybe, and since it's still so damn hard just to think with him standing so close, I nod slowly.

"Yeah, time would be good. Is that alright?"

"Of course it's alright," he says gently. "Like I said yesterday, I'm not going anywhere."

"Don't you have a Bureau to run?"

"I quit."

If there was anything in the world that still could have surprised me, that would be it.

"You *what?*"

Blair shrugs—he *shrugs,* like what he just said isn't certifiably insane—and fiddles idly with one of the vines on the gazebo. "It was time for me to move on."

I turn to face him, mouth opening, then closing, then opening again as I come up completely at a loss for words. This is Blair. Ewan Blair. Director Blair. Thinking of him as anything else is... absurd.

"There were more important things I needed to focus on."

I shake my head in immediate denial. "Please don't tell me you quit because of me. That's insane, Blair. Truly. I—"

"No, not because of you," he says, then thinks for a moment. "Well, maybe a little because of you. But also because it was time. And I left the place in good hands."

"I can't imagine the Bureau without you. Or you, without the Bureau."

"I'm not sure I can, either. But I'm ready to find out what that might look like."

Standing here, feeling the sheer magnitude of everything that's changed in the last half-hour, it's suddenly... not so impossible.

Given how completely unrecognizable my whole life seems right now, maybe it won't be so hard to see him as something new, too.

"I just... god," I say in a rush of breath. "I don't even know how to process any of this."

"Take all the time you need. I'm—"

"Not going anywhere," I finish for him, and he laughs softly before pulling me into an embrace.

"That's right, em—Kenna."

I don't know what to do with all this tenderness. Not from him. Not with how much time we've spent at odds, always burning, always challenging and dancing around each other, taking care not to get too close.

This ease and gentleness, the way he strokes a hand up and down my spine and presses his lips to the top of my head, it sends the world tilting even further off its axis.

Combined with everything he's told me, the fact that he somehow now believes I'm his mate, all of it makes me want to retreat. Not out of anger this time, or pride, but pure, choking overwhelm.

I take a step back and he lets me go, watching me carefully and following my every cue.

"I'll see you," I say. "I mean, if you're planning to stay in town..."

"I'll find you," he assures me, reaching up and tucking a curl behind my ear. "Always."

42

Blair

Some of my equilibrium has returned by the following morning.

Some. Not all.

I suspect I won't be feeling anywhere near balanced until matters between Kenna and I are settled.

Not that I have any idea when that will be as I wake up, shift from my dragon form back to my human one—something that's been surprisingly easy to do these past few days—and walk to my car to get a clean set of clothes.

I've been staying out in the brush near Kenna's parents' home, sleeping in my dragon form with the supplies and clothes I've gathered stuffed into my rental Jeep.

When Kenna refused me use of her cell phone, I had to get creative. Even though I nearly exhausted myself with the round trip to Seattle and back, it was worth it. I arranged for a rental car out here, clothes and money to be waiting when I got back, and special overnight delivery of a surprise I hope Kenna allows me to show her later.

But all of that can wait right now.

I haven't seen my mate in almost a day, since I left her yesterday after our conversation. I know she needs her space and time to process everything, and I'm more than willing to give it to her, but there's no part of me that can resist seeing her at least for a moment. Just to check in and make sure she's alright.

It's easy to find her as I climb in, turn on the Jeep, and start driving toward Glensbrook. I felt her leave her parents' place earlier this morning, and that same tug in my chest leads me to her now as I make my way into town and find a place to park.

Strange, so strange, to be drawn to her this way now that I'm allowing her in. And probably another in the long list of things my ember should rightfully be annoyed at me about, but I have too much hope in my heart this morning to let that bother me too much.

Getting out of the car, I breathe the fresh air deeply into my lungs and concentrate on finding her scent. It's faint, but there, calling me down a block from where I've parked.

Starting off down the street, I let my eyes wander over the scenery around me, imagining what it must have been like for Kenna to grow up here.

It's a quaint little town. Quiet and homey, with a single-block Main Street and plenty of houses with white picket fences. Sleepy and comfortable, typical, average...

Absurd, to picture Kenna here, somewhere so quiet and unassuming.

It's no wonder she would have stood out in a place like this. The narrow streets and tranquil banality aren't nearly enough to contain her.

Arriving at a small coffee shop, I follow her scent inside.

Kenna is sitting in a booth near the front windows, with sunlight spilling over her fiery hair and her sketching tablet propped up in front of her.

She doesn't notice me right away. It gives me a few stolen moments to study her, savor her, watch her where she's sitting with her brow furrowed and her head bent low over whatever it is she's working on. She's lost in it, entirely focused on what she's creating, and the sight of her makes my heart constrict in my chest.

How the hell did I ever mistake this feeling for anything but what it is, what it has been since the beginning?

I take a few steps toward her, and Kenna spots me when I'm half-way across the room, head snapping up and eyes fixed on me as I approach.

"Good morning," I say, sliding into the bench seat on the other side of the booth.

She doesn't answer right away, just stares at me with one brow quirked up and an expression on her face I can't quite read.

"Should I go?"

It just might kill me if she says yes, but she'd be well within her right to tell me to take a hike.

Letting out a long-suffering breath, she shakes her head. "No. You can stay."

Despite that small victory, silence falls again as we continue our staring match. Feeling the strain of that awkwardness, I glance down at her tablet where it's resting on the table. When she sees me looking, she reaches down and grabs it, pressing it to her chest so I can't see what's on the screen.

"What are you working on?"

She holds the tablet even closer for a few seconds before

relenting. She lays it back on the table, and opens up an image gallery.

"Some illustrations," she says, sliding it closer so I can see.

I flip through a few of the images, each one more fantastical than the last. Bursting with color and emotion and whimsy, they all feel like precious pieces of my ember's heart splashed across the screen.

"These are wonderful, Kenna," I say softly.

She relaxes a little, looking down and watching me scroll through the images.

"I was just offered a contract," she says, almost shy. "Working with a monster romance author, designing her book covers."

"I'm not surprised," I tell her, meeting her eyes. "You're incredibly talented."

A gorgeous blush climbs up her cheeks at the compliment, and the smile she cracks makes my heart ache. At least until I glance back down at the tablet and my finger swipes over the screen. Kenna's eyes track the movement, then go wide.

"Wait—don't—"

Too late, I flip to the next image.

There, staring up from the screen, is a golden dragon with his wings spread in flight, eyes nearly glowing with as magnificently as she's captured them.

"Ember…" I can't stop myself from using the nickname she's already told me to drop, nor can I stop myself from pulling the tablet closer and studying the image more carefully. "When did you draw this?"

Kenna doesn't answer right away, and when I tear my eyes from the screen and look at her, that flush has climbed all the way to her hairline.

"A while ago…" she says, then lets out a short laugh. "I actually started it the day the story about me came out in the

Whisper. Before I got ambushed an became a Twitter celebrity."

The day the story came out… so, the morning after I came home with her. When she first trusted me with the privilege of seeing her, touching her, bringing her to her pleasure.

"Why?"

Kenna's wry smile widens, and she rolls her eyes before she answers.

"Why do you think?"

Gods above, if I could take her into my arms right now and taste that smile, hold her close and carry her out of here, shift and take her some place far away where I could…

"They're remarkable, Kenna," I tell her, handing the tablet over. "All of them."

She shrugs, a little self-conscious. "Thanks. It's what I'm planning to do now that I'm not working at the Bureau. The contract I got will tide me over for a little while, and I've already gotten some additional business out of it on referral."

I fight back a flinch at the reminder of how much I've already cost her, but tuck the problem away for later. There must be something I can do when we get back to Seattle, some way to make things right and get her job back if she wants it.

Well, *if* we both return to Seattle. I'm still not sure what Kenna's doing here or what her plans are, but if there's a chance I can fix this for her, I will.

"Are you getting breakfast?" I ask, looking for a change in subject.

"Just coffee." She gestures to the empty cup next to her. "I was actually about to head out."

I nod, throat tightening at the thought of being parted from her again. Serves me right for imposing on her in the first place, but I'd do just about anything to have a little more time with her.

But it turns out my ember isn't quite finished with me.

"Would you..." she says. "I could show you around town a little, if you wanted."

"I'd like that."

Kenna gives me another smile that warms me from the soul outward, and I wait for her near the front door while she pays for her coffee at the counter. When we walk outside into the already balmy day, I rest a hand on the small of her back. Though she shoots me a pointed look, she doesn't move away or tell me to stop touching her, and the dragon in me roars his triumph at the small victory.

As we walk down the town's main street, she keeps up a running commentary. She points out places she used to come with her parents and sister when she was a kid, where she got in trouble as a teenager, little pieces of her life she trusts me enough to share.

The rest of the awkward tension between us melts away as we walk. When we reach a small park just off the end of downtown, we wander through until we find a bench to sit and enjoy a few minutes of sunshine and peace.

"Do you plan on staying here?" I can't help but ask, breaking the comfortable silence. "Or are you coming back to Seattle?"

Kenna glances sidelong at me. "And if I said I was staying here?"

"Then I'd ask if it was alright for me to stay, too."

Her eyes widen a little at the response, darting back and forth across my face as she processes.

"You're... really serious about all of this, aren't you?"

"I am. I know I have a long way to go in convincing you, but yes, Kenna. I am absolutely serious."

"Maybe not such a long way," she murmurs, and that ache in my chest grows even more pointed. "It's all just... so confusing. You know? Trying to square what we had with what you're telling me now."

Regret and shame course through me. "I know."

"Especially because..." she starts, and then pauses, like she doesn't want to finish the thought.

"Because you knew before I did?" I murmur, daring to reach over and brush a strand of coppery hair behind her ear.

A small shudder runs through her, but she doesn't shy away from the touch. Kenna leans minutely into my hand, and I'm not sure I'm breathing when she speaks again.

"How's that even possible?"

How, indeed. I've never known the gods or the fates to bestow much kindness, and I'd be hard pressed to guess at their machinations now.

"It happens that way for humans sometimes. It doesn't take a claiming bite for them to know and feel the bond."

Kenna's head snaps over to look at me. "A claiming *bite*?"

Grimacing a little at the detail I didn't mean to let slip, I nod. "Yes, a claiming bite. I'm not sure if you've noticed... fangs, when I've been half-shifted."

"Oh, I've noticed them."

Is that some humor in her tone? Likely not, but I press ahead anyway.

"Well... that's how a dragon claims a mate. With a bite."

She absently raises a hand and rubs it over the soft, tender flesh at the side of her throat.

The things seeing that simple touch does to me...

I can almost hear the beat of her pulse beneath her skin, imagine what it would be like to tip her head back and lower my lips to her, sink deep and...

"And you really do think I'm... I'm your... mate? After everything?"

"Of course I do, Kenna. If I'd been less selfishly wrapped

up in my own stubbornness and misguided belief that it wasn't possible, I would have never made all the mistakes I did."

She falls silent for a moment, considering, and when she speaks again her guard is back up. It's there, in the tension she's holding around her beautiful green eyes and the little furrows of worry on her forehead.

She's retreating, and I don't know how to pull her back from whatever edge she's teetering on.

"I should get going," she says softly, shifting a little in her seat. "I told my parents I was just going for coffee."

I nod and stand, offering her a hand to help her up. "Do you need a ride?"

To my surprise, she takes it. "I was going to call my mom to come back into town and pick me up when I was done at the cafe. But I suppose I could save her a trip if you wanted to drive me back out to their place."

Agreeing to drive her home, I lead us off toward where I'm parked.

But the closer we get to the vehicle, the more intolerable it becomes to think about leaving her. There's an instinct coursing through me, one that's whispering in my ear and telling me retreat isn't the path to take. Not now.

It'll be her choice if she still wants to go home. But the knife's edge we're balancing on can't hold for long, and something tells me my ember might just need me to make the next move. To show her what I mean, when words haven't yet been enough.

Inspiration striking, I step in front of her when she goes to reach for the passenger door, crossing my arms over my chest and looking down at her with a deliberate thread of challenge in my gaze. I don't have to say anything at all for Kenna to pick up that thread and pull it, mimicking my posture and giving me a provoking little smile.

Gods, it stirs my blood. That small flame, the light shining from her emerald green eyes.

"Was there something you needed?" she asks.

You. Just you, ember, I want to tell her.

"Can I take you somewhere?" I ask instead. "There's something I wanted to show you. A surprise."

Kenna tilts her head, considering the offer.

I'm certain she's going to say no, that we're going to move back a couple of steps for the few we've just taken forward, but my ember surprises me.

"Fine," she says, letting out an irritated breath I'm not sure is directed at me, or at herself. "Fine. Yes. I'll come with you."

There she is.

My brave, beautiful mate. My ember, not quite ready to let our spark die.

43

Kenna

"Is this the part where you drive me out to the middle of nowhere and murder me?"

Blair chuckles at the question, and the fact that he doesn't give me an immediate 'no' should probably concern me more.

I'm not concerned, though, not really. Just annoyed beyond belief with myself that I even agreed to this.

We drive north out of town in the Jeep he got from god knows where, toward the patch of open land he found me in two days ago. Blair still looks pleased as hell that I accepted his offer to see whatever surprise it is he has for me, but I'm staying closed-lipped, stewing over whatever insanity made me come with him.

When he offered me more space, I should have taken it.

I shouldn't have agreed so easily, shouldn't have gone anywhere with him. Even now, I'm not really sure why I did.

It's just... whenever he's close, nothing else in the world feels so right. I can't think, can't be logical and objective about any of this, can't stop myself from leaning into him, aching to touch him, trying to get just a little closer.

I'm still brooding when he pulls off the paved county road. But as we head down the gravel toward the middle of nowhere, I can't deny the pulse of curiosity that moves through me.

"But seriously. Where are we going?"

"So impatient, ember," he says, and it's just one more thing I should probably be mad about.

But how can I? God, I love when he uses that nickname.

Just a little ember, aren't you? Ready to spark a flame and burn me to ash.

Every time he says it, it's a reminder of the power I've always had over this dragon. Since the very beginning, it's *me* he's lost his mind over, and I'd have to be a much stronger woman for that not to thrill me in some deep, dark corner of my psyche.

Blair stops the Jeep at the dead end of the dirt road and glances over at me when he reaches for his door.

"Wait there."

I don't have the chance to ask him why before he lets himself out and crosses in front of the Jeep. He opens my door with a pleased smile spreading over his face.

Rolling my eyes, I let him help me out. I hold a hand up to my forehead to shade my eyes from the sun and survey the area.

"This is the surprise?"

"No," Blair says, walking around back to open the tailgate. "This is the surprise."

When I join him there, I'm not sure what I'm looking at. Some kind of contraption made of buckles and straps and a broad expanse of leather that looks like…

"Is that… a saddle?"

Blair chuckles. "Didn't you once ask if you could ride me?"

He shifts it further out of the Jeep's back end, laying it on the grassy ground. It looks complicated and expertly made. Expensive. Like something he would have had to order a while ago for it to be here, now, in all its improbable beauty.

"I… you…"

I stutter a little as he crouches and gets to work arranging all the saddle's complicated mechanics, and he shoots me a provoking grin.

"Nothing to say, ember?"

A challenge will get me every damn time, and he knows it.

"Won't it just piss off the big, scaly guy, to be wearing that?"

"If you're the one riding him, I think he'll cooperate."

The idea of that—of the ancient, mythical beast in Blair bowing to my control—sends a fresh round of heat coursing through my veins, but I make myself focus.

"So… the dragon," I say, genuinely curious. "Tell me about him. Are you… in there, when you shift? Or does he take over?"

Blair thinks for a moment. "I'm there, in some capacity. But the dragon also takes what freedom he can. He's at the forefront."

"And what does he think of me?"

The slow, devastating grin that breaks over Blair's face makes my heart stutter, then race.

"He likes you. He's almost as protective of you as I am."

"Is that right? He's got a strange way of showing it."

Apparently satisfied he's got everything where it needs to be, Blair stands. He's still got that ridiculously handsome smile on his face, and a glint of teasing in his eye that makes me sway closer to him when he comes to stand in front of me.

"You just have to learn to speak his language."

"What does that mean?"

Blair curls a hand around my cheek. "He wants to protect you, Kenna. He wants to make sure you're always safe. If there's ever any threat, anything at all that could hurt you, he's going to want to step in and put himself between you and the danger."

I'm honestly not sure if we're still talking about the dragon as Blair's voice dips low and he leans in close.

"You're the most precious thing in the world to him, ember. The greatest treasure. Worth more than any hoard. Worth more than his own life."

I take a deep, shaky breath. Mad at him. I'm supposed to be mad at him right now. I'm not supposed to give in this easily.

I take a step back, and the spell of Blair's soft words breaks.

"So, what?" I ask, reaching for something, anything, to pull me back from that ledge. "He'll just let me hop right on and go for a ride?"

I almost expect Blair to be disappointed in the answer, disappointed in *me* for pulling away. If he is, though, he doesn't show it.

"Yes, I think he will."

It's not fair, the way he's looking at me. Washed in summer sun, with kindness and patience shining in his golden eyes.

He's so fucking handsome like this. Happy, light, more relaxed than I've ever seen him. Even in his human form, he radiates a soul-deep magick that makes him feel infinite.

And it makes me feel infinite, too. Ready to face my dragon head-on. Ready to be brave.

"Alright," I relent. "Alright. Let's do this."

An expression of pure joy, of relief, of dragon-sharp victory crosses his face, but he covers it quickly as he turns back to the saddle on the ground.

He gives me a quick explanation of what goes where and how the saddle works. When I've got the gist of it, he steps back and starts unbuttoning his shirt.

I turn my back to him, pointedly ignoring his deep, knowing chuckle. When I feel the touch of his hand on my shoulder, though, and glance back to see what he wants, his eyes are soft with concern.

"If this isn't something you want to—"

"No," I assure him. "It is."

"Or if the dragon makes you uncomfortable—"

I can't help it, I laugh. "He doesn't. I mean, yeah, he's pretty fucking scary, but I think I like him better than I like you most of the time."

That earns me another wide, devastating grin. As he strips off his shirt, then his shorts, I don't turn away this time.

How could I? The man is a work of art, truly.

He takes his time, putting on a show that's just for me. When he rolls his shoulders, flexes all of those muscles and transforms into his half-shift, I can't stop myself from stepping a little closer to reach out and touch.

"Last chance, ember," he says, voice low and graveled as his pecs bunch beneath my fingertips. "If you'd like to bow out."

"Not a chance," I whisper, then step back again, every single nerve in my body tingling in anticipation of what's coming next.

Blair does the same, moving back until there's ten feet of distance between us, twenty, until he shifts again and I'm standing face to face with his dragon under the clear blue

Idaho sky.

When the dragon approaches me, there's something almost playful about him. Relaxed. Happy to see me as he nudges his nose against my outstretched palm and huffs a breath against my skin.

"Alright, big guy," I say, swallowing over the sudden, inexplicable tightness in my throat. "Just like last time, you're not going to kill me, right?"

His amused huff of breath is my only answer, but I suppose that will have to do.

The dragon is surprisingly helpful and patient as I awkwardly get the saddle on him, even rolling over and showing me his golden belly so I can get the straps secured around him.

When I've done as good a job as I'm going to with getting everything tightened and buckled, I go to the Jeep to get the goggles and helmet Blair brought for me. Putting them on, I walk back to the dragon with my heart hammering in my throat.

He watches me the whole time, golden eyes blazing. When I reach his side he dips down low—almost a bow—giving me plenty of room to climb up into the saddle.

"Don't make me regret this, alright?" I ask in a shaky voice as I get settled and tighten the helpful straps Blair included in the design across my thighs. "Blair seemed to think this was a good idea, so I really hope you don't prove him wrong about that."

The dragon gives his head a shake and lets out a short, chortling roar. With a few running steps and a mighty beat of his wings, he launches us both from the ground.

I let out a startled yelp against the sudden sensation of being airborne, clutch tighter to the saddle, and lean down low over the dragon's back. But he's not letting me go anywhere. His wings stretch wide and his body levels out as he stops climbing, and even though I'm shaking like a damn leaf and still scared half out of my mind, I make myself sit up in the saddle and look around.

It's… incredible.

A dream.

With the wind streaming past me and a bubble of near-hysterical, awed laughter threatening to break from my chest, none of it seems real.

Rugged mountains stretch out in the distance, and rolling plains pass in a blur as we fly fast and far, over rivers and roads and little farmsteads spotted across the land.

Every beat of his wings echoes through me, and when I pull one shaky hand from the saddle to lay it against his scaled neck, I swear I can feel the magick of him beneath my fingertips. Warm, fierce, free. It's a lick of flame that burns through me, all the way from where I'm touching him to the center of my chest.

The world spreads out from horizon to horizon beneath us. From way up here, on the back of this dragon, it feels like anything might be possible. Absolutely anything.

In some distant corner of my soul, the last brick falls.

Everything that wall has been holding back comes rushing in hard and fast and unbearably, exquisitely painful. Everything I've tried not to feel for him, every bit of longing and joy and desire I'd almost managed to convince myself I could survive without. It all washes over me in a cascade, taking the rest of my doubts and defenses with it.

Barely able to withstand it, I lay myself down over the dragon's back, pressing my cheek into the side of his scaled neck as we soar.

The flight lasts a little longer—short, but the first of what I have no doubt will be many—and he circles lazily back to where we started, coming down for a graceful landing in the grassland.

Tears stream down my cheeks as I stumble out of the saddle. I pull the helmet and the goggles off, tossing them to the ground and taking a few steps away from him. My breath is coming in hard gasps, emotions all over the place as I try to come to terms with everything I'm feeling.

Distantly, I hear the sounds of clinking metal and a heavy thud as the saddle hits the ground, but I can't really focus on any of it while I'm reeling like this.

"Ember." Blair's voice...

No, not Blair. *Ewan*. He's Ewan right now. My Ewan.

Ewan's voice is rough and strained behind me, and the heat of him washes over my back just before he lays a hand on my shoulder. "Are you alright?"

"No." My voice is just as raspy as his, and I scrub at the tears on my cheeks with the back of my hand as he takes me by the shoulders and turns me to face him.

Ewan curses under his breath when he sees me crying, and moves my hands gently away as he wipes my tears with the pads of his thumbs, curling his hands around my cheeks.

"I'm sorry," he says. "I shouldn't have... this was a terrible—"

"It was wonderful," I croak. "Thank you. For thinking of it. For asking me to come out here. Just... thank you."

Before I can think better of it, I throw my arms around his neck. He freezes for a heartbeat before his arms close around me. He lifts me off my feet and pulls me into the solid wall of his chest, and I've never felt closer to another person in my whole damn life.

"I believe you," I say in a strangled whisper. "About us. About being your mate."

How was it ever a question?

"Kenna," Ewan rasps, pulling me even closer.

"You're still sure you want me?"

"There's not a single doubt in my mind."

I hiccup a small, wet laugh at the impossibility of it all. "You barely even know me."

"I know who you are, ember. I know your vibrancy and your passion. I know the softness of you, and all the sharp edges. I see you."

"But—"

"I don't know everything about you," he gently interrupts. "But I want nothing more than the time to learn and know it all."

My heart is still racing, but something in me settles at the words.

"And are you... alright with it? After everything that happened with Lizzy? Are you alright with the idea of having another mate?"

It's a question I haven't been brave enough to ask, but one I need to know the answer to. Ewan's arms tighten reflexively around me, and he's silent for a few long moments before he leans back, putting enough space between us so he can meet my gaze.

"I'm more than alright with it. Even if some part of me is always going to love her and miss her," he admits, eyes darting back and forth across my face like he's worried how I'll react.

"I know."

His eyes stop moving, holding mine with that same burnt-gold intensity that used to scare me.

"I know you'll always love her," I tell him, the words coming as easily as the realization did the night he told me about her. "I wouldn't ever expect otherwise."

"And you're... alright with that?"

"Of course I am."

I mean every word.

Lizzy is a part of him, someone he loved and lost and carries with him still. The time he spent with her was short, yes, but it's left a mark on his soul that's made him the person he is today. And there's no part of me that would ever ask him to be anyone but who he is.

A dragon. My dragon. Flawed and infuriating and wonderful. Broken and healing. Impossible and real.

"I just need to know if there's enough room left in there for me." I press my hand to the center of his chest and feel the thundering of his heart beneath it.

"Of course there is, ember."

I believe him, I really do, and his words make a fresh round of tears gather in my eyes.

Still, there's a lingering pulse of guilt and uncertainty in his expression. He's holding back, leashing himself, not quite able to give in completely.

What's he waiting for?

I don't need any more time. Not when some part of me has been so damn certain for so damn long and I've had to convince myself otherwise over and over again.

We were always headed here.

From that very first day at the Bureau.

From the moment his golden eyes locked onto me.

I'm breathless, reckless, standing on the edge of the cliff between what is and what could be. It should scare me more, make me want to turn and run and stand on my pride, but I push all those doubts aside as I meet his golden eyes once more.

If there's ever been a time to be absolutely committed to a potentially life-ruining mistake, it's right now.

"Claim me, then."

Ewan's eyes widen, black pupils dilating and nearly eclipsing all of that gold. "Kenna..."

"Please. I'm here. Right here. I've been here since the beginning, and I'm not going anywhere."

He tangles a hand in my hair, clasping roughly and tipping my head back to expose my throat.

"Do you know what you're asking for, ember? Hundreds of years, shackled to—"

"Bound to you," I whisper. "Hundreds of years by your side."

Ewan's fangs lengthen as I speak, and my heart rate ticks up in response. His eyes drop to my throat like he can see the pulse of hot, needy blood beneath my skin.

"No matter what else we need to figure out," I say, "I love you, Ewan. I—"

My words cut off with Ewan's mouth crashing into the side of my throat, and with the sharp, shocking slide of his fangs into me. A hot jolt of pain follows, but in seconds it's melting into a smooth warmth that flows from his bite, down my neck and into the center of my chest.

I swear I can feel the very moment our bond latches on, and if Ewan's groan against my skin is any indication, he can, too.

He draws deep, taking me into him, savoring the feel and the taste of me until he pulls away with a rough gasp.

"Kenna," he growls. "Gods, I can *feel* you. I can—"

Whatever else he has to say is lost in the crush of my lips on his. There will be time to talk later.

The warmth of his skin is mixed with the sharp copper of my blood and the rasp of his fangs over my lip as I devour him. I might not be able to mark him in the same way he's just marked me, but that doesn't mean I can't let him know in no uncertain terms that I've claimed him, too.

When we come up for air, Ewan's eyes are blazing, his wings drawn forward to wrap around me. He tightens his grip on my hair and tips my head back so he can get a look at my neck.

"My mate," he whispers, and there's no holding back the tears now. They fall freely, and he leans in to kiss each one, murmuring it over and over again. "My brave mate. My vibrant, beautiful mate."

"Mine," I whisper in reply, catching his mouth in another deep kiss.

It might go on for hours, days, weeks, and when we finally pull away, Blair's eyes are lit with triumph and possession, a dragon who's captured the crowning jewel of his hoard.

"You're moving in with me," he says gruffly, leaning into my neck to kiss the mark he's left and sending a jolt of white-hot arousal through my veins. "When we get back to Seattle. And I'll talk to Cleo at the Bureau to see if you can get your job back."

Bossy. So bossy, my dragon.

I shake my head slowly. Ewan's eyes narrow and he opens his mouth to speak, but I silence him with a finger against his lips.

"I'll move in with you," I say, agreeing to the first part of his dictatorial request with absolutely no hesitation. Fuck it. His place is incredible, and the idea of spending another night without him feels pretty damn intolerable. "But I'm not going back to the Bureau."

Again, he looks like he's going to say something, but I keep my finger where it is, even when he nips it in frustration.

"Let me figure it out?" I ask him, and he nods.

"Whatever you need, and whatever you want to do, I'm here to support you."

More than pleased with that answer, I lean up to press a kiss against his lips before nestling into his neck.

"So..." I say with an unbearable lightness bubbling up in

my chest. "What do we do now?"

44

Blair

"What do we do now?"

I've never known it was possible to be so broken and so whole at the same time.

But standing here with my mate in my arms—having marked and claimed her and bound her to me for the rest of our lives—both things are true at the same time. My soul feels as if it's been shattered like glass, scattered across the surrounding plains, but also like my mate has picked up every last piece and put me back together.

I'm still cracked, still fragile, but with Kenna pressed against me, I've never known the depth of peace and certainty coursing through me.

I also can't stop the wide, embarrassing grin that breaks across my face. "Now? Now you're with me, ember. And now we figure it out."

It's exhilarating, and terrifying, and wonderful. Everything all at the same time.

"Now I make it up to you, just like I promised." I lean in to run my lips over my claiming mark again, and the breathy moan she lets out sends flames racing through my veins. "I'm going to spend the rest of my damned life doing everything I can to make you happy, Kenna."

She sighs and relaxes into me, and a few more of those cracks fuse themselves back together.

"All of this is insane, isn't it? Like, actually insane."

I chuckle against her hair. "Perhaps. But I still wouldn't have it any other way."

"Really?"

"Well," I allow. "If I could change anything, I might go back and pull my head out of my ass a little sooner, but… yes, really."

"How soon?" she teases. "That very first day at the Bureau?"

"If I'd acted on instinct that first day at the Bureau, my tenure as Director would have come to an even more abrupt end than it did."

Kenna laughs. "Oh yeah? What would that instinct have made you do?"

My own laugh is deeper, darker, a promise and a warning all wrapped up in one. "I would have claimed you right then and there. Carried you off somewhere I could hoard you and be greedy with you, ember."

The shiver that runs through Kenna has nothing to do with the temperature, and the answering surge of arousal in my blood reminds me where we are right now. Out in the middle of nowhere, under the clear blue sky, with the summer sun beating down on our backs.

Kenna must have the same thought, because when she

leans up to murmur in my ear, her voice is husky and thick with desire.

"So, do you have somewhere around here you can hoard me? Where are you staying?"

Laughing again, I grasp her ass and lift her up against me. I kiss the gasp off her full lips and groan at the warm press of her thighs on my hips, her plush body tucked against mine.

"I've been... roughing it a little."

"What does that mean?"

The back end of the Jeep is still open, and I set her down inside. It's a tight, awkward fit, especially while I'm still half-shifted, but if I slide her right to the edge, I might just be able to...

"Ewan," she says impatiently, reminding me she's still waiting for an answer.

"I've been sleeping outside. Well, my dragon has."

"And *where* have you been sleeping outside?"

"Near your parents' house," I admit. "It was as close as I could get to you while still giving you some space."

Her eyes widen a little at the confession, right before she throws her arms around my neck and drags me down for a long, hot kiss. My hands fumble with the snap of the denim shorts she's wearing, tangle in the hem of her t-shirt, and she helps me wriggle them off of her until she's just as bare as I am.

I pull her to the edge and wedge myself between her thighs. Kenna curls her hand around my cock, bringing me right up to her entrance, but I pause before driving into her.

"I love you, Kenna."

She already said it first, when she was pouring her beautiful heart out to me, when she had enough courage to bring us over that last hurdle together. And even if she's not ready to say it again, I want her to know how I feel.

Kenna is mine. Mine to love. Mine to keep.

Those emerald green eyes are staring up at me in disbelief, coated with a sheen of silver tears.

"Talk to me, ember."

She blinks her tears away, and I lean in to kiss the one that escapes from the corner of her eye. "You... love me?"

"I do."

"I love you, too."

I slide deep into her, and the very last pieces of me stitch themselves back together. Patched, but whole, and all belonging to my bold, brilliant ember. My impossible, incomparable mate.

45

Blair - Yule, Six months later

I don't remember the last time I had a holiday where I could actually relax, enjoy the company of my closest friends, and not have the worry of work or the sharp tug of grief draining all the joy from the day. But that's precisely what I've been gifted with this yuletide.

Elias and Nora are hosting this year. Their lovely home is decorated and sparkling with the cheer of the season, and the festive coziness of it all sits on my shoulders like a warm blanket.

It feels like luxury, to have so much peace after so many years of going without.

We're a small group, just Elias and Nora, Kenna and I, Elias's longtime housekeeper Marta and her wife Maud, Elias's head of security, Travis, and one more to round out the party.

Ruthie was a last-minute addition to the guest list when I stopped by the Bureau to meet with Cleo and found out she didn't have anywhere to go for the holiday.

She's currently sitting at the side of the large living room, leaning over a chessboard. Travis is seated across the board from her, and although I don't know the demi-fae all that well, I'm fairly certain it's not a normal occurrence for him to have such a soft, awed expression on his face that he does whenever he glances over at Ruthie.

I catch Elias's eye and he shrugs, obviously having noticed the two of them as well.

Turning away to give them some privacy, I come face to face with my mate.

Kenna has two glasses of wine in her hands, and is wearing a delectable little green dress I can't wait to peel off her later.

"Here you go," she says, handing one over.

I take it, then wrap my free hand around the small of her back and tug her closer. She comes to me easy, with a small laugh and a glimmer in her eyes that matches the splendor of the holiday around us.

This is luxury, too, having her here with me, having this time.

"Thank you," I murmur, catching her lips in a quick kiss.

"Gross," a voice from behind us says, and I turn my head to grin at Nora as she walks over with a tray of appetizers. "The newly mated bliss still hasn't worn off?"

"Absolutely not," Kenna says, taking one and popping it into her mouth.

"As if you're one to talk," I say, pulling Kenna even closer. "When that kraken of yours is still entirely moony eyed over you."

Speak of the kraken... a pair of arms wrap around Nora from behind, and Elias rests his chin on her shoulder. They're just as disgustingly happy as my mate and I.

I meet Elias's eyes for a moment as Kenna and Nora share a laugh, and the soft knowing in his deep blue gaze just adds to all of that sappy ache. Who would have thought, all those centuries ago, that this is where we'd end up?

"Is Holly going to make it?" I ask Nora, clearing my throat to dislodge some of the unexpected tightness there.

Nora shakes her head. "Not this year. She's on a hiking trip, of all things. Winter backpacking."

Kenna glances to the soft snow falling outside and shivers a little. "She's a braver woman than I am."

We move into the dining room a few minutes later and sit down to eat. The entire meal is loud and merry, with enough laughter to fill the room all the way to the rafters.

"Are you happy?" I ask my mate, leaning in close and speaking softly enough so only she can hear.

A smile like sunshine breaks across her face, and she lets out a contented little hum in the back of her throat before nodding.

"Good," I tell her, tasting that smile with a brief kiss. "And don't forget, I've got one more surprise for you at home."

"How could I forget?" Kenna glances meaningfully toward the door. "How soon do you think we can leave without being rude?"

"Patience, ember," I chide her, leaning in to place another kiss in the spot I know will drive her wild, right over the claiming mark on her neck. I stifle a grin at the needy little noise that lodges itself in her throat.

"It might be the holidays," Kenna whispers, breathless, "but don't think that means I won't get revenge on you for teasing me like this."

To prove her point, she drops a hand beneath the table and grips my thigh, sinking her nails in a little to let me know she means business.

"I wouldn't expect anything different, my mate."

Kenna

I'm so damn ready for whatever this surprise is.

Ewan's been teasing me with it for weeks, secretive as hell about whatever he's been doing in one of our spare bedrooms. It's been a strictly no-Kenna zone while he's worked on it, and it's been driving me out of my mind.

Still flushed and full and happy from our evening at Elias and Nora's place, I step into my dragon's embrace as we take the elevator up to the penthouse. It's late, the city is quiet, and soft snow falls outside as the glass-walled elevator carries us up.

The city lights sparkle so far below, and as we step into our home a sense of soul-deep peace moves through me. I'm still more than ready for my surprise, but as Ewan leads me inside I find I'm not so impatient for it anymore.

This, right here—these quiet moments and the soft glow of joy that's settled over us—is more than enough for me.

It's been that way for the last six months, and at times it's still hard to believe all this peace and happiness is ours.

Ewan still hasn't quite decided what it is he's going to do with his time now that he's not at the Bureau. However, between providing any support Cleo needs while she transitions into the Director position, taking a more active role volunteering with the Paranormal Advancement Society, and even doing some light contract work with Morgan-Blair, he's kept himself busy enough.

Him not having a 9-5 to rush off to every day also means we've gotten to spend a ton more time together than we would otherwise, and I'm not complaining about that for a single moment.

It hasn't been perfect. I'm still a mess and he's still stubborn as hell sometimes, but falling into this new life together hasn't stopped feeling like it was always meant to be. I've got a sneaking suspicion that for as long as we have together, we'll never stop challenging each other, never stop driving each other up the wall, and never lose that spark that makes us *us*, and I wouldn't have it any other way.

Taking my hand, Ewan leads me down the hallway to the spare bedroom. When we get close, he moves behind me and puts his hands over my eyes, body pressed up against mine as we walk toward the door.

"Keep them closed," he murmurs into my ear as he draws one hand away, and a shiver of pleasure races down my spine.

The sound of the door opening follows, and he brings his hand back to my face as he walks me into the room.

"Can I open them?"

"Not just yet. Stay right there."

He moves away, the light shifts behind my eyelids, and I wait with growing impatience as his footsteps echo deeper into the room.

"Alright. You can open them."

My breath catches in my throat as soon as I open my eyes.

A studio. He's turned it into a studio for me.

And not just any studio, either, but one that feels like someone reached directly into my brain and pulled it out. A space that feels like me, like all my favorite things in the world.

The entire room is decorated in golds and jewel tones, from the paint on the walls, to the light fixtures, to the curtains and rugs and all the other decor. It's warm and maximalist, and makes me feel like I've stepped into a jewelry box.

It's exactly my style, every piece I look at is something I absolutely would have picked out myself.

I take a few slow steps into the room, mouth falling open in awe.

"Do you like it?" Ewan asks, a little uncertain.

"Are you kidding?" I lunge for him and throw my arms around his neck. "I love it!"

For good measure, I use my hold on him for leverage and pull myself up so I can wrap my legs around his waist. He bands an arm under my ass and pulls me tighter against him, growling low in his throat as he takes my mouth in a swift, breath-stealing kiss.

Without breaking the kiss, he walks us over to the emerald green sofa at the side of the room and sits down, bringing me with him so I'm straddled across his lap. The flames between us grow hotter and more urgent the longer the kiss goes on, and I'm just about to rip his clothes off when he pulls away.

"If any of the supplies aren't to your liking, or if you'd like to change anything in the room, let me know. I can order whatever else you need."

He sounds absolutely serious, like he hasn't already gone way over the top. Supplies for every medium I've ever mentioned working in are stocked on the wide worktable at one side of the room. Every inch of this place is carefully arranged and decorated, put together with so much obvious care...

A sudden realization makes a bubble of laughter rise in my throat. "Ewan. Are you trying to hoard me?"

He's silent for a few seconds before he answers, and my grin grows even wider.

"I just like the thought of you here," he says gruffly. "Happy. Safe. With everything you need."

"Oh, my god," I laugh. "You're totally trying to hoard me."

With a low growl as my only warning, he flips me onto my back and presses me into the plush cushions.

"And if I am?" he asks, leaning down to brush his lips over the proud claiming mark he left on my throat all those months ago. "Would you let me hoard you here, ember?"

There's a dark promise in his words, threads of possession and need, something ancient and dangerous and so absolutely fucking hot I don't have to think for a moment before answering him.

"Always. You can always hoard me here."

This time, there's no denying the intent in his eyes or the urgency in his touch. Neither of us are gentle as we tear at each other's clothes. Neither of us has any patience as we strip each other bare and Ewan half-shifts, running his fangs over his mark in an act of deliberate provocation.

"Enough," I whine when he does it again.

"Never enough," he shoots back with a grin. "It will never be enough."

He moves us again so he's sitting on the edge of the sofa, wings spread wide behind him, and settles me over his cock. Lifting his hips to meet me, he presses the tip of himself just inside before pausing. I let out a needy, frustrated little whimper, and he growls in response.

"Look at me, my mate."

I do, and the possessive, satisfied gleam in his eyes steals the breath from me. It's a glow that turns utterly molten as he sinks deep, pulling me down onto his thick length until he's bottomed out inside me and I'm stretched to my limit.

Panting, I thread my hands into his hair and tug, tipping his head back so I can drag my teeth over his throat. He growls again, taking my hips in a firm, commanding grasp and lifting me almost all the way off his cock before slamming back into me.

We're both wild after that, moving together, pushing each other higher, harder. I stroke his wing, and the groan that slips from him echoes all the way down to where we're joined. I do it again, and he leans in to nip at my bottom lip.

"Not without you, ember."

Those four little words do me in.

Well, that, and the burning gold in his eyes. The power of him beneath me. The delicious spice of his kiss. The wonder of the room around me and the absolute knowledge of how very much I'm loved.

Ewan's hand drops between us—stroking me, pushing me over that edge right with him. I shatter, coming with a low scream and my arms banded around his neck, holding his gaze the whole time.

It might be five minutes or an hour before we finally catch our breath. I come down from the high that's still sparkling through my veins like starlight, and when I do, all I feel is peace.

Slumped in sated bliss against his scaled chest and basking in the warm, steady connection of our bond, I'm reminded once more of the unbearable joy of it all.

Of this. Of us. Of the dragon I call mine.

Made in the USA
Coppell, TX
13 April 2025

48243744R00194